I0539011

Praise
and other words
about the book and author

"Chuck who?"
-Trey Anastasio, Phish Guitarist/Singer

"Quirky, like a male Zooey Deschanel but with more
facial hair."
-Nancy Rhodes, International Woman
of Mystery

"In Destiny Unbound, Chuck Howe weaves a colorful
tale of the world of traveling Phish tour-heads who
are interesting, flawed and compelling characters.
The rituals, secrets and community of the touring jam
band scene and the caring relationships between the
characters grow and fade, much like the main
character's acid trip. Described by someone who
knows how to play an instrument, music is the
constant motif throughout the book. Nostalgia is
painted here with words like brilliant hues of color,
transporting you to a time when a ticket to a show
and a way to get there mattered."
- Erika Swartzkopf, Stand Up Comic

"Hippie philosopher faggot genius sweetheart"
-Mike Garvey, Sex Kitten/Internet
Personality

Chuck Howe

"Mr. Hyde's quick-witted, loving, warm-hearted, musically-inclined, Yankee fan, stoner brother"
-David Anania, Drummer/Performer
Blue Man Group Berlin

"Chuck Howe is a natural storyteller telling extraordinary stories. Take note! Destiny Unbound has so much heart and so much blood pumping through its veins, you'll wonder why most other books don't feel this alive."
-Bud Smith,
Writer/Publisher/Boilermaker

"Never Heard of him"
-Maya Angelou

@Chuck - Phish loving history nerd.
Joseph

"Not too shabby for a Yankee fan."
-Sophie Jolie, Superstar/Oddsmaker

"I wish he would spend less time writing, and more time on yardwork."
-Chuck's grandmother

Czuch Republic
Dept. of Arts and Literature presents:

Destiny Unbound

a novel

by Chuck Howe

Chuck Howe

Czuch Republic Dept. of Arts and Literature

for more information, please contact:
the Czuch Republic
czuch.destinyunbound@gmail.com

First Edition 2015
edited by Emilie Rappoport
front and back cover by Erin McParland
(erinmcp.com)

ISBN:
978-0692411667

"My balls are always bouncing, to the left and to the right,
It's my belief that my big balls should be held every night"

Big Balls
-B. Scott/A. Young/M. Young

Chuck Howe

Destiny Unbound

Dedicated to Phish fans everywhere

Chuck Howe

Destiny Unbound

prelude

Though you rehearse tomorrow's verse
Forgive me if I don't sing in your key

NICU
Anastasio/Marshall

Chuck Howe

Destiny Unbound

I was first introduced to the jam band phenomenon by my older brother Jackie, when he came home from college. The very first thing he did on his first visit home was to play me a tape called "Blues Traveler." It blew me away.

I had no idea what instrument the guy was playing, but it sounded amazing. Even after my brother told me it was a harmonica, I still wasn't sure.

It sounded like an accordion or organ. I had never heard a harmonica sound like that before. Rapid fire individual notes on a harmonica was just not done. I was used to Bob Dylan or Neil Young blowing and sucking sloppy chords on a harmonica strapped to their neck while they played guitar.

Then he played me a bootleg of a band called the Spin Doctors. They had played on his back porch, and they let him record it all. I had heard Grateful Dead allowed bootlegs before, but this was super impressive.

I had seen the Grateful Dead at Giant's Stadium, where I also saw the Who and Pink Floyd. The idea of a band playing on your back porch, and a good band at that, was beyond my comprehension. Soon I was being introduced to bands like Max Creek, the Zen Tricksters, the Authority and New Potato Caboose. New bands that were playing old school psychedelic rock.

People remember watching the Beatles on the Ed Sullivan Show, or where they were when the Space Shuttle blew up or when the Berlin wall came down. What I remember is where I was the first time

1

I heard a Phish song. It wasn't even Phish singing it.

It was during an overnight field trip to the Catskill Mountains for the Advanced Geology class during my senior year of high school. It was the fall of 1990 and though I had already been introduced to some newer bands, my favorites were still the old bands.

CSNY, Traffic, Jethro Tull and Jefferson Airplane were on heavy rotation on my car's tape player. Led Zeppelin, Pink Floyd. Real music. Not like the pop and rap that was on the radio. I couldn't stomach that stuff. I would have even picked 80's hair metal over that stuff.

Grunge music, or more specifically, Nirvana, had not been widely introduced to the public yet. The Red Hot Chili Peppers, Jane's Addiction and Primus were starting to make a scene for themselves, but they were all a little heavy for my liking.

Only the real alternative kids, and only a small group of kids were truly alternative at that point, even knew who they were. Metallica was getting big, but they were even heavier. They were good, but definitely not my thing at all.

Dance music and rap dominated pop music and it looked like it was going to be the future of music, whether we liked it or not. Sting and Paul Simon were still releasing good music. Good, not great. They were past their prime. I needed something new and different. I didn't know it yet, but I needed Phish.

There was a spot on a cliff near our campsite with a view of the entire Hudson River Valley, from Albany all the way down to New York City. A small group of us decided to check it out in the middle of the night. It was a bit of a hike, but the weather was beautiful and we were young, happy and high.

During the hike, Julia and Sarah, two girls I had been friends with for awhile, started singing. Their voices sounded great together as they sang songs by the Grateful Dead, Traffic, Cat Stevens and Crosby, Stills and Nash. I knew everything they sang until we got to the cliff.

The view was amazing. It was cool to sit way up in the sky and see all of the bridges that crossed the Hudson River as it made it's way south. You could almost see the cars on the Tappen Zee and Newburgh Bridges. The girls suddenly started singing in perfect harmony. It was a song that I had never heard before.

"The tires are the things on the car that make contact with the road," they sang over and over, their voices sounded great together. They finally hit the end. "Bummed is what you are when you go out to your car and it's been towed."

The song caught my interest immediately, in the same way that Thick as a Brick did the first time I heard it on the car radio with my father when I was five years old. It had a Nursery Rhyme sound to it, with a bit of a modern, mature edge. I needed to know what I was hearing immediately. I wanted to hear it again and again.

"It's Fish!" the girls screamed, again in perfect unison and in harmony.

"Like Country Joe McDonald and the Fish?" I asked. I had heard of them. They had sang that "What are we Fighting for?" song. These weird nursery rhyme lyrics could be his, but it was something that I had never heard before.

"No, Phish, with a PH." They answered, again

in perfect harmony.

They made sure I went the next time Phish was in town, and I never looked back. I became a Phish fan for life. I went to as many shows as I could through the rest of the 90's. I became a junkie for Phish. I was living in Oregon when they released the Rift album in 1993. Barely anyone on the west coast even knew who Phish were.

But there I was, on the album's official release day, waiting at the door for the record shop to open. The clerk couldn't understand why I was there so early, and had to search to find one of the two copies the store had ordered. He thought I was crazy, but Rift is still one of my favorite albums today.

It was Phish's attempt at a concept album. It followed the night's sleep of a man in a troubled relationship. The cover was a beautiful blue and black painting with great images of winter and cold sadness. At first I didn't even realize that every song on the album, except The Horse, was represented. There was so much about the album that I loved.

The album before, Picture of Nectar, had a lot of very different sounding songs on it. One was Bluegrass, the next a rocker. Rift seemed to attempt to combine all of these elements together in each song throughout the album.

By 1998, I didn't travel as far to see Phish anymore, and I was only going to one or two shows a year. Part of the problem was that my girlfriend at the time did not like them at all. We were on vacation in Rhode Island during the spring when I saw that they were playing nearby. She had never seen them so she agreed to go. It was an amazing show, part of the legendary four show Island Tour that many

Phish-heads still consider their best four show run ever.

I loved every minute of it. They jammed out a version of their standard song, Cavern, that was just unreal. Everything they played was super funky compared to the versions that I was used to. They also threw some great covers and some brand new songs that I loved.

My girlfriend didn't get it at all. She knew strange music. She was a bit of a Zappa fan and even played some guitar herself. It wasn't really her genre, but she usually liked when musicians played good music. I really thought she might get into it if she saw them live, but she didn't. I never even brought up the idea of going again.

At the time I was working at the best record store in town, and turned a lot of people on to Phish. Whenever they released a new album, I would order far too many copies of it. We would eventually sell them, but my managers were never too happy about it.

The shows became less and less frequent for me and eventually stopped altogether. The music was still great, I still loved to listen to them, but the band themselves just didn't sound like they were having as much fun playing live as they did in those early years. The live shows were gigantic productions that no longer had the same spontaneity that I used to love about them anymore.

Eventually they felt it wasn't the same anymore, too, and they split up in 2004. When they announced their return in 2009, I didn't get too excited, but after hearing their reunion shows online, I had to check them out for myself.

The first show I saw was in Hartford, and sure enough, Phish was back and they were having fun playing music again. So I started going to see them as often as possible again. It felt just like old times.

I didn't travel as far as I used to anymore, a couple of hours at most, but I did that a few times. By the time the Super Ball was announced, I had been to 10 or 15 shows. I had gone from Great Woods to Bethel, and from Amherst to Atlantic City.

For the first few shows back, I started a new tradition. My friend Bob Afetti was a little bit afraid of Phish shows. He was a big fan of the music, but I had a reputation for going a little crazy at shows and I think I might have frightened him out of ever going to one with me. He figured everyone partied as hard as I did. He had a point. There were a lot of people who were a lot more fucked up than I was at most Phish shows.

Bob had a period of his life that he didn't really like to go anywhere outside of his safety zone, or even leave his house really. Since then, he has gotten a lot better and we went to see a few shows, like Steely Dan and David Byrne, over the years, but he still wouldn't go to see Phish with me.

I knew I wasn't going to get him to go. I gave up trying and decided the next best thing would be to scare him even more. At least that way I could have some fun with him not going to shows.

The tradition started very naturally, after that first show back in Hartford. There were always people selling balloons of nitrous in the parking lot. Basically, it was laughing gas, also known as hippie crack.

Inhaling gave you a great, short, spacey high,

but it had the added benefit of dropping your voice to a much lower register, the opposite of helium. The only problem with nitrous was the amount of brain cells that it killed. Too much nitrous, and you would wake up feeling especially stupid the next day.

So I called Bob right as I was starting to take my hit. I knew he wouldn't answer the phone, especially if he knew that I was at a Phish show.

Sure enough, his voice mail picked up before the first ring. When I heard the beep I would let out a low, guttural, nitrous induced, primal scream. The next day he called me to ask if I remembered doing it. Of course I didn't, but I made sure to do it at every Phish show thereafter.

Every Phish show, that is, until the one where I figured out that I really shouldn't do nitrous anymore. Waking up in the parking lot with a bump on the back of your head will do that to you. It's a sad day, the day you realize that you can no longer do nitrous, but it is a rite of passage in every hippie's life.

I was a fan of music, even before I started listening to Phish. As the first decade of the 21st century came to a close, it was a good time to be a music fan. Digital files meant that you could collect and store thousands of songs in one tiny place.

Not only was there a lot of good new music, but the "rare"older tracks were no longer rare. The ease of home recording meant that there was a lot of crap out there, but there was also brilliance that would never have had a venue to shine otherwise. The casual fan no longer needed to leave the house to become a music expert.

For those who did leave the house, the live

music scene, which was always an easy target for ridicule, was thriving and as vibrant as it had ever been. There were venues popping up specializing in just about any genre imaginable. It seemed like you could catch a good band, even in small towns, any night of the week. Not only that, but the festival scene made a huge comeback as well.

Festivals have been around for as long as there has been entertainment. The Greeks and the Romans were famous for their festivals (and orgies), but they weren't the only ones partying in the ancient world. In China, Japan, and even in the ancient America's, humans just loved all day celebrations of the arts, sports or human sacrifice.

Some of these festivals carried over into modern times. We still have Shakespeare and Mozart festivals. The tradition is being kept alive. The 1900's saw the rise of jazz, folk and blues festivals all across America.

The Newport Folk and Jazz festivals of the 50's kicked off a whole new era of great live music. Genre specific festivals offered the fans all of their favorite performers in one spot.

Of course, the pop music festival was a staple of the 60's. It seemed like there was a different festival every week. Monterrey, Woodstock, Altamont, and many more that have been lost to history and drugs. They were all the rage.

The seventies saw their share of festivals too, and in the seventies the festivals started having purpose. There was a "No More Nukes Festival". There was a "Save the Whales Festival." If there was a worthy cause, there was a festival for it.

The festival scene died out a bit in the early 80's. There was Live Aid and the Us Festival, but the only other festivals were huge and needed corporate and TV backing to survive. Each festival had to outdo the last, and how could you outdo Phil Collins playing at the same festival, on two different continents, on the same day. It seemed like there was no such thing as a festival for the sake of music anymore.

That wasn't entirely true, the folk scene still had a fair share of festivals across the country. The Clearwater Festival was a perfect example. Based around the cleaning of the Hudson River in New York, the conservation of the sloop named Clearwater and our environment, the Clearwater Festival was started by Pete Seeger and had become a great yearly Father's Day Weekend event in Westchester County. The location changed every few years, but the spirit always stayed the same. Love and respect, for our land, our music and ourselves.

For a few years during my childhood, I would go to the Clearwater Festival with my family to celebrate father's day, and every year we got to see a variety of amazing acts.

From Odetta and Richie Havens to Ani DiFranco and Toshi Reagon. There was always something new as well as a good old fashioned jam led by Pete Seeger himself. As a kid I didn't realize how special it was to have Pete Seeger sing to me, because that was how it felt. But those memories helped kick start a life long love of live music.

The Clearwater Festival helped lead me to the Grateful Dead. They were like a festival experience all to themselves. In fact, their shows probably inspired the modern Jam Band Festival more than anything else. But by the end of the 1980's, they had almost become a nostalgia act, one that every college kid in the country felt they had to experience. They still toured like mad men, but the music wasn't the same. Their jams were a bit slower. Their voices couldn't hit the same notes that they used to, but for awhile they were the only game in town. In their wake came a whole new generation of musicians that lived for the live show, and they became known as the Jam Bands.

By the time the 90's rolled around, the music festival started to make a comeback. But now, the festivals would travel to you. First there was Lollapolooza, an alternative rock jamboree which even had it's own sideshow. It made its way across the nation every summer with two stages and a full day of music. It was quickly followed by festival tours like the Warped tour, Ozzfest and many other genre specific shows.

My personal favorite of these boutique festivals was the HORDE tour. It was led by Blues Traveler and was the first celebration of what the Jam Band scene had become. In the first year it also featured Col. Bruce Hampton and The Aquarium Rescue Unit, who were a personal favorite of mine, Widespread Panic, the Spin Doctors, Bela Fleck and Phish. The Allman Brothers joined the second year, officially bridging the gap between the Jam Bands and the bands of the late 60's, early 70's.

In the late 90's I went to the Tibetan Freedom Festival on Randall's Island in New York City. There were a lot of bands, including the Beastie Boys, that I was excited to see. I really didn't know the band Rancid at all, but they played an amazing set. They were punk, they were ska, they were fun. It was great to discover music I would not have heard if not for a festival.

The festival circuit was in full swing by the time the second Woodstock happened in 1994. That was a corporate success, and corporations flooded back into the festival market in a major way. Each year there would be more and more Festivals. They must have made money, because they just kept coming.

Finally the second great festival era seemed to come to an end with the disaster known as Woodstock 99. If the theme for the first Woodstock was "Peace, Love, and Music," the theme thirty years later was, "Shut up and give us your money like a good little consumer."

The crowd turned on the organizers, the sponsors and the entire legacy of the name Woodstock. Ten dollars for a bottle of water can bring out the worst in people.

While the rapes and sexual assaults were, as always, just fucking wrong, the tearing down and burning of the vendor booths was a a release of pure frustration after 3 days of price gouging and profiteering. But the events also ended the corporate sponsorship of the huge festival. That was fine by me at the time, they had defiled the very meaning of the original Woodstock.

Now Pepsi didn't want to be known as the official sponsor of price gouging and rape. When all was said and done, it wasn't the rioters who got the blame, or even the rapists. It was the organizers, the sponsors and the vendors.

People still wanted music though, and smaller craft festivals started popping up all across the country. Between the Gathering of the Vibes,

11

Bonnaroo, and Coachella, bands could do entire tours of just the festival circuit. None of them were as large as Woodstock, and that made them even better. Even small towns like Pleasantville, New York, in my area of Westchester County, could have their own music festivals, and they could bring in some really good acts, too.

The only way a festival could be a success would be if it were driven by the music. Phish knew that. They had played plenty of festivals through out the years. Between the HORDE tour, playing with Santana, the New Orleans Jazz Festival, Austin City Limits, and Bonnaroo, they learned what worked and what didn't over the years.

In fact, every few years they would throw a festival of their own. It was usually in the Northeast, but there had been festivals in Florida and California as well.

In the spring of 2011 Phish announced Super Ball IX, their ninth official festival, for the Fourth of July Weekend at Watkins Glen International Raceway. It was a place that once hosted a legendary Grateful Dead and Allman Brothers Band show. I made sure to get my tickets as soon as possible.

A few months before the Super Ball, a group of people I knew only through the Internet, met in the apartment of Heather Smith in Brooklyn. I didn't go. I was at the Phish shows in Bethel New York that weekend. I had never planned on going to Heather's party. These were people I only knew on-line, not real life friends. Besides, Phish.

These were all people that I had first met on Myspace, in my earliest days of social networking.

We were all bloggers. Some of us were writers, some artists, and some just observers of life. Looking at the pictures posted on-line, I realized that these were all people who I had grown to know and love, even though I had never met a single one of them.

It would have been really nice to actually meet them in person, and I had missed my opportunity, or at least I had missed that particular opportunity. I vowed that I wouldn't miss the next one.

I had never really planned on ever meeting any of the people I had met on the Internet when I first joined Myspace. That life seemed different to me. That was my computer life, not my real life. Phish was my real life.

A year or two earlier, David Byrne had played a free show in Brooklyn. When I mentioned it on-line, Heather immediately wanted to go. I never went, and it turned out that neither did she, but that was the first time I had ever "almost" met with any of my Myspace friends.

Another writer, Joseph Allen, was also at the party. He had been a favorite writer of mine on Myspace, but he was much younger than I was. He would invite me to go out drinking down in the city with his buddies, but not being a big drinker, and knowing he was young, didn't make it all that appealing to me. He had then disappeared on Myspace for awhile only to reappear on Facebook. Older and wiser, but still writing great stuff.

One of the best things to come out of that weekend was the idea to put together a book of stories, poems and art from all of us. I was thrilled to be included in the group even though I wasn't there for it's inception. I wanted to write the best story I had ever written.

I thought that it shouldn't be too hard, I had never really written anything very good before. But these people came from all over the world. Some of them had books out already. I had done some funny blogs back on Myspace, but nothing great. I needed great if I wanted to be a part of it. Luckily the deadline to submit wasn't until the end of July.

I had plenty of time. Even when it came time to head out to the Super Ball, I still felt like I had plenty of time. It was only the end of June. I had a month to write a story, hopefully enough time to come up with something great.

Except that there was a problem. I hadn't been writing like I did back in the Myspace days. In fact, I hadn't written at all in months. The last time I wrote anything was when I went on a huge acid trip. After that I wrote for about three weeks straight. Maybe that was all I needed, and what better place to trip out than at a Phish Festival.

Destiny Unbound

Wednesday June 29, 2011

When I first jumped off
I had a bucket full of thoughts
When I first jumped off
I held that bucket in my hand
Ideas that would take me
all around the world
I stood and watched the smoke
behind the mountain curl
It took me a long time to get back on that train

Back on the Train
Anastasio/Marshall

Chuck Howe

Sabrina's car was all ready to go. I was just waiting for Reed to come and get me so to pick it up. I had wanted to drive it around for a bit, and make sure it was up for the five hour drive to Ithaca. It was getting old, and even though Honda's were supposed to last forever, it had lived a tough life. I really didn't want to get stranded in western New York.

I had been trying to write my story when I got the call about the car. Writing was still not going very well for me. I was staring at the screen, with nothing on it. Maybe a weekend away would help inspire me. There was going to be plenty of drama, of that much I was sure.

Reed had been down in Atlantic City at a Dave Matthews show with Sasha when Sabrina and Sam had their blow out. He hadn't seen Sabrina since she announced that she had a new boyfriend. It would be interesting to see how Reed would take it.

I went outside and lit a cigar while I waited. Cigars were always good for passing time. Cigars and chatting with my yard pets.

In the summertime the dragonflies would come and sit on the lilies in my backyard. The same ones came every day. They would get to know me after a while, and knew that I was just out there to smoke my cigar and enjoy all of my yard friends.

Sometimes I would sit on the stone wall and play guitar, and they would fly around me. They

17

didn't bother me, and I didn't bother them. They did frighten some of my friends, just because they were so big, and, after a time, they had become friendly. Unfortunately, most humans didn't understand dragonfly affection very well.

There were honey bees in my yard too. They didn't bother anyone, but I could see how they might be a little scary, but not the dragonflies. The honey bees could care less about humans though. They might sniff a person for pollen, but they left when the didn't smell any.

I never thought that dragonflies had personalities, but they did, and over time I was getting to know them personally. The golden one would come right up and land on my finger, and so would one of the three red ones. Those two had no fear at all. The other red ones were a little shy, but never flew away from me when I would study them up close.

The shyest among the dragonflies I had named Powder. He never came to close to me, but he didn't exactly hide either. He had a light blue body and dark wings with a little puff of white at the tips. When he was flying, he looked funny because you couldn't see the dark part of the wing, and the white part looked like there was a big cotton ball on the end of each wing.

I didn't own a pet. Growing up I had cats and dogs, but it had been a long time since I had an official pet. There was a spider that lived in the corner of my bathroom for a while. She never left the corner, so I left her alone. She would probably still be there but I think I may have accidentally vacuumed her up at one point. I felt like I was Reed's cat Maxwell's godfather, but I didn't have a pet of my own.

My yard pets were as close as I had to owning a pet. There was a stray cat that would hang out on my porch. I would always see his paw prints on the hood of my car, but like with all of my yard pets, I never bothered him and he never bothered me. I can't say I was happy when he left me a dead chipmunk. I appreciated the thought, but the chipmunks were my yard pets too.

He was just a cat, doing cat things, so I couldn't blame him. I never named him though, he was always just Cat to me. He had been gone for a while. I hoped he had just moved on to a new spot with new chipmunks, but it was a hard world for a stray cat in the wild.

The only one of my yard pets that ever caused me any trepidation was the skunk. I always made sure to make plenty of noise when I left my place at night, sometimes singing the "Hello skunk, please don't spray me" song, just in case he happened to be around.

He had never been right at the door when I opened it before, and I don't know what would have ever happened if he was, but he was always cool when I pulled into the driveway in the car and saw him. He had never sprayed in my yard as far as I could ever tell.

He lived in a drainage pipe that ran between my neighbor's yard and mine. He was an odd looking skunk. His white stripes were very wide and very low, making it look like he was a white skunk with a black stripe running down the middle of his back. Because of that, I named him Cracker.

I was sitting on the stone wall with a couple of dragonflies, plucking away at my guitar when Reed pulled up. Writer's block never seemed to affect me on guitar, of course I could always just play tunes other people wrote whereas I couldn't really write stories that other people had already written.

Reed must have been in a rush and waved me over to the car. Sometimes he would come and hang out, but he was going up to Sasha's house for the night. She hated it when he was late, and he was always late. He was already late coming to get me.

I thought it was ridiculous that he was going up to her house for the night. That would add almost an entire hour to their trip up to Ithaca the next day. I often thought Reed's plans were ridiculous, yet somehow he always made them work out eventually.

I could tell right away that Sabrina's car drove much better than it had when I had brought it in. The brakes actually worked. The only problem was that the windshield was still so dirty that I could barely see out of it. When I got it home, I busted out the hose and soap and gave the whole car a good washing. We were going to ride up to Ithaca in style.

I hadn't slept at all the night before. I hated when my friends were fighting. I should have been used to it, Sam and Sabrina hadn't dated in years, but they still argued like they were all of the time. This time they were trying to get Reed and I involved.

Well, Sabrina wasn't. She preferred that we had nothing at all to do with it. Sam was trying to get us involved though. I didn't appreciate it at all, and felt like once I was involved, I was involved. It weighed heavy on me.

I was also excited for the festival. That always gave me trouble sleeping too. The time leading up to a show was always exciting. It didn't matter how many times I had seen them. The first show wasn't even until Friday, but I was already pumped up. I hoped that I would sleep at least a little in the meantime.

I called my drummer, Diamond Jim and made sure he had a replacement on bass for me. We ran an open jam night every Thursday. I had given him plenty of warning, but I wanted to make sure he knew it was that week that I was going to be gone.

Luckily, he remembered. Our friend Don, who was a really good bass player, was going to fill in. I felt better, that was one less thing that I had to worry about.

I finished packing Sabrina's car. I really wasn't bringing much of my own stuff and Sabrina had already packed it with her tent and a bag of clothes, so it didn't take me very long. I had clothes, an air mattress, an acoustic guitar and my laptop.

The laptop would be the last thing to get packed in the morning. I was still hoping that I might end up writing something, but the words just weren't coming. That was fine, I had plenty of time before my story was due, and a weekend of crazy Phish induced hi-jinks might spark my creativity. It certainly was in the realm of possibilities.

I realized, after completely packing the car, that all of my weed was in my suitcase. I meant to leave some aside for that night, and some for the trip itself. I didn't want to have to unpack the suitcase while we were driving. I was bringing a lot more weed than I needed, especially considering that Sabrina would be bringing up some, and Reed always had more than enough.

There would probably be a lot of weed for sale

21

in the parking lot, too. Still, I wanted to make sure I didn't run out. That would be the worst. I unpacked the car and got my suitcase out. The weed wasn't in my suitcase. I went back inside and found it in an unusual spot. I took some out and put the rest in my suitcase before repacking the car. At least I had a nice little reward for when I was done.

I already knew the way to Ithaca, but I had a map marked up with the route just in case. Sabrina would be doing the bulk of the driving, and she might be a little unsure of the directions. It was good to have them anyway, just in case I fell fast asleep. I would drive as much as she wanted, but she usually wanted to drive. She was a good driver, and a frequent designated driver, so it worked for me.

Neither one of us had smart phones, in fact, I was starting to think my phone might have brain damage, but it was a pretty straight run. Five hours exactly. That was what it had always been. I knew Sabrina drove fast, but I used to go that way with my brother. He drove faster.

On the way we would actually be going right passed Bethel Woods, where I had seen Phish over Memorial Day Weekend. It had been my first time at that venue, right next to the site of the original Woodstock, and it was an amazing show. That was supposed to be my last show before the Super Ball, but Reed had lost his wallet there and in his wallet were two tickets for the PNC Arts Center show in New Jersey.

Reed had been really upset. He lost his money and his tickets. He had called security at the venue, but no one had turned in a wallet. He wasn't expecting to hear anything about his wallet ever again.

The next day his phone rang. His wallet was found and turned in to security. There was no money in it, but there were the two tickets for the show in New Jersey, that night. There was probably a lot of money in it when he lost it, but Reed was happiest that the tickets were still there.

Reed needed a copilot, and since he thought the tickets were lost, he didn't have anyone to go with him to the show either, so he dragged me along. It was five hours of driving for a concert that was only an hour away, but it was a free concert. I had nothing to complain about.

I tried to go to bed early, to make up for my lack of sleep the night before, but sleep only came in small doses. I was too excited for the Super Ball. I never slept long enough to dream. I tossed and turned until I got up and tried to read myself back to sleep. I reread the entire Notes from Underground before I decided it was light out enough to warrant getting out of bed. It was almost time for Phish.

Chuck Howe

24

Thursday, June 30, 2011:

Here comes the joker
we all must laugh
cause we're all in this together
and we love to take a bath

Bathtub Gin
Anastasio/Goodman

I knew she wouldn't be on time, Sabrina, like Reed, was never on time. I only hoped that she wouldn't be too late. I was waiting for her to call and say she was home. She had dropped off the car before heading up to Cape Cod with her new boyfriend.

He would drive her home in the morning, and then I would pick her up, in her car, at her place. The drive back from Cape Cod could be brutal for her, but hopefully most of the traffic would be headed the other way for the holiday weekend

Reed and Sasha were planning to be in Ithaca by the time we would get up there. Once again though, using past experiences, I figured they would get there a lot later than they had planned to. I was hoping that Sasha had gotten Reed up and on the road early, but even she could only do so much to get him moving.

I was dreading the trip up. I hadn't been to Ithaca in twenty years and the last time I was up there I was in love, and that may have been the last time I was in love, too. It hadn't ever felt like love since, or at least not close to the way it had with Michelle.

There had been a knot in my stomach ever since Reed first floated the idea of going to up to the Super Ball. The concert itself was in Watkins Glen, but we would be staying right down the road, in Ithaca, the town where Michelle and I had spent most of our time together.

27

I decided to go for one simple reason. I always had fun at Phish concerts. A few years ago, at the Gathering of the Vibes, I had come to the conclusion that it was OK to have fun again. For a long time I didn't think it was alright, I would feel guilty just because I was having a good time. Michelle's passing away had something to do with it, and so did Al's death.

I had been fighting depression for awhile already when I started playing music with Al. He had a little home studio set up in his basement, and we had a great time writing, playing and recording music together. I would add bass lines to his dance tunes, and he would engineer and program drums for some of the songs I was writing at the time.

Al taught me a lot about music, but he taught me even more about being a friend and he did it with his actions. Al loved his friends and would do anything for them. It was obvious to everyone who ever met him. There were two things everyone knew about Al, he was loud and he was caring.

Al was always looking to help. If you told him anything, his mind was already spinning trying to figure out the best way that he could help. It didn't matter if it was good or bad news, he wanted to help. Every time we would talk on the phone, I would have to hear how everyone in his life was doing.

He kept track of everyone he knew and made it a point to talk to them all at least once a week. He talked to me about friends of his that I had never met, as if they were one of my best friends. In his mind, we all were. He loved us, so obviously we loved each other.

He was married to Kate, and they had a son named Roger. They would be the lead story every time we talked. His family meant even more to him than his friends, and his friends meant the world to him. His mother had passed away just a little while before I met him, but I felt like I had known her from all of the stories that he had told me about her. His father had worked in the Italian Embassy in New York City and every old world Italian you would ever meet spoke the world of him.

Al's house was a refuge for me, a place I always felt warm and welcome. Kate and Roger always made me feel welcome, too. I helped Roger record a rap song once. It wasn't really a rap song as much as spelling out swear words.

He was seven, and it was the most controversial thing he had ever thought of. I pressed record, and then burned him a copy. I guess I became a bit of a hero to him, until a teacher heard it and he got detention.

After a few years of working together, Al passed away. He had cancer and it attacked him hard and fast. He was gone within a month of the diagnosis. He went from back pain, to cancer diagnoses to the grave much faster than any of us expected.

That sent me into one of my worst periods of my life. I didn't write, I didn't play music, I really stopped having fun entirely. Eventually Phish reunited, and Reed forced me to start going to shows again and something clicked. I knew Al would be pissed at me for being so depressed. Shows were fun, so I had no choice but to go to shows.

Sabrina now lived in the same neighborhood where Al had lived, but it never bothered me to go to her place. It felt comforting in a strange way, just by going in that direction again. I was hoping Ithaca would bring back good memories and not bad ones. There were plenty of both. I was not sure how I would react.

The last Phish festival I had been to was also the first official festival that Phish held. It took place on an old Air Force base in Plattsburg, New York, just across the lake from their home town of Burlington, Vermont. They called it the Clifford Ball after a sign they saw in an airport once extolling the heroics of early aviation pioneer Clifford Ball.

Phish decided then and there that they were going to throw a Clifford Ball, an aviation themed weekend of musical bliss. The name sounded familiar to me, so I went back and looked through their older albums.

Sure enough, their 1994 release, A Live One, recorded live at various shows in 93 and 94, had "Recorded at the Clifford Ball" in the liner notes. In other words, they had released a live album two years before the concert took place.

Of course Phish fans could tell you where each track on that album was actually recorded. The only one I remember now is that the Wilson was from Madison Square Garden. It was the first time an Arena crowd chanted the intro to the song.

Phish had been known for their long concerts and their long party sets. There had been unofficial weekend-long parties in the early years, but the Clifford Ball was an all out festival. The first to be called a festival, and it was all Phish.

Vintage airplanes flew over our heads all through the weekend. There were art exhibits, including one where glass blowers showed off their talent. The glass blowing booth was actually manned by an old neighbor of mine from when I lived in Oregon.

Sculptures were everywhere. More and crazier sculptures popped up as the weekend went on, too. The former runway served as both the parking lot and as a campground. There were tents as far as the eye could see. It was not the most comfortable accommodations, but at least there was enough room for the 80,000 Phish heads that descended on Plattsburg.

There were many musical highlights from the Clifford Ball. Phish only shared their Clifford Ball stage before they came out on the second day. They had the Vermont Youth Symphony performing the Stravinsky Firebird Ballet, one of Trey's favorite compositions.

Not only was the music stunning, but there were two silent gliders that looked like they were dancing with each other high in the air above us, while the orchestra played. The choreography was perfect.

The orchestra was conducted by Ernie Stires, who had been Trey's Music Composition teacher in College. Their festivals now have many lasting traditions, but they always pay tribute to the past, the future and the present. They were never afraid to break old molds or cast new ones.

Another highlight of the Clifford Ball became known as "The Flatbed Jam." At two in the morning the band climbed on the back of a flatbed truck and played an ambient jam while they drove through the campground. There were Christmas lights draped all over the truck, and no one was really sure what was going on at first.

This started a tradition that they repeated at

most of their festivals, the secret late night set. The Flatbed Jam didn't last long, or not very much of it was ever recorded. Later jams seemed much longer and much more structured, but always had the looseness that a 2 AM jam should have.

There were low points at the Clifford Ball as well, and unfortunately the whole weekend ended on a low note. No one got hurt, things just didn't work out as planned. That is one of the dangers of taking the risks that Phish always liked to take.

For the encore on the last day, they played their epic song Harpua. It was the story of a dog and a cat who went to war. The song often featured a long narrative in the middle of it that guitarist Trey Anastasio would usually improvise.

The story always ended with Harpua the dog killing Poster Nutbag the cat. The father of Poster's owner would then have to tell his son, Jimmy, that his beloved cat had died. Jimmy, of course, now wants a dog to replace his cat. The dog he wants is Harpua. Sad and comical at the same time.

Since the Clifford Ball was an aviation themed event, the Clifford Ball version featured Harpua and Poster Nutbag getting into fighter jets and having a "dog fight" over the crowd, and of course they had actual jets flying and dog fighting with fireworks over the crowd.

At first it seemed like Trey was directing them with his words, but out of nowhere one plane "shot" down the other, and a huge fireworks display went off with the band still mid song. The band ended up just walking off the stage and letting the fireworks end their festival. It was a great contrast to the gliders and the ballet, but overall the weekend was a success.

Originally I was supposed to go with Rebecca, who was my girlfriend at the time. She couldn't get the time off of work, so I ended up going with my roommate Mugsy instead. When I got back home afterward, Rebecca broke up with me.

Going without her was sited as a reason, but there were plenty of other, much better reasons, too. I was still glad that I went. I had already bought the tickets, was I supposed to not go just because she couldn't go? It had been a great experience, and that festival had only been two days long.

The Super Ball was going to be three days long. Watkins Glen was a racetrack, and they were having fun with the racing theme in the days leading up to the Super Ball. There was an announcement that pit crews would be patrolling the grounds to help assist the fans throughout the weekend.

It was also Fourth of July weekend, so patriotism might be a theme for the shows. The Grateful Dead and the Allman Brothers had played a famous show there in the seventies, so the 70's might be a theme, too. I was hoping for an All-American Race Car weekend. It was hard to tell what they might do, and that was how they liked it. As long as they played some good music, and that was almost guaranteed, I would be happy.

In the mid-nineties they would play a song called "The Big Ball Jam." Four gigantic beach balls were thrown out into the audience. Each band member would follow his own ball, and played along with it's actions on their instrument.

It was a great live moment, but it always sounded horrible on tape. It was another one of those things that Phish fans loved, and non-fans just couldn't understand, especially if only heard on tape. They hadn't done it in years, but the Super Ball would be the perfect time to bust it out.

    I was dreading the conversation I was going to have with Sabrina on the ride up. We had been very good friends for a few years already. Things had always been very light between us, there was never much reason for seriousness between the two of us. We had never had any romantic attraction between us at all, even though sometimes Reed acted as if he had wanted us to be together.

    Sabrina Goncalves was a beautiful girl. There was no doubt about that. She was tiny. Both in height and in size. She always acted tough, and was a pretty tough girl, but part of it was a Napoleon Complex for sure. She had long straight dark brown hair and was always perfectly tan, even in the winter.

    Personality wise we had always gotten along very well, but that might have been because there was no romantic feelings between us. There was no reason to argue about the small stuff.

    The same things that I enjoyed about our friendship would probably really piss me off if we ever did try to date though. She was much more demanding and combative with her boyfriends than she ever was with her friends. Plus she had never given me any indication that she was interested in me in that way at all. So the point was moot.

    A few weeks earlier she had given me a scare. She had started asking me all sorts of questions about a brief relationship I had with an old friend from high school. It hadn't lasted very long, but it was fun, it ended well and we had stayed friends afterward.

The way she was asking questions about going from being just friends to more worried me a little. I had thought that maybe she was wondering about us. I was relieved when, a few weeks later, I learned that she was starting to see an old friend of hers from high school and it had nothing to do with me.

Of course this caused other problems, even though it really didn't have to. When I first met Sabrina she was dating Reed's friend Sam. She was very young at the time, and I remember thinking that she seemed like a little brat to me. She was a brat, she was only 18, but over the years she really impressed me with her intelligence and humor.

She was a big reader, and that was always a plus in my book. It seemed like she could keep up in just about any conversation that we had, so it didn't take long for me to consider her a friend. Every now and then, the brat would come back out. But she had long grown out of that phase.

She and her family were originally from Portugal. Her parents first moved to America when she was 13, but they left her behind with an elderly grandmother. For a year she had the run of the house, and then her parents came back and dragged her off to a foreign country.

She had grown up in Lisbon, the capitol and largest city in Portugal. At first when she heard that she was moving to New York she wasn't too disappointed, she thought she would be living right in Times Square, in the heart of the greatest city in the world. When she found herself in a small house in the middle of the woods in Westchester county, her heart sank. While we were only an hour from the city, it was not what she had expected.

You would never know that English wasn't her first language when talking to her now, though she pretended not to understand it at all when she was in high school. She was finally busted by a teacher while she was chatting with friends in flawless English. The first time I heard her speak in Portuguese it was weird, like she shouldn't be speaking a foreign language so easily.

It had been a long time since she had been with Sam, and I now saw her a lot more often than I saw him. She was soon a much closer friend than Sam was, to me at least. Even so, I think she was afraid that Reed and I wouldn't like her anymore if she started dating Brendan, so she never told us. She was afraid we would stay loyal to Sam and drop her.

Reed had always been very close to Sam, but he wasn't one to just abandon any friend. Still, she felt uncomfortable telling us. She and Reed had butted heads before, but then again, so had Reed and Sam.

Part of the problem was that she had been so vocal about swearing off men for such a long time. We knew it she would find someone eventually, but she acted like that would never happen. After Sam, she had a relationship with a guy who ended up sleeping with one of her good friends. That convinced her that all men were scum.

So she would tell everyone and anyone that she was completely done with men. No more guys ruining her life for her. I think part of it was just to keep Reed, Sam and I from hitting on her, but I also think that she needed time away from men. The problem was that she was so vocal about being Anti-men, that when she found one, she didn't know what to say, so she didn't say anything.

She really didn't need to say anything to me. I wanted to make sure that she knew she could tell me anything that she wanted, but that she did not have to tell me a thing. Reed had taken it differently. He took it that she was hiding something from us, or even worse, lying to us.

Part of my job for the ride up would be to smooth things out between them. I was kind of dreading that. They were both great people who I liked a lot, but they were also both very stubborn and sure that they were right and the other was wrong. It would not be easy.

She called as she was getting close, so I left to meet her at her place. I had already loaded everything I needed in the car, now including my laptop and all of the weed. She was already at home when I pulled in, and the new boyfriend had already left. I got into the passenger seat, and she jumped behind the wheel.

When she got in, she saw I had a Snapple bottle with a single red rose in it. Sabrina immediately asked about it. I knew that she would, but we had a five hour drive ahead of us. There was plenty of time to tell her that story. First I wanted to hear about this new Brendan guy.

It turned out that I knew Brendan's brother, Jack, and they were both good friends of my drummer Diamond Jim.

Jack had been a regular at a coffee shop that I had run a few years back. He was a good guy. We were both chasing after the same girls but I still liked him. That in itself said a lot about him.

I knew that being brothers wasn't always the same. Though we were both good people, my own brother and I were the perfect example of that. Coming from a good family was a definite plus for him right off the bat though. I was trying to keep an open mind, even though I kind of really wanted to hate him.

Sabrina and Brendan had gone to high school together. He used to ask her out all of the time back then, but she always refused. She claimed to be too young to date, and as soon as she was finally old enough, she had moved in with Sam. Poor Brendan had missed his chance back then.

Sabrina and Brendan had ran into each other a few weeks earlier and when he asked her on a date, this time she said yes. Brendan's time had finally come. That was when she first started asking me about dating a friend.

Sam had caused a commotion when he went to Sabrina's house to do some work and found Brendan there. Sam had thought that he and Sabrina were in the process of getting back together. They may even have, I don't know, but it seemed obvious to me that Sabrina was over him even before news of Brendan broke. Of course Sam claimed otherwise, and he may have even been telling the truth, but it didn't matter. She was over him.

He wasn't ever a really a close friend of mine, but I had known him for years and we always got along fairly well. I had worked with him a few times over the years doing odd jobs, too.

He worked doing jobs for others, but he was also always doing work on his own apartment, and would give me a call if he had a two person job to do.

Destiny Unbound

He lived in an old mansion that had been subdivided into eight small apartments. Sam lived on the second floor.
I had never met his downstairs neighbor. I had once talked to the police after they were called because we were walking around too loud. At noon. On a Saturday. The neighbors were basically insane. At first Sam tried to be nice, and he even tried to be quiet for them whenever he was home.
After the tenth time they called the cops on him for walking, all bets were off. He would turn his stereo up loud and leave it on when he left for work in the morning. The mother was Korean, and she would scream at Sam in Korean. He didn't know what she was saying, but he got the impression that she did not like him very much..
One Sunday morning, I was helping him put a new floor in his kitchen. We had completely pulled up the old floor and sub-flooring before taking a break to smoke a little weed. The kitchen floor was gone. It was completely stripped to just the rafters. We had to carefully step from beam to beam to get around or we would end up falling through his downstairs neighbors ceiling.
I was joking about how the police had not yet been called, even though we had been making a ton of noise. I guess we smoked a little too much weed, or maybe the weed was just a little too good.
Because the second we went back to work, I fell right through the floor into the apartment downstairs.
I wish I could say I slipped, or missed the rafter. The fact of the matter was I walked right into the kitchen without ever bothering to look down. I didn't fall all the way through the floor. Luckily I caught one of the rafters with my arm, but both of my

39

legs went right through the sheet rock and were dangling into his downstairs neighbor's kitchen.

I looked down and saw the kitchen table, with a completely finished four course Sunday dinner on top of it. It looked great, but now it was covered in pieces of sheet rock and dust. I must have almost kicked the mother when I fell through, because she was right there, screaming in Korean and punching my legs as they dangled from her ceiling.

I pulled myself up as fast as I could. My leg was all scrapped up. In fact my whole left side was scrapped up, but I really lucked out that I didn't do any more serious damage to myself.

We immediately threw a piece of sub-flooring down and screwed it in so that the hole would be covered before the police showed up. Then we went to work hiding the bong and anything else incriminating, because sure enough, 20 minutes later, the police were there.

I thought the police would yell at us a little bit. Maybe they would write a ticket for something, but when they came upstairs, they were laughing and just talked to Sam at the door without even coming in. Apparently the woman spat at them, so they were in no rush to do anything for her.

They told us that they would leave it up to the Home Owners Association. The Home Owners Association eventually told Sam to just pay for their ceiling to be fixed, which he had offered to do anyway.

The neighbors wanted all kinds of other stuff too, but they had done something to piss off the head of the Home Owners Association, so he was in no rush to help them either.

Sam was a bit of a hoarder and he lived in a

very small place. So he often had to find other places where he could keep stuff, and Sabrina had a huge basement. Reed, in order to help out both friends, offered to pay Sabrina a bit of her rent to keep some of Sam's stuff in her basement.

Unfortunately Sam began to feel a little too at home when he was at Sabrina's, and he would go over all the time. One day Sam showed up and Sabrina refused to let him in. Soon he discovered that she had a friend over and flipped out. That was when we first learned about Brendan.

There was another problem with the whole situation, and it was that Reed had always had a crush on Sabrina. He had for years and she knew it. He wasn't subtle about it, even when she was dating Sam.

Reed had only just started dating Sasha and that was going really well, but we weren't sure how close they were. I had known Sasha for awhile, and really liked her. They seemed like a really good fit. Even though he was with Sasha, Reed felt a little betrayed that Sabrina never said a thing to us about Brendan.

"Why should I have said anything? I have no idea if it will last, besides, what business is it of his?" She snapped back, and she was right. But they had become good friends over the years, I didn't want them to lose that, and I could see it happening just because they were both so stubborn.

"OK, you're right. But now that you two seem like you're going to be together for a bit, why don't we all go out sometime? Besides, even if Reed is pissed, he still loves you and only wants you to be happy," that much was certainly true. Reed was a giant teddy bear. He was harmless, but he did like to yell and scream a lot.

Once he got it out of his system, he was back to being a teddy bear. The problem was Sabrina would take his yelling personally, yell back and get him even more worked up. They knew how to piss each other off and they weren't afraid to do it.

The best I got from her was a "yeah, sure" under her breath, followed by an even quieter "It's no business of yours either." We were getting close to the Roscoe Diner. I figured that would be a perfect lunch stop. I had been there many times back when my brother and I went to college in western New York. I called Reed to tell him where we were.

"I know man, look behind you, we've been following you for a few miles now." Sabrina and I were so deep in discussion, neither of us had noticed him sneaking up on us.

"Pull off at the next exit for some lunch, there's a good diner there," I said and hung up.

"Sounds perfect!" Reed liked to eat a big meal. When he went out to eat, he wanted big portions and lots of sides. From what I remembered, the Roscoe Diner would be perfect for him.

Reed Tanner was an impulsive, instant gratification loving, madman. The thing about Reed was that he always accomplished his missions. He even got a whole group of us to drive five plus hours to go to a concert in the middle of nowhere.

Reed always took very good care of his friends, whether they deserved it or not. It was true for me as it was for many others, Sabrina and Sam included. He was very protective of his friends. They were his tribe.

In his home life he had his mother, and a cat named Maxwell. His mother worked hard her whole life, she always took great care of Reed, whether he deserved it or not. That was where he got it from most likely.

Nancy wasn't his birth mother, but she was his mother in every way possible. She had adopted him right at birth. Reed's birth mother was a very young girl from Florida. Her doctor was a college friend of Nancy and her husband. He knew they were looking to adopt, and worked it all out before Reed was even born. Nancy always thought that it was funny that her husband had called her to tell her that they were parents. How often did that happen?

Even now it was funny how controlled he was by impulse and instant gratification, I could only imagine what he would have been like as a child. Nancy and her husband didn't last for too long after the arrival of Reed. So for most of his life it was just the two of them. As loyal as he was to his friends, he was even more loyal and protective of her.

The best way to get something done was to tell Reed that you needed it done. He would come up with a plan and attack it right away. Unless, of course, he just ate. Then he would need a good twenty minutes to sleep before he got to work.

To both Sabrina and Reed's credit, not much was brought up at the diner. I was a little worried, Reed wasn't known for his tact, but he did love his friends and didn't ever go looking to cause problems. Reed did make a joke about us keeping her away from her boyfriend at one point, but that was it. Sabrina, luckily, didn't take the bait, or more likely she didn't hear him. It was unlike her not to take the bait, too.

The food itself was nowhere near as good as I had remembered it. I like to have breakfast when I am at a diner, no matter what time it is. The waitress made it perfectly clear that I was an asshole for wanting eggs at 3 in the afternoon. She made a huge deal over the fact that I could only get fries with them, and not hash browns.

I ended up just getting a bacon burger, it was just easier. I still really wanted a good diner breakfast though. The bacon on the burger wasn't enough for me. The portions weren't as big as I remembered either, and it didn't taste the same. Maybe I had just gotten used to better food, or better diners.

I had known Reed for over ten years, and over the last few we had become really close friends. I often joked that he was my "Viking Spiritual Adviser" but he really was. Usually his advice to me was "Do more!" and usually it was pretty good advice.

At least it usually wasn't bad advice. Although, sometimes it was really bad advice, but most of those times it was my own fault for listening to him, I really should have known better. It might have been great advice for him, but he could always handle more. Not all of us can.

In his high school days, Reed was a beer drinking offensive lineman for the football team. He still had a bit of that look to him, except now his beard and concert shirts said "Road Trip" more than "Road Game."

At some point he started smoking pot and he had found his true calling. That ended his heavy beer drinking days for good. Now if he ever has a beer it would be a Heady Topper before he ever considered having a Coors Light again.

Reed, even in high school, was always his own person and never cared what anyone else thought. If he liked something, he liked it with all of his heart. He was a big fan of anime and cartoons. He really loved one cartoon called Captain Harlock in particular.

At one point he commissioned a glass blower to make him a pipe in the shape of the ship from the cartoon. He didn't give a fuck what anyone thought of it. He had a pipe of Captain Harlock's ship and no one else did. In his mind, as far as pipes went, he won.

When he first started getting into the jam band scene, he dove in head first. One thing he loved about the jam bands was all the bright colors. People wore all sorts of great clothing, and the more acid he ate, the cooler it looked. He had a hair wrap. Back in those days everyone had a hair wrap. Reed's was put in by a cute girl in the parking lot of a Grateful Dead show. Of course she gave him the full rainbow of color.

Reed loved rainbows. How much more peace and love could you get than rainbows? He suddenly got a great idea. He had an old pair of pants that he used to wear to raves. The cuffs were worn, but he loved the pants. He took the same rainbow string that his hair wrap was made out of, and sewed it into the cuffs and seams of the pants. Soon enough he had his own hand made rainbow pants. He was ready for the next show.

He didn't have to wait long for a Blues Traveler show at the Wetlands. So an 18 year old Reed, complete with his rainbow pants, made his way downtown. The show started, and Reed, like a true viking spiritual advisor, was dancing like a mad man.

Halfway through the show he started to notice that all of the guys around him were being really nice. One of the guys even bought him a few beers. Reed thought nothing of it, he was never big on subtlety. He just thought that Blues Travelers shows were awesome and their fans were the best.

It took a couple of more shows before some guy wanted a little something from Reed for all the beers that he had bought for him. It was then that Reed learned that the rainbow was a gay symbol. He didn't have a problem with gay men or anyone else really, but he never wore those pants to another show.

Reed's girlfriend, Sasha Rosen had been around for years. She went to school with Sabrina, and while they got along in school, they didn't really become friends until later. Reed always had a bit of a crush on Sasha, but all they ever did was go to the occasional movie. As far as I knew, nothing had happened between them until a year earlier. I don't know how he finally wore her down, but he did.

Their relationship was great for Reed. She was a big music fan, even more of one than Reed. She loved Frank Zappa and Jaco Pastorius and all the right musicians. Reed was getting into all the right musicians, and now had someone to go to all of the shows with.

She forced Reed to go see all of her favorites and Reed forced her to go see Phish and the Dead. Forced may not be the right word since they both enjoyed the shows that they saw together. She loved reggae and funk, so Phish was a perfect fit for her.

It could be hard to get people into Phish sometimes. Though I had became a fan right away, they are an acquired taste for most people. Sasha didn't know very much about the Dead or Phish at first, but being with Reed she was learning fast.

She picked up on their vibe right away. Plus she loved to drink and she loved to smoke, so she fit right in with the rest of us without a problem. At first she was a little more reserved than most of our friends, but as time went on, she opened up and let loose a little more.

Like Reed, she knew what she wanted and she went after it. Unlike Reed, her path was mostly on the straight and narrow. She had gone to college. She had a good job. She owned her house and a house in the mountains of Jamaica, where she more or less fed an entire local family.

Her parents were Jewish, but only in heritage, not practice. Sasha wanted to explore her religion, so she enrolled herself in a Hebrew school and got a Bat Mitzvah on her own, with no help from her parents. Like Reed, she knew what she wanted, didn't care what anyone else thought of it, and did what was needed to get it.

When we finished our lunch Sabrina and I got back into her car. "I told you about Brendan, so now it's your turn, who is the rose for?" Sabrina, like Reed, was never very subtle. We still had a couple of hours left on the road, it was time I told her about Michelle.

I had never told Sabrina, Reed or anyone else very much about Michelle. She had passed away before I had become friends with either of them. Actually I think I met them both fairly soon after she had passed away. But I hadn't ever told too many people who I knew back then about her either. Very few of my friends had even met her.

I met Michelle during my first attempt at college, and I never saw too many of the people I knew from that period ever again, except Michelle. When I did go to visit her after that, I always went alone. It wasn't like I was going to party.

We went to Hobart College about 30 minutes away from Ithaca. Well I went to Hobart, she went to William Smith. It was basically the same school, Hobart for men, William Smith for women. The only reason they were separate was because men had penises. At least that was what I was told by the school (Hobart, not William Smith) President during orientation.

I thought it was stupid. I had known that I had a penis long before I went to college, but my high school was better than most. At one point I heard that we were separate schools to show that men and women were equal.

I didn't get that at all. All I knew were that Hobart's team colors were purple and orange and William Smith was green and white. It all seemed very much like "Harry Potter and Slythern vs. Griffendor" years before Harry Potter was even written.

Michelle and I would go down to Ithaca on most weekends. I wasn't too happy with the school and she just wanted to get away every weekend. Nothing ever happened between the two of us sexually, but not for my lack of trying. One night, on the way back to school from Ithaca, we stopped at an old yellow barn on a darkened country road.

I had hoped that maybe I was going to get

lucky, instead she told me that she was HIV positive. We both left school shortly after that. Over the years I would go to see her whenever I could. She was in a bad car accident a few years later and never fully recovered. She passed away a few years after the accident. I had not been to Ithaca since the night that she had told me.

"I looked on the map, we aren't going to be too far from the yellow barn," I said as I finished telling Sabrina the story. "I was going to ask you or Reed if I could borrow your car and head out there, tonight or tomorrow, just to leave the rose."

"Yeah, of course you can. If we get there early enough go tonight, or whenever," she answered. I was happy. Leaving the rose and having fun were my only two missions for the whole weekend. It would be nice to get the rose out of the way that night. It was a mission I was dreading, but for some reason, it was one that I felt like I had to get done.

We finally pulled into the Hotel right as the sun was setting. Chris and John were already there, grilling food in the hotel parking lot. Since Reed had set everything up and reserved all of our rooms, we couldn't check in until he got there, and somehow, though we left the diner at the same time, he said he was still at least 20 minutes out of town. He had a smart phone. That's what had kept him.

I had only met Chris's girlfriend, Kerry, once and I had never met John's girlfriend Linda before. They hadn't been dating for very long.

Chris and John were both pretty good friends of Reed and I had gotten to know them pretty well over the years. A few years before, Chris had been dating a different girl named Kerry. The first time I met her, she puked in my car. I didn't like that Kerry too much. It turned out that no one really did. At least I knew Reed and Sabrina didn't like her either.

Then, a few months before the Super Ball, we had all gone to that PNC Arts center in New Jersey for a show. When I heard Chris and Kerry were going to be there, I wasn't very excited to see them. I didn't mind seeing Chris, I always liked Chris, it was Kerry I wasn't excited to see. It turned out to be a very different Kerry. This Kerry was fun and vibrant and sweet. The last Kerry was a complete downer. I liked this Kerry a lot more.

By the time Reed and Sasha showed up, I was downing my second gourmet hot dog. Sabrina was still cooking her first. She didn't think it was ready until it was a crispy, charred black, when most would throw it out as burnt. Reed checked us all in, and gave Sabrina and I our key cards. We made our way to the room on the second floor.

It took us a few swipes of the key card in the lock to open the door, but we got settled in pretty quickly. We had two huge queen sized beds. Like every hotel room, there was a table with two small chairs right next to it by the window. The window only slid open about a foot. Enough to blow the smoke out when we smoked my orange alien pipe to christen the room.

Kleborp, my pipe, was blown by a guy named Down Neck and looked like a one eyed orange alien. Everyone in the hotel was there for the Phish show, we really didn't need to be too sneaky about smoking, but acting sneaky was kind of fun.

After we got settled in, Reed called. Everyone was going to meet up in Chris and John's room. I was dreading going out to find the yellow barn, but I knew that there wouldn't be a better time.

I wasn't sure how far away it was, but I knew it could not have been too far out of town. I wouldn't be gone very long. I got the keys from Sabrina and went down to the car as she went to join the others.

Before I was even two minutes out of town, I knew that I was close. I drove passed a familiar darkened police station that looked like it closed at 5 o'clock every afternoon, and it probably did. Everything came back to me, especially with it being in the dark of night again. Five minutes later I was pulling over and parking at a sign that said "Yellow Barn Road."

I was definitely at the right spot. I pulled into the same rut on the side of the road that I did twenty years earlier. I looked around, but of course the old yellow barn was long gone now.

It had been falling down back then. I had known it was unlikely that it would be standing anymore. I was hoping that maybe a new barn had been put up in it's place, or maybe there was still some trace of it, but it was completely gone.

Instead, there were three long steel buildings with the words "Self Storage" written on them in giant letters. It was funny to me, we were in the middle of nowhere. There was nothing but open space, yet still, there was a need for self storage.

It was disappointing for sure, but I wasn't going to let anything stop me. I had a job to do. I took the rose out of it's Snapple bottle/vase and looked for the best place to put it. There were no markers or any indication of where the barn used to be, or at least not one I could see in the dark. There really wasn't a perfect place to put the rose.

Finally I just lay it on the ground if front of the middle building. I held my head low. I wanted to say, or at least think, a few deep and meaningful words. Nothing came to me, so I just turned around, got back in the car and headed back to the hotel. I needed a drink or two or five.

No tears had come to my eyes. I didn't feel the waves of sadness that I had been expecting at being at that sacred spot, but I did feel better. I turned the radio on and some seventies anthem rocker came on. Before I knew what I was doing I was belting right along. I was grinning from ear to ear.

I had always treated her right when she was still here. I did not need to leave a flower or anything else for her. I had mourned her passing already, but I was glad that I did it anyway. She was a special soul, and that was a special spot. I had to recognize being back in some way. I felt better, but I also felt drained. I hadn't slept well for days, maybe this would help. Plus, now I could concentrate on all of the amazing music I was about to see.

When I got back to the hotel, everyone was in Chris and John's room. I walked in the door, and Sasha immediately handed me a bottle of Jack Daniels. Sasha could always be counted on to have a good strong drink nearby. The long swig I took felt great. I had really needed it. Between the ride up and the trip out to Yellow barn road, I felt drained.

Chris and John's room was right next to Sabrina and mine and it looked exactly the same. The screen in their window was ripped and Linda was half hanging out, smoking a cigarette. That must have been why the windows barely opened. To keep people from jumping out.

Sabrina and I weren't smoking any tobacco in our room, but our screen hadn't been ripped open. If we could half hang out of the window we probably would have smoked in our room, too. Non smoking rooms were just wrong to me, but at least it was summer so we wouldn't freeze our asses off when we went outside.

Sabrina wasn't as big of a Phish fan as the rest of us were. She thought they were OK, but she had only been to one other Phish show. She had been a rave kid back in the day. She liked dance music and pop stuff that the rest of us couldn't stand.

We had been able to get her to go to the Gathering of the Vibes with us, a four day Grateful Dead inspired festival, and she really enjoyed that. Sabrina liked to have fun, and these things were all about fun. It wasn't the same as going to a Phish festival, but it was close.

I felt bad that she was always going to see our favorites, so I had tried to win free tickets to the Jingle Ball for her one year. I didn't know what the Jingle Ball was, but I knew she wanted to go. We kind of owed it to her. I didn't win the tickets, so really we still owe her.

She really enjoyed the scene at Phish shows. She liked the freedom, but also liked laughing at the Wookies and watching all of the crazies running around. So she was there more for the fun of it than the music.

The only song she really liked was Possum and she called it "Awesome Possum," because she was sure that they were singing the word awesome leading up to the Possum. They weren't, but we didn't have the heart to tell her that.

Kerry really liked Phish a lot, at least she had

a blast at the show we went to earlier in the summer. She was the youngest of us, almost 15 younger than me, the oldest of the group. But she didn't give off a kid vibe at all. She seemed very warm and loving. I liked her from the start.

Phish hadn't played a show in Vermont in years, yet they were still considered a Vermont band. That was where they had formed, it was where all of their early shows were. She had grown up in Burlington, the band's hometown, even if not any of the members hometown. I think that would either make you a fan for life, or make you sick of them. Luckily she was a fan.

I knew Chris was a big fan of music. All of it. Even crappy music. Chris just liked music. He liked good music, too. He really liked Phish. What he liked most about them was that they had introduced him to other music.

He got into bluegrass because they played a lot of bluegrass. He got into progressive rock because some of Phish's songs had a real prog rock feel to them. And he got into the Talking Heads because Phish had covered them.

That wasn't true. He got into the Talking Heads because the Talking Heads were so amazing. Although anyone who was a Phish fan and didn't know the Talking Heads, became a Talking Heads fan the minute they learned that Cities and Cross Eyed and Painless were both Talking Heads songs.

Where Chris and Kerry were very lively, energetic and enthusiastic, John was much more mellow, sarcastic and skeptical. It seemed like he had a "better than" story for everything.

The truth was that he had been to a lot of great shows and had done a lot of cool things in his life, but it still came off a little bit smugly. Chris and John had known each other for years, Reed had known them both for awhile, but I really didn't know either of them very well.

A year earlier, Reed had been on Phish tour with both Chris and John. He called me after a few days begging me to meet him in Amherst, Massachusetts. He had already bought me a ticket if I would drive him back home to New York after the show. I was off of work for the night, and he was offering a free Phish show, so I jumped in the car.

I drove for three hours and still got to the parking lot before they did. I was starting to get pissed while I waited for them. I had a crappy old cellphone and had bad reception, so I was afraid that I had missed his call. He was already a half hour late and I was still sitting at our meeting spot.

Ten minutes before the scheduled start of the show, my phone finally rang. He was twenty minutes away. John had made them pull over for a drink at some bar right outside of Amherst. They sat in the bar for hours and now they were stuck in traffic.

Reed had enough. He would have loved to have gone up to see the rest of the shows in Maine, but Chris and John, well, mostly John, were pissing him off too much. He liked John a lot, he really did. That was why he wanted to go home, before he stopped liking him.

Reed was a pot smoker above all else. He wasn't a drinker, and Chris and John were both heavy drinkers. John would even end up buying a beer store. So Reed sold his ticket to Maine for my ticket to Amherst. It worked out well for me. It turned out to be a great show, but of course John had seen better shows, and he told us all about them before

Reed and I jumped in my car and headed back to New York.

John's sarcastic nature could be funny as hell when he was drunk. He could get very mean, but at least he was funny. One night he had me cracked up while he was ripping on every person who walked passed my car. We were waiting for Reed to grab some food after a night out on the town.

But John could be a little bit too much of a downer the rest of the time. For the Super Ball, I would have to give him the benefit of the doubt. I was judging how he was before he had met Linda. I hadn't seen him since they had been together.

I was hoping that maybe if he was happy in a relationship, he would be a little happier with his life in general. It was a lot to ask for, but I hoped so, for all of our sake.

At one point Linda said "Hello." I think that was the most I heard her say the entire weekend. I couldn't really blame her. She didn't know any of us, and we were definitely a weird group of people. I should have given her credit for not just running and hiding from us.

She and John had not been dating for very long, and they spent most of the weekend huddled up whispering to each other. I never really could tell if he was any happier, but he wasn't complaining about everything, at least not to me.

As the weekend wore on, I did hear him complain more and more, but I tried to block him out, and I was usually pretty successful. Most of his complaints came in the form of a joke, At least he was usually funny. It was hard for me to be pissed off when I was laughing.

After we had consumed enough alcohol and

marijuana and we had told enough stories of Phish shows past, it was time for us to all head to bed.

Sabrina didn't drink at all. She never had in the entire time that I had known her. She smoked cigarettes and weed like a human chimney, but she never drank.

For a long time she had been working in bars and restaurants, but never even had a glass of wine at the end of a shift. It might have been watching the drunks around her that convinced her.

It worked out well for us, she was sober after every show we had ever been to, and she could always be counted on to be a designated driver. She didn't mind it either. For a few years she was "less than a legal resident" and didn't have a license, so she didn't drive at all.

It made her a little nuts. Driving was required in Westchester, plain and simple, and she couldn't do it. When she finally got her citizenship and her license, she couldn't wait to drive everywhere.

Reed and Sasha were in a Suite on the third floor, but they were in their room and in bed long before Sabrina and I got in our room right next door to Chris and John. I tried my key card at least twenty times, but the door just would not open at all.

Sabrina, of course, figured that I was just doing it wrong, so she tried with her card. It didn't work, she tried again and again and again. Then she took my card and tried. She looked at me like it was my fault, but I knew it was just general anger.

She was getting frustrated. Not only was the lock not working, but her cellphone hadn't been working either. Her phone was getting no reception. She had yet to call Brendan to tell him she made it safe and sound. She was trying to play it cool, but I could tell she was starting to lose it.

Finally I gave her my cell phone to call Brendan while I made my way to the front desk. My cellphone was just as old and crappy as hers, but at least my carrier worked out in western New York. The woman at the front desk worked some black magic behind the scenes to get the cards to work again. With a suspiciously fake smile, she explained that the locks were getting old. The cards needed to be reprogrammed a lot and she apologized for the inconvenience.

It was a long walk to the front desk and back, but it wasn't really an inconvenience, yet. It would be soon enough though. When I got back to the room, it took a few swipes, but I got in easily enough. I looked out of the window, and could see Sabrina smoking away outside of the back door, still chatting on my phone.

She saw me inside, and eventually came back in. Once she was back, I went out for a smoke of my own. That way she could let me in if the card didn't work again. Of course, since we took precautions this time, it worked perfectly.

Sabrina liked to sleep with the TV on. I usually liked to sleep with a fan or some other type of white noise. It had been a long time since I had slept with a TV or Radio on. I stopped because I would find myself concentrating on the music or the sounds of the show, and then had a hard time falling asleep.

I had always loved music and sound since I was a child. I started playing instruments at a young age, but was always disappointed that I couldn't get the sounds that my musical heroes could get.

I was always very good with writing the music

and playing the notes, but I never really got the concept of tone and sound mixing until I met Al. He was great at mixing all of the instruments together perfectly and adding just the right amounts of the perfect effects. He made my music sound the way it did in my head.

It is always important to have a good sound man. During most of their musical career, Phish had Paul Languedoc. Not only did he work the soundboard, but he also built Trey and Mike their instruments and speaker cabinets. Mike eventually switched to a Modulus Bass, but even Paul Languedoc himself was not surprised by that. He knew that he couldn't build a better bass than Modulus.

Trey would not only stick with a Languedoc guitar, he would get a few new ones, too, including his newest guitar, affectionately named "Ocedoc" after the Ocelot inlay on the head piece.

When Phish broke up in 2004, Languedoc set up shop and began making guitars full time. When they got back together, he decided to stick with his new career as a luthier and passed along the reigns of soundman to Garry Brown. Though the fans were down on him early, the sound at the shows was as good as it ever had been leading up to the Super Ball.

The sound of the TV was annoying, but after the restless night the night before I fell right to sleep. I woke up a few hours later to a woman's high pitched voice, screaming. "No matter what she says, every woman wants a man with a bigger, well... you know." A bikini clad woman was giggling and prancing on the TV in front of me.

It was late enough so that whatever station we

were watching had switched over to infomercials and I remembered suddenly why I never liked going to sleep with the TV on. I got up and turned the TV off. Later on I woke up to the same woman screaming from the TV again, Sabrina must have woken up and turned it back on. This time I just left it on and fell back to sleep.

Destiny Unbound

Friday, July 1, 2011:

I would choose my own religion
Worship my own spirit
But if he ever preached to me
I wouldn't want to hear it
I drop him a forgotten god
languishing in shame
and then if I hit stormy seas
I'd have myself to blame

Sand
Anastasio/Marshall

Chuck Howe

I still vividly remember holding my first Phish CD. It was Picture of Nectar, an album that many Phish fans still say is their best. It was their first release on a major label. They went from being a Vermont band to having a national release and advertising to go with it.

It was their first album to come out on CD. Their self-produced White Tape, and the professionally produced Junta and Lawn Boy had only been available on cassette tape; they would be re-released on CD after Picture of Nectar came out. Fans had been recording all of their shows from very early on, but those were all on tape as well.

The Picture of Nectar album would launch them into the future, but it also paid nice tribute to the past. Nectar's was a bar in Burlington that helped give Phish their start. They would play at Nectar's as often as they could and for as long as they could each night. Many nights were three set shows. Tapes of their third sets were usually hysterical, if not musically the best. Nectar's was where they really formed their sound, their humor and their showmanship.

For the cover, they took a picture of the owner, Frank Nectar, and super imposed it onto an orange. The grainy image would leave the newer fans wondering who it was supposed to be. It could be Einstein or maybe even Hitler? It was really hard to tell, but old school fans knew it was a Picture of Nectar.

With the CD release of Picture of Nectar came

their first appearances on TV. The very first was on MTV back in the days when MTV still had some music. The Real World had already started, but there were still long blocks of music videos and there was still live music, too. In the afternoons there was a show called "Hanging with MTV" which featured a bunch of kids hanging in the studio as the host chatted with a current musical act.

Phish appeared on the show the day that they played at the Roseland Ballroom in New York City. It was their first time playing at one of New York's larger venues. The appearance was mostly short clips of bad interviews where all that they told the studio audience, a mix of Phish fans and club kids who had no idea about Phish, was that they were weird, and they were from Vermont. Finally they would play small clips of them jamming while going into commercials.

There was a clip of Trey and Mike playing while bouncing on trampolines. There was a clip of Fishman playing the vacuum, but there wasn't really anything to tell you what a Phish show was really all about. It wasn't a great appearance, but it was Phish and it was MTV. We were proud of our band, we few Phish Heads of the world. There was a mix of joy and dread that they were being recognized outside of their own world.

That morning, with the TV blaring, Sabrina and I were woken up by Reed pounding on the door. "If you guys want the free breakfast, you'd better get up!" I looked at the clock. It was only 10:00. Even free bacon didn't usually get me up by 10:00, but it was the first day of the festival. We had to get there early so that we could set up our tent in a good spot.

At least now the TV was playing the Daily Show, instead of that crappy late night infomercial.
I let Reed in and looked around for Sasha. She was next door getting the others up. Waking up must have been her idea. Reed was not a morning person either and he would have slept all day if it was left up to him. Sasha worked a regular 9-5 job. 10 AM was a nice late morning to her.
"Did you guys get breakfast yet?" I asked as I turned the TV off and Sabrina started getting up. Sabrina always looked super pissed off when she woke up, but it was a really cute pissed off look.
Reed immediately grabbed Kleborp, packed it and handed it to her. That was the best way to get her to cheer up a little. It was the Purple Kush, my favorite. She sparked it and passed it to me.
"Not yet. We can walk around from the outside if you guys want to smoke your cigs though." We each took another hit from the pipe, but I needed coffee more than anything else. Sabrina and I just threw on robes, grabbed our key cards and smokes and headed out.

The breakfast buffet was a pretty nice spread. Nicer than I had expected. They had all the basics. Pancakes, French toast, waffles and hash browns in the giant Sterno heated trays. They had bagels and cereal.
They had coffee and Juice. They had sausage and bacon. Both kinds of bacon. Real and Canadian. Best of all, the real bacon was actually good. It was nice and crisp, the way it should be.
Everything that I had wanted at the Roscoe Diner the day before, was now in front of me. I started off with the hash browns. They were never

my favorite before, but having been told I couldn't have them the day before made them taste even better. The buffet was the greatest thing ever, or maybe that was just the purple kush.

We took up a big table and it was only then that I noticed other than the 8 of us, everyone else in the room was a senior citizen. We found out later that they gave seniors a plate for really cheap. That made me feel better about the place. At least they did something nice for the community. None of our fellow Phish fans were there. Either they ate early, or didn't understand what free breakfast meant.

Before going back to the room, Sabrina took a bagel and an orange and put them in her robe pocket. It was a good idea, it would be a long day, we could nibble on stuff on the way to Watkins Glen, so I did the same. Then she started loading a napkin full of bacon. A lot of bacon. I gave her a funny look.

"What?" she fired at me. "So I like bacon."

I nodded and followed her lead. We walked back to the room, but of course the key cards didn't work. This time after she had tried for five minutes, I was sure she was doing it wrong. I tried my card and then her card and then mine again.

She handed me her bagel, orange and three pigs worth of bacon and grabbed my key card. "My turn." She said stumbling off to the front desk.

After waiting for a few minutes, I realized I still had my cigars with me. I went outside and smoked away, it was an absolutely beautiful day out. It was nice and sunny, but not too hot or humid.

We had really lucked out with the weather, and it looked like our luck would hold out all weekend. July first and I wasn't sweating balls. I took a deep drag from my cigar and smiled as I exhaled.

Super Ball IX was about to begin, and I was there for it.

Soon Sabrina was in the window waving me up to the room. She was holding both key cards and she didn't look happy when she opened the door for me. "I tried this one twenty times and it never worked. This one worked after ten tries."

I was still in my bathrobe, and wanted to get ready for the show. "OK, let's get ready and hit the road. We'll deal with it when we get back tonight." I was really looking forward to the show, I wanted to get there as soon as possible. Besides, one card worked. We would probably be able to get back in later. Sometimes the cards even worked on the first try.

The drive to Watkins Glen from Ithaca was beautiful. It took about 20 minutes, and we drove passed a Finger Lake, then through some scenic farmland and a few cute small towns. One old town had a beautiful waterfall that seemed to cascade directly behind the town hall. We had to stop and take pictures.

John and Linda had gone with Reed and Sasha. Chris and Kerry were with us in Sabrina's car. We could feel the excitement growing and Kerry kept snapping pictures of everything. We were about to get three solid days of Phish.

The traffic at the racetrack was better than any concert that I had ever been to before. Granted we were getting there very early, but even so, it seemed like we zoomed right in. Part of leaving early was to give us extra time for traffic. The road leading to the racetrack was busy, but everyone was moving. The ride was absolutely painless.

Security pulling in to the venue was very relaxed. We expected a bit more of an inspection, but they just looked in the windows, saw we were somewhat decent and respectable folks and they waved us right in. I couldn't believe that I was actually passing for decent and respectable. They gave Reed's car a little more of an inspection, but he was quickly waved through too.

A map of the Raceway and where the campgrounds and parking lots were going to be, was released online a few days before the festival. Experience had taught me to prepare, so I knew to scout out the layout ahead of time. There were several huge parking lots for people staying and camping. The problem was that once you brought your car in, you were stuck there until the end.

We needed an "in and out" lot. Almost everyone there left their cars alone for the weekend, so they could be parked next to tents without trying to get the cars in and out.

We might take the bus in one day, the hotel did provide free buses, but we thought we would end up driving in most days. We also had Sabrina's huge tent that we planned to set up somewhere as a base of operations. A great place to hang out between sets and we could even stay there overnight if we wanted.

I found the perfect "in and out" parking lot where we could easily set the tent up nearby. We would be in the "Alaska" Campground. Just from studying the map, it looked small enough to be overlooked, but close to all of the action.

You couldn't park your car right next to your tent in Alaska, so even though there was the lot right near it, most people stayed away. We ended up having an almost private camp ground with a beautiful lawn. Occasionally when people walked by we would hear them wondering how much extra we had to pay to camp there. Of course we didn't have to pay anything. We just read the map before we went in.

It took us almost an hour to put the tent up. Sabrina, Kerry, Reed, Chris and I ended up doing all of the work. John just sat there complaining about how hard it was to put up a tent.

He was right, it was a monster of a job. There were two bedrooms, a living room and a front porch. It made our little private camping area look even more officially bad ass. Since it was Sabrina's tent, it became known as Chateau de Goncalves.

Just as we finished putting it up, my phone rang. I didn't recognize the number. Usually I would let it go to voice mail, but I had told a lot of friends on Facebook that I would be there.

"Hey Chuck!" I recognized the voice at the other end even though it was one that I had not heard in almost twenty years. It was Danny LeMaire. I had last seen him when I lived out in Oregon, just before he moved out to Hawaii.

He had moved there with two other friends from high school. One, Tim Kravitz, I had also been good friends with. The third, Sean Trembell, I didn't know very well but I had always liked him. He was an outdoorsy type of guy, like both Tim and Danny.

I could easily picture all three of them out in Hawaii even back when I was in high school. Sean had lived in Oregon when I was out there, only not in Eugene. He lived about an hour away, but I saw him at all the good musical events. And I had once run

Chuck Howe

into Tim at a Jerry Garcia show in Portland, though I have no idea where he was living at the time.
The three of them had formed a band together once they all got out to Hawaii. They played reggae-infused bluegrass and were an immediate hit. Anytime musicians went out to Hawaii, they would end up jamming together.
Bill Kruetzman, former drummer for the Grateful Dead, moved out there and played with them all the time. They even ended up playing with Mike, the bass player from Phish, when he was out there visiting. I kind of hoped that Danny might still have an in with the band, but if not, it was going to be great to hang out with him.

We had been to a whole lot of Phish shows together back in the day. From the Wetlands Preserve to the Roseland Ballroom to The Capitol Theater and beyond. Even before that, Danny and I had been good friends. It was going to be great to see him and rehash some of the old stories again.
The Capitol Theater had been host to some of my all time favorite Phish shows. It was only a twenty minute drive from my hometown, and it was a beautiful old theater where the band obviously enjoyed playing. It was a perfect spot on their rise to the arena circuit. For a couple of years in a row they had played there during the Thanksgiving weekend. I even flew back to New York from Oregon for Thanksgiving one year in part because they were playing at the Capitol Theater.
The balcony used to bounce when they played and it would scare the fuck out of me. If you sat in front and turned and watched it, the center seemed to move up and down about 10 feet. I

almost didn't like taking acid there, thinking about what a bad trip it would be if it collapsed. Even if it didn't collapse, it looked like people might be thrown off at any time. As far as I knew, no one had ever flown off and it held every show.

By their final visit to the Capitol, I had learned the secret. There was a window in the second floor bathroom that was always open. By climbing on the dumpster in back of the theater, and having a friend in the bathroom to help out, you could climb up and into the window. My last two Capitol Theater shows were free, and that only added to the mystique of the venue. Years later, when they reopened, they had gotten wise and the dumpsters had been moved. I checked.

Right near the Capitol Theater was 7 Willow Street. It was really just a large bar, but it was perfect for bands that weren't big enough to fill the Capitol yet. I had seen the Spin Doctors there about one week before they exploded into pop culture. The Wetlands Preserve was where I first saw most of my favorite bands and was the top spot for all music growing up.

The first thing anyone would notice when they walked into the Wetlands, after the little person working security at the door, was the old grandmother style lamps and lampshades. The next thing was the VW Bus parked right in the middle of the floor. There it was, like it was ready to take a bunch of drunk hippies home. It was actually used as the place to buy band and bar merchandise. I think of all the times I looked at the Wetland's T-shirt never thinking to buy one, and how I wish I had one now that the place is gone.

Surrounding the bus was the Wetland's

Activist Center. If the FBI has my name in its files, it all started with the petitions I signed at the Wetland's Activist Center. There were posters up with all the reasons why you shouldn't buy anything from Home Depot or Staples or why you shouldn't buy the New York Times.

Yes, the newspaper that was thought of by conservatives to be the bible of the liberals, was actually boycotted by the most liberal of liberals. Before I left for Oregon, I never really looked at the activist center, after coming back, I always made sure to check it out while I was there. I had to make sure I was hating the right people. I had always been a bit of an activist, but living in Oregon taught me that something could be done to change the world if the right people got to work.

The bar itself was huge, and zigzagged along the back side of the room. There were plenty of spots to jump in to order your drink, so there was never too long of a wait for a bartender. Which was really good because the place got extremely hot, even in the winter. They packed the place and there was no air conditioning at all. I think I even left one or two shows simply because of the heat.

The bartenders were definitely alternative. Even in the days before alternative. They were even alternative to alternative once alternative became mainstream. Whether they were scary looking, sexier, or an odd mixture of both, they were surprisingly good, and quick with your drink. My drink was usually just a Sierra Nevada, but they were so big on the details, that even the coasters were made from recycled materials.

As for the music, that was always top notch. They offered a little bit of everything. It almost didn't matter who was playing, if I was going to the city, I wanted to go to the Wetlands. They always had the best music on any given night. It was always in my top choices of destinations at least.

I somehow lucked my way into shows by Grey Boy All-Stars, Robert Hunter and moe. I didn't go to see them, they just happened to be there. It was a place where I always had fun.

There were certain nights that didn't appeal to me as much. Sunday was the hardcore night, and I usually kept away from that. For awhile my friend Steve was really into bands like Murphy's Law, so I went a few times. The bar looked the same, but it was a completely different place depending on the music.

It seemed strange to see a bunch of hardcore kids moshing under the mural of the hippies dancing in the sunshine. It was high energy, it just wasn't my type of energy.

I had been forced by friends to go down for the Concrete Jungle a few times. I was told that it was always the best DJ around spinning all the hottest music and I later learned it was considered the birthplace of Jungle Music. It was not my thing either, but it was always a fun night, and there were always beautiful half naked women dancing in a really hot room.

I also later learned that Roots hosted the jam night once a week there, years before anyone had any clue who they were. They would bring in some amazing rappers and RnB singers who would later go on to be big stars in their fields, but I really don't know who. That really wasn't my thing either, though I think I was there once or twice when they played.

My favorite night was Dead Central. They had

Grateful Dead cover bands playing all night. Most of those nights ended with a drum circle at sunrise. A lot of guys who would go on to rule the Jam band scene got their start there.

One of the early draws of the Wetlands was that it was usually 18 and over. Everywhere else was 21 and over, and they were starting to crackdown, but I kept going to the Wetlands even as I got older. The downstairs lounge was the real star of the place. There was a small bar down there, and a bunch of couches and big puffy chairs. Everything was covered in tapestries and it seemed like every hippy's college dorm room times ten.

For a few years, "The Inner Sanctum" at the Wetlands made High Times top 10 list of places in America to smoke a joint. It was always the scene of a drum circle on Dead Central nights. Later on they pulled out some of the couches and had bands play down there, too, but it was still the smoking haven.

The last time I was there, I had a friend who had just gotten back into town from Amsterdam. We headed down to The Inner Sanctum with one of his last joints of pure dutch beauty. The couches were gone, but there were still people sitting around in groups on the floor. We found a spot and sat down. He pulled the joint out and was holding it up when a security guard came up behind him and tried to grab it from his hand saying, "Thanks for rolling me a joint, fellows."

We started to laugh, thinking he was kidding. Nobody would actually stop us from smoking a joint in the Inner Sanctum, would they? My friend wasn't laughing, and he wasn't letting go of the joint either. He and the Security guard both held on for a good ten seconds. Finally the security guard snapped at him. "Let it go right now."

He looked right at the security guard and spoke softly, but very determined, "Look, I'm sorry. I thought it was cool. I won't smoke it here, but there is no way in hell you are taking this from me without getting the cops in here." The guard looked at him, looked at us, and decided it just wasn't worth it and let go. That was the only time anyone ever said anything about us smoking in the Wetlands, and we did wait until we left the place to smoke, but we left a lot earlier than we ever had before.

The Wetlands was also a great place to bring the nannies that flooded Westchester county. Whether they were foreigners or from elsewhere in America, it didn't matter because the Wetlands was truly a New York experience. The World Trade Center was the perfect backdrop right as we drove downtown. The bands would usually play until two or three in the morning. We'd head out for food, and just be coming out as the sun started to rise.

A few times I actually did the tourist thing and went all the way down to the world trade center, just so they could take pictures from underneath looking up. If it was late enough, the coffee shop at the foot of one of the towers would be open and I could get an espresso for the ride home.

September 13th and 14th 2001 were supposed to be the last two shows before the Wetlands closed it's doors for good. Bob Weir, from the Grateful Dead, was a great score to be the final act.

On the night of Monday September 10th a mix of guys from some of the great bands of the day were playing together. The jam lasted all night. Mike Gordon was living nearby. He had been part of the jam and was just leaving when he saw the planes hit the World Trade Center. It was so close that the area around the building had to be evacuated for weeks.

The owners of the property allowed the Wetlands to re-open for one night only about a month later. I never heard about it but Robert Hunter, Grateful Dead lyricist played. About a month after that I decided to look and see who was playing there. The minute I saw no listing for the Wetlands, I knew it had closed. It was a surprise that it had stayed open as long as it had. Rumors that the Wetlands was going to close had been circling for ten years. I had hoped the day would never happen.

Danny had been to a lot of those early shows with me, I had almost forgotten that he told me that he was going to be back in New York for the Super Ball, but it was great to hear his voice. "Where are you, dude?" He asked. Danny was kind of a surfer bro back before he had ever gotten on a surf board. Not much had changed.
"We just finished putting up our tent in Alaska, where are you?"
"Hawaii," he said with a pause, then a laugh. "Hawaii, the camp ground, of course. I have a map, you aren't too far, I'll be right over."
Danny had flown into New York from Hawaii, and then took a party bus from Manhattan up to Watkins Glen. It had been years since he was back on the east coast, and he really didn't know anyone else at the Super Ball.
He came just for the music. He was always a very friendly guy, so he must have met plenty of people on the bus, but still, it's always nice to see an

old, familiar face. He hadn't even gone to see his family yet, but there he was at the Phish festival.

As I waited for Danny, a few other groups came by and set up tents, but we all had plenty of room and what seemed like plenty of privacy. Everyone was excited and intermingling and discussing what songs might be played and what surprises might be in store. Reed got a call from a friend who was camped on the opposite side of the raceway, in the North Dakota lot. It turned out that all of the lots were named after states that Phish had yet to play in during their career.

I didn't know the guy they wanted to meet too well, but everyone else did, so they took off. They wanted to check out the ground too, and I didn't blame them, there would be lots of cool stuff to see on the way. I stayed back to wait for Danny. I knew we would be there a long time. I didn't have to rush to see everything on the first day. I had my air mattress, so I worked on blowing that up while I waited for him.

Danny showed up about ten minutes later. He looked just like I remembered him, with only a few years of time added to his face. Hawaii looked like it agreed with him. I couldn't tell if his hair was a lighter blond, or his skin was just a darker tan. It could have just been because it was cut short. I had never seen him with short hair before.

Even growing up in Bedford, Danny had a total surfer vibe to him. In high school we all liked to think of ourselves as Jeff Spicolli, Danny actually was. Now he actually had the surfer pedigree to go with the vibe. I don't know if he actually surfed, but he lived in Hawaii, and that was close enough. He was wearing a Hawaiian shirt and drinking a beer. Also just like I remembered him.

We sat down and immediately got into chatting about old times, and folks we hadn't seen in awhile. Danny told me all about Tim and Sean and their band. I told him about Bob Affeti and other guys from high school that I had seen in the last few years. The list wasn't very long for either of us though.

Instinctively I grabbed Kleborp and packed it up. Back in the day Danny had smoked more than any of us. "Oh man, I haven't done any of that in a long time." He said looking at the pipe. He could see that it was good weed too, not like the crap we had smoked back in high school.

"Oh sorry, I don't have to smoke, I can put it away if you want." I didn't mean to make him uncomfortable or anything, but I started to laugh a bit. I didn't ever remember him once turning down a hit throughout all of high school. We even called him Moon Man, because if you couldn't find Danny, chances were that he was on the moon again.

"No!" He answered a little too fast. "I mean no," a little slower and more composed this time. "That's cool. I'll give it a try." He grabbed the pipe and either took a much bigger hit than he was planning on taking or couldn't hold his weed like he used to, and immediately started to cough his brains out.

He took a sip of his beer, got the coughing under control and then took another hit that was way too big. When he stopped coughing the second hit out, he handed the pipe back to me. "Wow that is good weed. Better than anything out in Hawaii, that's for sure." So he had smoked, just probably not that often anymore.

I was a little surprised to hear about their weed though. I always had a romantic notion about the weed in Hawaii being beyond belief. "Really? Better than Hawaii? I thought Hawaii was supposed to have the best weed in the world. No way this could be better."

"Well, it grows everywhere out there and it is good, but no one takes care of it. They just let it grow wild. Good pot needs some loving too. No one gives it any loving." That was good to know. I knew that what I had was really good, but to hear it from others was always nice. "So when was the last time we actually saw each other?" He asked.

"I think it was in Oregon, back in 1993." I really couldn't remember him coming home since then. "Right after Phish tour. You stayed with us in Eugene before heading out to Hawaii."

"Oh man, I remember now. You lived with Lenny and Rico in that huge house on the mountain." His voice trailed away as he was thinking and then suddenly grew loud again, "Oh my god, that Phish tour was crazy."

It really was, it felt as if I knew every single person who was on that tour. They were either from Eugene or New York. And if they weren't, they were friends of my friends and we got to know each other quickly. "Do you remember when Rico got arrested in Portland?"

I sure did. Rico was a friend of ours from high school who had dropped out and moved out west with Lenny after I had rented a huge house with several other friends. He had been pulled over after the first Portland show with no license, driving a car that wasn't his, and the owner wasn't in the car. He was also speeding, driving down a one way road the wrong way, with his head lights off. Basically he was screwed, but that wasn't the worst of it.

"Did you know he moved back to New York without going back for the court date?" I asked. Danny hadn't heard this part. "Yeah, Five years later he goes back out to Portland to visit a friend. He gets pulled over the very first day he's out there, warrant for his arrest, off to jail."

"Ah man, that sucks. Did he ever get out?" Danny asked.

"I think so," I answered, but I wasn't entirely sure. "Actually, I haven't seen him since, so maybe not. But I didn't see him much before that either."

"If you lived in Oregon, where did you meet up with us, because I remember you at the Arcata show?" Phish had made there way through California before hitting Eugene, Portland, Seattle and Vancouver. I had gone from California up to Portland before heading back home to Eugene.

"Yeah. I met up with you guys in Sacramento for the Gamehendge show." Gamehendge was Trey's Senior project in college. It was basically a concept album, like the Who's Tommy, with lots of narration. The musical saga gave Phish their own mythology to work with.

Characters like the evil King Wilson, the noble Colonel Forbin and the valiant if unintelligent knight, Rutherford the Brave, were all well known to Phish fans. As were the creatures of Gamehendge, like the Unit Monster, the multi-beasts, the famous mockingbird and the spotted stripers.

Almost every song from Gamehendge was a fan favorite, and they would usually play at least one song per show, but a complete telling of the story was very rare. But every now and then they would bust it out for the pleasure of all the die hard fans in the audience. Anytime there was a festival, people were sure that they were going to play Gamehendge. Of course, they hadn't played it in years now, but everyone still expects it. The Sacramento show was the only one I had ever seen.

"I think you were traveling with Sarah and Julia, right?" It was hard to remember, but the more I thought about it, the more it came back to me. "Didn't they jump on the bus with Phish and give you and Rico her truck to follow the bus around?"

"That's right, and I don't even think I had my license either and I know Rico didn't, it was Sarah's truck that he was driving when he got pulled over." Danny was a few years younger than me, but I didn't realize that he hadn't gotten his license until he moved to Hawaii. When we were in high school I used to pick him up and drive him to school every morning, but I was one of the first of my friends to start driving. "Holy shit those were crazy times."

I remembered a funny story from that tour that I didn't ever remember telling Danny. "So at the Eugene show that tour, there was a little rope separating us from the back stage area and I saw Sarah back there. I think you were staying at our place or something, so I called to her and was like, 'Hey, where's Danny?' The next thing I know, I hadn't noticed since he wasn't in his dress, but Fishman must have been standing next to her with his back to me. He turned around and was like 'Danny? I just saw him back there near the keg.' And he pointed to where you were. I thought that was so cool that Fishman not only knew who you were, but where you were."

Danny started cracking up. "That is awesome,

you definitely never told me that one. I have a good story that goes with it, too. The night before that, we were in a hotel in California. Sarah and Julia were there and I was tripping my face off staring into space. Next thing I know Fishman starts fucking with me. He didn't know me at all.

"So he's like 'Why are you here? Who the hell are you?' and I'm all freaking out, not sure of what's going on. He was kind of joking I think, but he was talking about throwing me out of the room.

"I'm freaking out, getting yelled at by Fishman, thinking I'm going to end up sleeping in the truck. The next thing I know Julia jumps up and starts yelling at him to leave me alone. I had been driving them all over, so she was like

'Danny has saved our lives countless times. Danny is the man, you don't talk to Danny like that.' Before I even realize what was going on, Fishman apologizes to me and says he was just messing with me. That's probably the only reason he knew who I was that day."

We sat there for what felt like hours, trading stories back and forth. Every story he remembered reminded me of one I long forgot and that, in turn, brought an old one back to him. I remembered the time he fell off of the roof of a cabin and landed flat on his back. We all thought he was dead, but he just jumped right up and started dancing.

Of course he remembered the time I drove our friend's parent's Maserati into a dry stream bed going at least 100 mph. We had somehow managed to get the car back into the garage in one piece. The next time the father took the car out, flames came out of the dashboard and he had to bail out, thinking the car was about to explode. It didn't and luckily he never figured out it had all been my fault.

By the time Reed and everyone else got back we were rolling in the grass cracking up, and we hadn't even smoked that much weed. Danny had always been a fun guy. It felt great to reconnect.

Danny had never met any of my friends, so I introduced them all. Later, right before we went to go see the show, a guy came out of a nearby tent that I had assumed was empty. He came over to me and shook my hand.

"Dude, you and your friend have some great stories. I was in the tent cracking up the whole time." The guy looked just like Shaggy from Skooby Doo, so that became his name for the rest of the weekend. Shaggy.

Sabrina came back pissed off. Although security wasn't too bad when we came in, going from the camping area to the concert field you had to pass through a check point. They were checking for wristbands, but they were also going through bags and being much more thorough. They found Sabrina's little bundle with her pipe and a small bag of weed in it.

She was lucky, all they did was take it from her. There was still plenty of weed and it was just a small cheap pipe, but she was pissed anyway.

Big Birch was a ski mountain only 30 minutes away from where I lived. Phish once opened for Santana there. The cops were walking around the parking lot busting anyone who they saw drinking a beer or smoking a joint. They grabbed one of my friends for drinking and then they found a tiny bag of weed on him. He never missed any of the show, but he got a ticket, and a big fine when he went to court.

Still the weed Sabrina had lost was the Purple

Kush, the best type we had, so that really sucked. By the second day we learned who's line to go through, and that they checked bags, but they didn't really check pockets. I would go into detail about the best way to sneak weed in, but I want it to still work the next time I go to a festival.

As the day marched on, we started getting psyched for show time. We slowly started making our way to the concert field. Security barely even looked at me as I went through the check point. I couldn't believe they actually searched Sabrina. I was clearly a lot more sketchy than she was. I think the security guard just wanted to check her out a little more for personal reasons.

I had been to plenty of places with horrible security over the years. Phish shows were never as bad as the security was at Grateful Dead shows. My freshman year in high school a kid from the neighboring town was killed by security at Giants Stadium during a Dead show.

Even before that incident, Giants Stadium had been notorious for their bad security. Danny had been beaten up pretty badly by the security guards at Giants Stadium at a Dead show. Giant's Stadium had bad security, it was a given.

I don't know why we kept going. While it was true that Danny had jumped down to the floor, that alone did not warrant such a violent beating. Danny's usually pretty face was bruised and swollen for weeks afterward. It didn't hurt his chances with the ladies at all: now he had their sympathies, even if his smile was a little crooked.

One of my favorite places ever when it came to security was the Luther Burbank Center in Santa

Rosa, California. Phish was not very well known in those days, so they didn't warrant the scrutiny the fans would get in later years.

The Burbank Center was an old church run by elderly volunteers. As I walked in the door, security was a 75 year old man asking me where I was from. When I told him he gasped and turned to the other 75 year old security guard. "This one is from New York!" He turned back to me. "Have a great time please," and I was sent off inside.

They had wine. I want to say that it was free, but I know that it wasn't. It tasted free, maybe because of the relaxed atmosphere. I spent most of the night on the floor, right down in front of the stage.

At one point Phish was playing "Take the A-Train," or one of their jazzier numbers, I danced with the 80 year old lady who was there to keep order on the floor. She did a great job, it was a very well behaved crowd, even if most of the crowd was on mushrooms. It was proof that tripping didn't mean out of control.

There was a small balcony along the back of the venue. At one point I thought it might be cool to look down on the stage in such a small room. I was right, it was cool looking almost directly down on them. There weren't very many people up there and they were all sitting down. There were a few kids smoking weed and a couple making out, and that was about it. The band was jamming, I couldn't help but move, so I started dancing.

An elderly gentleman came up beside me, "Excuse me sir, if you would like to dance, I would encourage you to dance downstairs, the balcony isn't built for it. I'm sorry," the look in his eyes told me that he really was sorry. He wasn't there to bust the kids smoking weed. He was up there to stop us from getting hurt.

He was right too. When I was down below I looked at the supports for the balcony. They could hold the weight, but they wouldn't be able to stand the rhythmic movement of everyone dancing. I imagined the balcony at the Capitol theater. These wooden supports would snap right away.

That was the most hardcore I saw security have to get all night. During the encore, Page did his usual amazing piano solo at the end of the song called The Squirming Coil. Lights had been set up behind the stained glass windows that were directly behind the stage, bathing us all in an amazing psychedelic light show.

At the Super Ball there were people dressed in all sorts of crazy costumes, even though it had been hot all day. The weather had been perfect. Hot, but not too hot. And not a muggy hot either.

Since we were coming up on the Fourth of July, I saw an Uncle Sam and a couple of Ben Franklins. There was even a guy with a shower curtain around him and a shower head hanging over him. I didn't look under the curtain to see what was holding it up. There was always at least one Waldo at a show. On the way in to the Super Ball, we passed three Waldos.

Reed came up to Danny and I and he had a small baggie with several tiny pieces of paper inside of it. Danny was never one to pass up acid back in the day, but the day was twenty years behind us. He politely declined, I enthusiastically accepted. There was no better place to trip than at a Phish festival. I felt safe. I was with my people.

Phish always did a great job of hosting festivals. For the Super Ball they had set up Ball Square, a fake town square that would host all sorts of events over the course of the next three days. It was also where the information booth, first aid booth and a giant disco ball, in case you needed one, were to be found.

True to past Phish festivals, there was a lot of interesting, evolving artwork going on as well. There was an area where people were making their own flags in all sorts of interesting colors and designs. There was also a giant spinning wooden wheel. A man would use giant branding irons and burn cool designs into the wood. It felt like I could watch him work for hours.

There was also a small building with a large wooden wheel in the floor. People would walk on the wheel, while holding on to the side of the building and the wheel would spin. This somehow activated a pump, and people could quickly fill balloons from spouts on the outside of the building.

It was really pretty neat, though seemingly pointless. It turned out that there would be a lot of balloons flying around all weekend, so it may have been wise to automate the blowing up process.

Everything had a "Frontier Days" or Pre-industrial Revolution feel to it. That was not something any of us had expected, but it was cool. With Phish you could never expect anything, because it was going to be different than you thought every time. It didn't matter what they did in the past, today was today. Maybe we would get a lot of bluegrass tunes, or an acoustic set.

They did always try to involve the fans in the show itself as often as they could. Even the average show had a lot of audience interaction. Over the years they tried many different things, some successful, some not.

One of least successful attempts, in my opinion, was the Audience Chess game. For an entire tour, the audience played a giant game of chess with drummer Jon Fishman. One move per show.

Part of my problem with it was that the audience move was chosen at random from fan e-mails. At that point the internet was a huge drain of time to me. I would get on to check e-mails or something, and a half hour later, half of a picture of a naked chick would be loaded onto the screen as I impatiently waited for the rest of it to load.

All tour long, a large chess board would pop up behind the band on stage. The audience move would be announced, Fishman would stare at the board for a few seconds, get on a stool, and move one of his chess pieces.

I never got to see the end, for all I know they never finished playing the game. To me it just seemed like a waste of time where they could be playing music. Plus it was one of those things that you really couldn't even listen to on tape. They may have even done it just to try to get people to stop taping shows, but it didn't work.

We were just getting to the concert field, past Ball Square, when the first notes of Trey's guitar hit. The acid hadn't kicked in yet, but it was about to. Sabrina turned to me with a huge grin. She didn't know much about Phish, but she knew they were opening with Awesome Possum. We all ran to find a good spot on the lawn.

Even though it was one of their more commonly played songs, I thought that Possum was a great choice to kick things off. It got the whole band warmed up and grooving together right off the bat. It gave Trey a chance to shred, Mike a chance to sing, and Fish and Page had to work hard to keep up the tempo. It got everyone going.

For those who didn't like Possum, it was a blessing as well. The band got Possum out of the way early. There was no avoiding it, everyone knew that they were going to play Possum at some point over the weekend anyway. Better early than as the encore the last night.

The next song they played was Frank Zappa's Peaches en Regalia, so Sasha was super happy too. It was her favorite cover that Phish played. She was a bigger Zappa fan than she was a Phish fan. It was as if Phish wanted to set the super good vibe tone early.

We somehow lost Danny on our way in. I don't know how or when it happened, but that's what goes on at festivals and shows. People sometimes got lost. Most of the time they reappear eventually. Most of the time.

He was a veteran of many shows. He would be fine, and he knew where our tent was and what my cell phone number was. Danny was a big boy. There was no need to worry about him.

The band was on fire from the start. Both the song selection and their playing were great. They were playing crowd favorites like NICU and Moma Dance, but they were also giving us rare covers like the Rolling Stones Torn and Frayed and Life on Mars? by David Bowie, a song I had first heard them play at the Clifford Ball.

They had started playing it the day that Bill Clinton announced that a meteorite from Mars showed signs of past bacterial life on Mars. They were great at modifying their show on a whim to fit the mood of the day.

As the show went on it started to get darker, and all of my friends all started to disappear. Soon there was no one I recognized around me. Thanks to the acid, it never occurred to me that I could have been the only one who was lost. That was fine though, I was a veteran of a lot of shows myself. I was sure I'd find people at the set break.

The music was kicking ass, and the acid was kicking in just right. I could sense that the first set was close to ending, so I made my way to the back of the field. Oddly enough, without even really looking for anyone I ran into Chris and Kerry. Soon Reed, Sabrina and Sasha were there too, appearing as if by magic.

At the very back end of the field was the Ferris Wheel. After playing one song, Trey asked the whole crowd to turn around and wave to the guy up top. Of course we did. Trey joked about how the guy should jump, and then immediately realized what a mistake that could have been.

The crowd really did listen to him. You never knew how seriously the fans would take what he said and he knew it. He saved himself, and the guy at the top of the Ferris Wheel, by saying at the next festival they will blow up giant air mattresses so that people could jump off.

As it got dark, I wanted nothing more than to go on the Ferris Wheel. Everyone else seemed to want to go as well. Everyone, except for Sabrina. She was terrified of heights. I had forgotten all about

that because I was tripping. Before anyone realized
it, Reed had bought tickets for us all. That was the
type of thing Reed did.
"No way!" Sabrina immediately protested.
"There is no way! I'm not going on that Ferris Wheel!"
Sabrina yelled over the music. The set was finally
coming to an end. Most of the people waiting on line
wanted to ride while the band was still playing, so
they left the line leaving us next to board.
First Reed and Sasha got on. Then John and
Linda. Our turn was coming up quick. Sabrina
pushed Chris and Kerry in front of us. I saw the
camera she always carried with her and got an idea.
"Think of the great pictures you could get. Come on,"
I grabbed her arm and got her in the basket before
she could really protest much more.
In all honestly, I thought that she would be fine
once we got started. She was usually a pretty tough
chick, but as the wheel spun and we climbed higher,
I could tell she was deeply frightened. She would
gasp each time we would stop to let more people on.
I tried to get her mind off of it. I pointed out things for
her to take pictures of off in the distance.
Her knuckles were turning white as she
clutched the hand rail. But by the end of the ride she
almost seemed comfortable. "There, that wasn't so
bad, was it?" I asked as the ride ended and we got
off.
"Oh hell yeah it was," she exclaimed,
smacking me on the arm just a little too hard for it to
be considered playfully. "I am never doing that shit
again!" Her eyes shot bullets straight into my head.
I thought that she would have been fine. I had
forgotten, part of the problem was that she was on
acid. What Sabrina really wanted was Ecstasy, and

there was never any of it around any more. I always kept my eyes and ears open for it even though it wasn't my thing. I knew that she wanted it no matter what. There was always the Molly powder around. Molly was one of the ingredients of Ecstasy, but Sabrina was an old-school rave girl. She liked her Ecstasy.

Finally right before the set break ended she got a text from a friend of hers who was there. He had something for her, or so it seemed. It was hard to tell, he was apparently pretty fucked up himself. He was going to meet her at the Disco Ball in Ball Square, that much she knew for sure.

On the way there, we passed a giant building that had a sign that said "Self Storage USA" on it. I took that as a very weird sign. It was made to look as if boxes were falling out of the place, but they were kind of built into the doorways. They were covered with brown paper and people had been writing things all over it. Mostly names,and where they were from, but there were some cool doodles too.

One small corner of the building was open, and there were several people dressed in what looked almost like Steampunk ringmaster garb standing all around. They kept pointing to a steel door, begging us to enter and see the future. A bunch of us lined up haphazardly. Sabrina kept going to meet her friend but Reed and Sasha were right behind me on line.

When the lead Ringmaster opened the huge door, a group of people came stumbling out looking dazed and bewildered. Someone in front of me asked a guy coming out what was inside. The guy just stared at him with a blank expression and then gave a small smile. "It's cool man," was all that he had to say.

The lead ringmaster started grabbing people at random and throwing them into the door. He grabbed me and stuffed me into a cramped room filled with smelly hippies. He then closed the door behind me with Reed and Sasha still on the other side, although I didn't realize it at first.

I couldn't even call it a room, it was more like a closet with 15 of us packed inside. The floor was completely uneven and sloped towards the back of the room at a very awkward angle. The ceiling sloped to a different corner at a different angle. It kept everyone completely off balance.

The very instant that the door closed, people started pulling out pipes and joints and lit them up. I didn't know anyone in the box with me. I had weed, and a bowl, but I was tripping hard, and with everyone else in there, I felt like I couldn't reach my pockets, but soon a bowl was shoved in my mouth, too. It wasn't bad weed, but it wasn't great weed either. I took the hit anyway. Soon enough, the air was thick and heavy with all kinds of thick and heavy pot smoke.

Suddenly there were strange noises and lights all around us. The room felt like it was spinning. All of our senses were under attack. A tiny movie was projected onto the door. We had to strain to see it, and even though I was up front, I could barely make it out.

There were shots of cells dividing. Time lapse shots of flowers growing and all sorts of craziness. Between the noise and lights and sloped floor and colors and smoke, I had no idea what was happening. The LSD didn't help the situation either.

The freakiest part was that I knew exactly

what they were doing to me. These were all CIA tricks. They were throwing us off balance, literally and mentally. It scared me a little, but everyone else in there was just smoking away and enjoying themselves, so I did, too. Before it was over, I did announce nice and loud, "Well, now that the FBI has us on tape, I guess none of us is running for office."

When the movie stopped, the door flew open and a bright white light came flooding in, blinding us. It was night time, but there must have been a light pointing right at us. Things just didn't look right.

We all came stumbling out, off balance and stunned by the sensory overload. The ringmaster had to help a few people steady themselves as they tried to exit. Everyone was just looking around, unsure of what just happened and disoriented.

When we went into the room, I thought the line was to the left of the door, but when we came out, the line was to the right. I never found out whether they moved or if I was just thrown off. I didn't see Reed or Sasha outside because the ringmaster had already pushed them in for the next show.

As I was waiting for them, a guy came up to the group of people who were behind me in the box. "How was it? What happened in there? What is it all about?" I think one of his friends was the person who put the pipe in my mouth. They must have thought I was their friend the entire time we were inside.

"You were there!" the friend kept insisting.

"No I wasn't, man. What happened in there?"

"Dude, you were totally there," the friend insisted again. I could tell that they were both fucked up and would never be able to hash this out, so I turned to the guy who wasn't in the box with us.

"We went to the future, dude. You were there.

Don't worry, you were doing fine." It was all that I could think to say to him.

He was really worried about what was in the box. He was too afraid to go look for himself. It was my random act of kindness for the day.

The guy just kind of smiled at me and then walked away with his friends. I could swear he had a bounce in his step. I was glad I was able to give him a little peace of mind. If he happened to walk in front of a bus later that day, I would have felt really bad, but I didn't tell him how far into the future we went.

I kept my eye on the door, to see if the room moved at all. Of course it didn't, and the line stayed on the same side of the door, too. It had all been perception.

Reed and Sasha came out a few minutes later, looking as disoriented as I must have looked a little while before.

"Wasn't that cool?" I asked

"Umm," replied Reed. "I have no idea what that was." He was blinking rapidly.

"Did everyone light up the second the door closed?" I asked already expecting the answer to be yes. To me it was a no-brainer. I figured everybody who went in there had smoked. That was probably part of why they built it.

"No man, why didn't we think of that? That would have been cool." Why didn't Reed think of that? I figured that would have been the first thing Reed thought of. But it was very interesting to see how everyone who went in the box had a different experience, but they were all strange. It was the perfect little side attraction to a Phish show, and almost a microcosm of the festival itself.

We found Sabrina, sitting on the grass near the Disco Ball, with her friend. He didn't have any ecstasy. No one at the entire festival did. He had a lot of Molly with him though. He was obviously already on a whole lot of it, too. He handed Sabrina the bag and then stumbled away right as the second set started. We searched but couldn't find him anywhere. It was like he had simply disappeared.

We figured that he must have meant to give us the whole bag. We tried it out. We had to. If someone hands you a bag of drugs and disappears, the polite thing to do is to sample the drugs. Molly wasn't one of my normal drugs. I had only tried it once. I was at one of Trey's solo band shows at the PNC arts Center in New Jersey.

I went with a guy I didn't know very well and two girls I didn't know at all. That trip was the last time I had eaten at McDonald's. I didn't want to, but when you are in a car with people who all want to stop at McDonald's, you get what you can because you don't know if you are going to stop again. I got the Chicken Sandwich. It sounded better than a burger. It wasn't.

One of the two girls had just had surgery on her foot and was given all sorts of pain killers. She was freely passing them out the moment I got in the car. By the end of the night I had no idea what I was on or what was causing me to feel what. All I remembered was that it was a fun night.

I rubbed some of the molly on my gums, It tasted like chemicals. I couldn't say that I knew how her friend's Molly stood up to any other Molly, but to me it felt good, and I really enjoyed the rest of the night.

We never found the guy, or Danny again that

night. I wasn't worried about Danny, he could take care of himself. The other guy was wasted and alone. I hoped he would find his way to where he needed to be, but he was a big boy. He'd have to do it himself. The other guy however, was fucked up. I didn't know him, but if he was a friend of Sabrina's I hoped for the best for him.

To me the second set that night felt like one long jam. I always liked when the second set worked out that way. At first we weren't even sure the set started. We heard weird noises and laughs as we made our way through Ball Square. It was the band, and a cool little jam led into the Talking Head's song Cross Eyed and Painless, that kicked the set off right. The first night really did bode very well for the rest of the weekend. The band was firing on all cylinders.

One of my favorite new characters was there, Stick Figure Guy. The first time I remember seeing him was at the Amherst show, where I had met Reed. Stick Figure Guy lined his clothes with glow sticks or lights of some kind. For the last few years I had seen him at every show. Surprisingly, no one ever copied him, at least they hadn't yet, but he made a great point of reference if you were sending a text to a friend. "I'm right behind Stick Figure Guy!" were the best directions you could give at a packed show.

One of the stand out songs from the night was Simple. Some nights it was played quick and straight forward, other nights it would work as launch pad for a nice long jam. Night one of Super Ball was one of those jammed out ones.

Simple was one of those Phish songs that had

ridiculous lyrics. They ended up devolving into nonsensical sounds by the end of the song, "Cymbop and Bebophone, Skyballs and Saxscrapers." While the lyrics to Simple were nonsense, many Phish songs had great lyrics, and most of those with great lyrics were thanks to Tom Marshall.

Tom Marshall is to Phish what Robert Hunter was to the Grateful Dead. Tom went to high school with Trey and co-wrote some of Trey's earliest songs. After Trey left for college and started playing with Phish, legend has it that he sent Tom a copy of the album Junta and Tom immediately offered to help start writing songs with Trey again.

He thought songs like "Dinner and a Movie" whose only lyrics were "Let's go out to dinner and see a movie," and David Bowie, whose only lyrics were "David Bowie" and "UB40" were sub par at best. It worked, because the lyrics from then on were much better. Even the songs written by others were better, because Tom Marshall had set the bar that much higher.

So the band was all set musically, and with Tom they were set lyrically. A lot of their songs even got pretty deep. Not Simple, of course. Although Simple was great in it's own right. The genius was in the music, not the lyrics.

The light show at a Phish concert was always top notch. Chris Kuroda was the best there was at what he did, and what he did was awesome. The ever evolving light show that has dazed and confused fans for years is all controlled and designed by one guy. Industry wide, he is recognized as a master.

When Phish wasn't touring, he designed and did the light for Areosmith, the Black Crowes, R.

Kelly and even Justin Beiber. He learned something new from each artist and then brought it back to Phish. He was always improving and always impressing.

Many acts have computer programmed light shows. That couldn't work with a band like Phish. They play the same song at a different tempo and play different jams each night. To run his lights right, Chris Kuroda would jam live with the band. That led to the nickname CK5, because CK was the fifth member of the band.

Much like the band itself, CK5 would master a lighting set up, and then start from scratch with a completely different set up the next year. At the Super Ball he had three giant circles surrounded by lights above the band. He was getting really good at the projections he was creating using only light. A year or two earlier, there had just been one circle. Evolving, CK5 always strived to be better.

When the show ended, I was with Sabrina, Reed and Sasha and we couldn't find anyone else. They knew where we were camped though. They should be able to find us no matter how wasted they might be. We had to go back through Ball Square to get back to the tent and car, we thought that we might even run into them on the way.

Near the Self Storage building, a group of horn players that I recognized were just warming up. The Primate Fiasco had played at the Gathering of the Vibes the summer before and, for me, they were the unexpected highlight of the weekend.

They called themselves psychedelic dixie-land and that is exactly what they were. There was a banjo player, a drummer and about 4 horn players. This time they had Christmas lights strung up around their instruments.

At the Gathering of the Vibes, they would lead parades around Seaside Park and kick things off every day. You might find them playing anywhere, at any given time. I became a fan from the first note. When I saw that they were jamming away at the Super Ball, I pulled out my camera and started taking pictures.

They were standing out in the open, in the middle of the square, jamming away with people walking all around them. I got really close and started snapping pictures with a little disposable camera.

I was sure that I was annoying and bothering them, but when I posted the pictures on facebook a few days after the festival, the banjo played loved them and tagged every member of the band. I may have been annoying at the time, but he was glad to have the pictures to show for it.

We stuck around for a few songs, then I noticed that Sarina, Reed and Sasha were heading back to camp. I could have stayed, but I got my pictures, and now that I knew they were there, I was sure I would catch the Primate Fiasco again. I quickly caught up with everyone before we hit the bridge covering the track.

In the first parking lot we passed a guy selling nitrous balloons and I couldn't resist, or rather, I didn't even try to resist. Nitrous was a tricky thing at Phish shows. It was what security was really looking for the most, which caused the sellers, who were already assholes, to become bigger assholes. It was the type of thing I normally wouldn't do out of principle, but it was a lot of fun.

I took a hit and called Bob. Sabrina was

cracking up after I screamed "Butt Licker!" into my phone at top volume. Of course my head was spinning so I almost fell over. After taking the hit I remembered that the last time I had done it, I had fallen over.

Luckily Sabrina was there this time. She may have been a tiny girl, but somehow she caught me and steadied me. After I hung up, I noticed she was looking at my phone. I knew she wanted to call Brendan, so I gave it to her. We were just getting to the tent, and the rest of the group was already there. She moved off, away from us and gave him a call.

There was the typical buzz of a first night of shows. Everyone was excited for what they had heard, and what we might still hear. John and Chris were popping open beers, and Shaggy even joined us for a bit before heading off to his tent. There was no sign of Danny, but his tent was set up in the Hawaii lot, so he was probably there.

When we got back to the hotel, everyone was having problems with the key cards. Chris and I took ours down to the front desk and there was already a line of people waiting. Every one of them needed their key cards to be reset.

We got to the front of the line and both clerks looked exhausted. They did their black magic with the cards and we made our way back to our rooms. Chris got into his room no problem. Sabrina and I took considerably longer. We both took turns with both cards, but we did finally get in.

That night we were smart and went out to smoke in shifts. This way one person could let the other one in if the card didn't work. The cards did not work even once for the rest of the night, but we didn't get locked out.

    Once again we fell asleep with the TV on, this time to the Dave Chappelle Show. That was not a bad thing. He was a funny guy and I liked his show. The problem was that this time I woke up to horrible xylophone music and young women screaming about how much they loved Girls Gone Wild.

    Then they would woo really loud. They always wooed. I hated the woo, even when it was accompanied by tits. But on late night infomercials the tits were censored, so it sucked even more.

    I was still tripping a little and I couldn't fall back asleep. I threw on the shorts I had been wearing all day, even though I could see the dust coming off of them when I picked them up, and grabbed my cigars. As I was leaving I wanted to jam the door with something so that I could get back in. Reaching into my pockets after a trip was always an adventure.

    I have no idea why, but I become a collector when I trip. Anything that gets into my hands goes into my pockets. I found plenty of used napkins. I threw them away before I left. There were singles and other bills that never made it into my wallet. I never took care of my cash when I tripped.

    There were a couple of small bags of weed, because I probably kept thinking I was going to need weed and couldn't find any in my pockets while I was tripping, so I would grab another small bag. My wallet and several lighters. They stayed in my pocket. I was going to need them. I found the butt of one of my cigars. Just the birchwood tip. I didn't know why I had kept it, it was smoked down to the wood.

    I had several fliers of bands who would be

playing all over the northeast over the next couple of months. People always handed you cards at shows, for another show that you would never want to travel for.

I was just about to use one of the postcard fliers when I found a matchbook. I stuck it in the door to keep it from locking as I left. I certainly didn't want to have to wake Sabrina up, or go to the front desk to recharge my card just to get back into the room.

I thought that Phish had gotten off to a great start but I know that Phish fans liked to over analyze everything. I was sure that people were complaining about the show online. They complained about everything online, they especially complained about not being at the show.

There were websites that could tell you every song that Trey teased in guitar solos for the last 20 years. I had to admit, I got caught up in that stuff, too. I would catch a little bit of Oye Como Va, or Third Stone From the Sun in one of the solos, and then when I got home I would check the website to see if it was credited. Half the time the song that I had heard was uncredited, but there were three or four other teases that I somehow missed.

Phish fans also loved to make up terminology, like teases. They liked coming up with categories, too. This lead to the phrases "Jam Type," Type I," and "Type II." These terms become confusing, even to die hard Phish heads.

Eventually I would come to understand that a Type I jam stays within the key and time signature of the original song. The easy way to look at it is, if you came into a song during a Type I jam, you would still know what song was playing. So you might think to yourself, "This is a great Chalkdust Torture Jam."

A Type II Jam leaves the structure of the song behind completely. The best Type II jams are long and change key and time signature a few times during the jam. When you walk into a room with a Type II Jam playing, you have no idea what song it is, and you may never find out. After a type II jam, Phish loved to leave a song "unfinished."

Phish had already given us both Type I and Type II jamming. I couldn't wait to hear what else they had in store for us. There were still lots of songs with a lot of room for jams that they could unleash on us.

The funniest thing about Phish was how everyone thought of them as simply an improvisational band. With their type I and II jams it was easy to see why. It was true, they were masters at it, but some of their longest and most loved tunes were fully composed. Trey wrote Divided Sky and You Enjoy Myself as traditional classical compositions.

Another thing Phish fans liked to do was to assign an MVP for each show. They were one of the few bands that could be taken over by any member on any given night. Usually they all played well. Most shows the idea of an MVP was subjective, but there were some shows that were obviously taken over by one band member. On the first night, Bass player Michael Gordon was my vote for MVP. It could have really gone to anyone, it wasn't a clear cut victory, but Mike was playing great and seemed to be singing most of the songs. He had come a long long way since I first started going to see Phish.

Back at my earliest shows, I always

remembered him in a black bowlers hat, like the one from Clockwork Orange. Sometimes he would wear bright neon pants. If not for the fact that the drummer was in a dress, he would be considered the worst dressed guy on stage. In the early years, it seemed like he was the weakest musician in the band. Not to say he wasn't good. He was always better than most bass players in other bands, but the guys in Phish were all amazing. He had to work hard to keep up, but he managed to do it.

He really improved during the band's five year break up. He started playing with his own band, and when Phish came back together he took more of a leadership role than he had in the past. His playing was now almost perfect, every night. He still let his bad fashion sense get the better of him on occasion. But now it would only be a scarf or neon shoes instead of an entire ridiculously bad outfit.

I always enjoyed his vocals, though he wasn't technically the best singer in the band. He usually sang the low bass parts, but he also could do a decent falsetto. The songs he wrote were a little strange and quirky. The covers he liked seem to range from blues to blue grass, to R and B.

As a bass player, he could always get funky with the best of them. In recent years he started busting out a bass synth pedal that gave him some super funkiness. He was usually very selective about when he used it, but it always caused a huge reaction in the crowd when he did.

I was happy to have my band back. When they originally broke up in 2004, no one thought they would ever get back together again. Phish was finished. Each member started their own career, and though all of their individual bands were good, they never captured the same spirit as Phish.

Guitarist Trey Anastasio not only had his own great band, but he also had hooked up with Les Claypool, bassist of Primus, and Stewart Copeland, the drummer for the Police, to start the Super Group Oyesterhead. Fishman played with the Jazz Mandolin Project and Page hooked up with the New Orleans band, the Meters.

Trey's own project, the Trey Anastasio Band had been around even before the break up. Many newer Phish songs got their start with Trey's solo band. It featured horn players that had appeared with Phish throughout the years, but the best addition to the Phish Phamily would come in the form of a trumpet player named Jen Hartswick.

Trey found someone who he trusted to create horn arraignments for his songs. And Jen was not only a writer and trumpet player, but she could sing with soul. She soon became the reason to go see a Trey show.

The problem was that Trey himself was not very happy, or at least he was projecting a troubled soul. I had seen his band open up for the Black Crowes at Madison Square Garden. Trey played his set and sounded great, but the whole time he had a strange look on his face.

The look said "This is my building, and I am opening for another band." He came out and played with the Crowes at Midnight, but it was not the same.

Drug addiction, part of what caused the strain and eventual break up of Phish, had taken a firm hold of him. One late night in upstate New York, Trey was pulled over. He was high and in possession of drugs.

He was arrested and went before New York's

drug court. He eventually got the help that he needed and he came out of it in much better shape mentally than he had been in years. He even thanked the policeman who had pulled him over for saving his marriage and his life.

Mike seemed to make the most out of his time away from Phish. One of his earliest projects was an album and tour with guitar virtuoso Leo Kottke. Working one on one with a master gave him an extreme amount of confidence.

Soon after, he put together his own band. He even got Scott Muranski, who Mike was a huge fan of back in the early days of Phish, to play guitar for him. Scott was the guitar player for Max Creek, the band that was supposed to be "the next Grateful Dead" in the 80's. Phish even used to cover their song Back Porch Boogie.

Mike also soon discovered two guys who called themselves the Benevento/Rousso duo, a drum/piano combo that was almost a complete band unto themselves.

Eventually Trey would join with them and Mike for a tour where they called themselves GRAB. It wasn't exactly Phish, but it was as close as anyone had come since the break up. Drummer Joe Russo would eventually join Bob Wier and Phil Lesh of the Grateful Dead as drummer of their band Furthur.

Then, one fine day, the four former members of Phish found themselves at the wedding of former stage manager, Brad Sands. At one point in the night, using the wedding band's instruments and equipment, Phish reunited for a brief set of their classics. The wheels began to spin.

Several months later it was announced that Phish would reunite for a three show run at the famed Hampton County Coliseum. It was a venue that already had a great history between Phish and the Grateful Dead. It was affectionately referred to by Phish fans as "The Mothership" due to it's strong resemblance to a UFO. The three shows in Hampton were great. So good that Phish offered them as free downloads. The boys were back, and they were better than ever. Soon, an album and a tour were planned.

I went outside and lit my cigar. It was my favorite time of the day. It was just starting to get light out, but there was still at least a half hour before the sun came up. I started walking without thinking about where I was going and I ended up on the main road. I wanted to go somewhere, and get something but I didn't know where to go or what to get. I could see an open convenience store down the street so I started walking toward it.

It was a lot further away than it looked when I started my walk. By the time I got there I was hungry as hell. I opened the door and was assaulted by the florescent lights and an 80's power ballad coming through the blown store speakers, neither lights nor song were particularly welcome while tripping. I already regretted walking in the door, but the buffet at the hotel wouldn't be open for at least an hour. Plus, the store had donuts and the buffet didn't. So I bought the donuts and juice. I was convinced that all I really needed in the world was donuts and juice.

The donuts sucked. I would have preferred Dunkin Donuts or Krispy Cream or even Entemans. These were the type of donuts that are tiny and come in a pack of ten and were probably made a couple of months ago in some far off factory. They come covered in either powdered sugar or chocolate. I bought the chocolate.

I started my walk back and immediately regretted my decision. The chocolate had melted and re-solidified a few times already in the young summer, I should have known to get the powdered ones. I took a big swig of the juice. It was supposed to be an orange mango pineapple blend of heaven.

It was horrible too. I didn't know if I was still tripping or if it was the worst juice ever. I looked at the label and it was only 10 percent juice. The only thing worse than fake fruit flavor was fake exotic fruit flavor. Damn those people at the Corn Syrup Beverage Corporation. They tricked a dude tripping on acid again. Those assholes.

Saturday July 2, 2011:

And if the moment passes
You should try it once again
For if you do it right
You'll find the moment never ends

Scents and Subtle Sounds
Anastasio/Marshall/Hermann

Chuck Howe

Waking up in a hotel room was far from the strangest place I had ever woken up in after a Phish show. At least I remembered falling asleep there. After one New Year's show I had woken up in bed with a girl I had never seen before in my life. That was a first. I normally wasn't a big drinker at shows, but that time I had been. It wouldn't have been too weird, except that Clockwork Orange was blasting on the TV. She made me breakfast, and I was parked right outside of her place. So it all worked out for the best.

One morning after the show in Santa Rosa, I woke up under a tree looking out over the Pacific Ocean. That was really nice. Even if I was covered in dew and bug bites, the view was amazing. There were several nights during that west coast tour that I woke up at a stranger's house. I had stayed with my friend Lea outside of San Francisco for a few nights. But I know I spent one night in San Francisco at a party and slept there, without knowing a single person in the place. The same thing happened in Santa Cruz.

Once, right near Ithaca, I had woken up on the floor of a strange dorm room. That was the same tour I was woken up with news that Kurt Cobain shot himself in the head with a shotgun. "Is he all right?" I asked, still not entirely awake.

Now, waking up once again in Ithaca, I felt bad for Reed. He was the one who really pushed for us to come up to the Festival. He reserved the rooms for all of us and made sure everyone had tickets. He made sure we all got the days off of work and that we were all able to get up there. Yet he failed to take into account Sasha's 90 year old great aunt.

Sasha's whole family was gathering at her Aunt Gertrude's house in New Jersey. I got the impression that she didn't get along with most of her family. Aunt Gertrude was Sasha's favorite relative, so she told Reed they should be there. He agreed, before realizing that it was the same weekend as the Super Ball. Reed, being the good boyfriend he was, set his alarm and was on the road before the rest of us were even thinking about getting out of bed.

Sabrina and I had almost missed out on breakfast again. Luckily for us, this time Kerry banged on our door loud enough to wake me up as they came back from eating. I was grateful that she was looking out for us. I really needed food and Sabrina and I had both forgotten to set an alarm.

I still had the fake juice and shitty donuts taste in my mouth. My stomach was tossing and turning with a mix of acid and the late night snack, but I was a heavy sleeper, so it probably wouldn't have gotten me up. Sabrina and I were both late sleepers, so we would have probably missed half the show if Kerry hadn't woken us up.

We rushed down to the buffet as fast as we could. I devoured as much of the pancakes, eggs and bacon as humanly possible, all the while chugging down cup after cup of coffee. The acid from the day before had been very clean, I wasn't hurting at all, but I was hungry and tired. The coffee was shitty, but it had caffeine in it, so the shitty coffee was perfect. I was almost recovered from the "juice" and donuts.

Reed had given me a baggie with a few more

hits of acid in case Sabrina or I decided that we wanted to trip at the show, but we both decided against it. Sabrina still had that huge bag of Molly from her friend, too. She had texted him, at least she could text on her phone. She wasn't sure if he meant for the whole bag to be for her and she would prefer to get it back to him, but he wasn't responding.

Danny hadn't texted or called either. I had wanted to let him know it was OK to crash in our tent if he wanted to, but he had disappeared. Both Sabrina and I were getting texts from other people, so we knew that there was a connection.

Danny had his own small tent, but we had the air mattresses. That made a huge difference when sleeping outside. Danny was a tough guy though, and he was used to camping out, even from our childhood. I was sure he was fine.

Phish was scheduled to play three sets that day, the other days were only two set days. I wanted to get back to the racetrack as soon as we possibly could. Once we finished our food, and loaded up on our pocket foods, we made our way back to the room. It was a miracle. Sabrina's card worked on the very first swipe. The day looked like it was going to be a good one from the start.

We jumped in the car and made our way back to Watkins Glen. Chris, Kerry, John and Linda all took the bus, wanting to get there super early for some reason. We wouldn't have all fit in Sabrina's car anyway, and they all wanted to drink and not worry about driving.

As we were pulling into the Raceway, I got a text from Danny. He had just finished running in the Runaway Jim 5K, a festival tradition. I still felt shattered from the night before. I couldn't imagine doing a 5K run. I let him know that we would be there soon, and to met us at the tent.

"So, what is Danny's deal," Sabrina asked. "He got really, really flirty with me at one point last night. It wasn't sleazy or anything, but it was kind of weird."

Danny LeMaire was a year younger than me, but in high school we were hanging out with the same group of people and got to be pretty good friends. Danny was always a smart kid. A lot smarter than he ever let on. He played the dumb, cute blond really well, almost to the point of the rest of us hating him because all of the girls loved him. But he was such a nice, happy guy that in the end you really couldn't hate him.

When he was staying with me out in Oregon, the second I saw the girl I was crushing on start to look at him, I told him it was time to pay rent or hit the road. He hit the road, and jumped on a plane. That was when he moved to Hawaii.

Happy go lucky was the perfect description for him. It seemed like nothing would get him down and because of that everything went his way. He was bullet proof, almost literally.

He fell off of some crazy things when we were younger. The roof of a cabin, a cliff, a few trees and probably a lot more that I didn't witness. A few of the falls I was sure would result in hospitalization, but every single time he would pop right back up as if nothing had happened.

"I'm sure that he would love to get you into bed if he could, but I don't think he needs to, if you know what I mean. Danny just loves the world, and likes to share his love." I answered as honestly as I could. "He always has. I don't think he ever means to hurt or freak anyone out. He's just Danny."

"Yeah, he was kind of funny. I just told him to quit it, he said OK, and then went on dancing and acting like nothing had happened." If Sabrina hadn't just started a relationship, I would have told her to go for it. Danny was physically pretty much her type. I didn't want to get involved in any of that though.

"Yeah, that's the way he is." As we were talking I got another text from Danny. He ran into someone. He'd meet us after the first set. Yeah, that was just the way that Danny was. Danny was an odd cat. He was a hippie in the Me generation. I didn't know where he got it.

His father was a former Marine. He was also a cub scout leader and that may have been where Danny got his love of the outdoors, but he went a very different direction than his father probably hoped he would. I had never met his father, and who knows, maybe he was a Marine turned hippie, but that was probably not where Danny's attitude toward life came from.

I had never met his mother either, but I had met his brother. Greg looked just like Danny, but he had been a complete jock in high school. He was a few years younger than Danny, so I never really hung out with him, but I got the impression that he was a bit more of what you might expect of the son of a Marine.

By the time we got to the tent, everyone else was already gone. I hadn't really explored the lot scene the day before, and Sabrina was more about exploring than she was about the music, so we went to find "Shakedown Street," the main area of

117

commerce in the parking lot of any show.

Everything, legal or otherwise, could be found on Shakedown Street. T-shirts, beers, chicken wraps, weed, pipes, kind Brownies, dresses, Molly, LSD, mushrooms, posters, tapestries, smoothies, jewelery, and just about anything else if you hung around long enough and listened carefully. The only thing we couldn't find was some real Ecstasy.

At most shows Shakedown occupied a small area at one end of the parking lot, usually pretty close to the entry of the venue. Festivals attracted all sorts of vendors, so Shakedown at the Super Ball was much longer than at the usual show. Everyone had something to sell, and everyone wanted to sell it on shakedown. We could explore it for hours.

What first grabbed my attention was the Mojito stand. It wasn't really a stand. More like the back of a station wagon with jars with rum and various fruits, vegetables and herbs steeping in them. I wasn't a huge drinker, and it was still fairly early in the day, but it was already getting hot and I was on vacation. They didn't look like regular Mojitos either.

There were cucumbers and limes and things other than just mint floating in the jars that made it look even more refreshing, not to mention there was a super hot chick pouring them. And so the Mojito won as my first purchase of the day on Shakedown Street. It would definitely not be the last.

Most people could go all day eating nothing but junk food at a Phish festival, but not me. I would usually eat better than I did when I was at home, if you didn't count convenience store donuts and fake juice. There were all sorts of good chicken wraps, and veggie burritos to be found, and even my Mojito had cucumber in it.

Destiny Unbound

When I was home my drinks never had a cucumber in them. You could always find just about anything you were in the mood for. In past years I had sold Bagels and Cream Cheese or Grilled Cheeses at shows, these days there were gourmet meals.

The show started, and though there was an exodus from Shakedown to the concert field. Plenty of people kept walking around checking out the goods and working in the booths. Sabrina was not there for the music, so she was in no rush.

They were broadcasting the show on the radio, so everyone in the lot was playing it. I heard every note. I was happy, and in no rush to go stand in a huge crowd in the hot sun either. There was still plenty of music to be heard.

There were a few large screens set up in random places through out the grounds showing what was happening on stage. It was really pretty cool. When the band wasn't playing, they had all sorts of other things on the screens.

One afternoon there was a Yankee game on. They were playing the Mets, a big game for New Yorkers, even way out in western New York. There were a whole bunch of people sitting in the grass, watching a baseball game. Some were rooting for the Yankees, some the Mets, and some were just watching a good game while sitting with friends, out in the sun. It was awesome.

At night, after Phish finished playing, they would have concert movies playing as people left the concert field. The first night they played the Talking Head's movie "Stop Making Sense," which was made even better since Phish had played Cross-eyed and Painless that night, too. There was plenty of entertainment everywhere you turned.

We were able to hear and see most of the set even though we weren't actually at the concert field, and the sound was great. We just explored around the perimeter. Anything with lights, or that glowed in the dark caught Sabrina's eye. She got all excited talking about how she was going to put lights into her clothing for the next festival.

Sabrina loved to dress up for festivals. She had three different outfits with her for the three different sets. For the daytime sunshine set she was wearing her bikini top and long white skirt. The skirt would be black on the bottom before she switched to her evening set outfit. She always got a lot of stares, whether it was because of the glow sticks in her clothes or her bikini top.

At the Gathering of the Vibes she was in her bikini top and jean shorts when she decided to go roller blading. I had my banjo with me, so I taught her two chords and sent her on her way, roller blading and banjo playing. For the rest of the weekend I heard tales of the hottie roller blading around, who was some sort of banjo master. I assumed that they meant, but I really hoped that they didn't, mean Sabrina.

Because of the acid I had taken the day before, and then adding the coffee and mojito in the morning, I was getting pretty dehydrated. Luckily there was a smoothie booth nearby. At a festival there is always a smoothie booth nearby. I drank two before we made it back to the concert field. The fruit was like an energy shot. I perked right up.

The biggest difference between the modern Phish festival, and the old outdoor show/party days, other than sheer size, was a lack of dogs. I hadn't noticed a single dog at the Super Ball. In the old days there were dogs everywhere. Phish even credited Trey's dog, Marley, as the head of security on their first few albums. Everyone knows that there is no better security than a golden retriever.

Every tape I had of the early days had dogs barking in the background. Usually it was Marley, and Trey would sing to him until he stopped, but most often there would be other dogs there to egg him on and he'd start up again during the next song.

Marley even starred in the only video that Phish had ever made. The song was Down With Disease, and the video was directed by Mike Gordon. It featured every cliché of a Phish show you could think of.

They all dove into a fish tank, Fishman using the Electrolux vacuum that he often played on stage, as Scuba gear of course. Poor Marley got pulled into the fish tank with them. He was even featured lip synching the chorus, barking out "Stop!" over and over. Marley passed away in the early 2000's, and with him went an entire era of Phish.

The only splash that the video had made with the MTV crowd was on Beavis and Butt-Head. They declared Phish to be cool, because fish poop where they swim. Phish-Heads could live with that assessment. The great Cornholio had spoken.

On the way back to the concert field , we found the hammocks. There were a whole bunch of them and almost no one hanging out in them. We jumped on the chance. As we lay in our hammocks, people with Hula Hoops and Devil Sticks and all sorts of fun toys went by. You couldn't really use those things in the concert field, but there was plenty

121

of room out here on the perimeter of the action.

Even during the show, there was a lot of activity going on in Ball Square. People started hanging the flags that were being made the day before on clothes lines stretching from building to building in Ball Square. There were hundreds upon hundreds of them. They seemed to come from nowhere. They were brightly colored and very psychedelic for the most part.

In just a few minutes, Ball Square went from looking almost Colonial to looking like it came out of a Dr Seuss book. There was always something new to check out at Ball Square. Even places where you thought you had already seen everything the day before, a trademark of a good Phish Festival.

We caught the end of the set from the hammocks. Surprisingly, they ended it with the Rolling Stones song Monkey Man. As far as I knew they had never played it before. Though I had never been a huge Rolling Stones fan, it was one of my favorite Stones songs. The hammock only made it sound even better.

Keyboard player, Page MacConnell, took care of the vocals on that one. To me, he was the heart of the band. The band relied on his performance show after show. He was the ultimate musician. For a band that was thought of by many to get by on the searing guitar solos, Page was highly influential in their sound.

One of the great things about Page was his abilities on all of the keyboards at his disposal. He was just as good on Piano as he was on the Organ, Clavinet or Moog. Lately he had been playing the hell out of a Rhodes electric piano, too. Just by changing instruments, he could completely change the feel of a song.

He had an amazing piano solo at the end of the song Squirming Coil. He played a great Clavinet in Moma Dance. His electric piano in No Quarter was unbelievable. He could flat out play any instrument with keys. He even busted out a Keytar on the rare Frankenstein.

He also had arguably the best voice in the band. He could be a little inconsistent at times, but he would usually make up for any flubs with amazing keyboard playing. There were a few nights that he just didn't have it vocally, but when he did, he was the best of the best.

For the song Lawn Boy, he would get out from behind the piano and give his best crooner impersonation. After belting out Monkey Man, I had to give Page the MVP of the set. As the set closed, Sabrina and I made our way back to Chateau Goncalves.

Everyone else, including Danny, was there by the time we got back. "Hey Danny, how did you do in the 5k?" I asked. Everyone turned and looked at him in shock. We had all been partying hard, it seemed strange to do something like run a race, but Danny was a Hawaiian surfer dude now. He had to get his exercise in.

They had all sorts of great events going on, the Runaway Jim 5k was just one of them. That had become a tradition though, and somehow it raised money for Phish's charity, The Mockingbird Foundation. I wasn't sure how, maybe they charged for admission. Even though there was one at every festival Phish had done, I had never even considered it before.

There were plenty of other things to do, too.

Every morning when we arrived, there was a large group doing yoga to Phish music. Most people passed by without even looking over, but the guy leading the event was trying to pull anyone who even looked over into doing it.

Most of the participants were beginners, following what the leader was doing. I didn't know Yoga very well, but it looked like they were doing fairly easy stuff. Of course there were also people who knew what they were doing, and they were doing their own exercises. One woman was on her head for a good 15 minutes straight. It was all set to great Phish jams from concerts past.

They also had a Bocci tournament, a Wiffle Ball tournament and a Kick Ball tournament, all on a field that had a big sign that simply read "Balls!" They were really playing up the whole "Ball" theme. If I had any motivation whatsoever, I would have signed us up for the wiffle ball tournament. That was the one sport that I could play.

There was even a bar set up that looked like a giant pinball game. The tables were the bouncers and flippers. I think that was where John and Linda were whenever we couldn't find them. I only went in once, and I kept waiting for a giant silver ball to come in and cause havoc on the place.

"Well, I finished it," Danny said with a smile. I had no idea how far 5k was. I was pretty sure it meant 5 times the distance to the moon and back, so I was pretty impressed. "But they probably won't be calling me up on stage to give me a trophy or anything." The winners from all the different age groups usually were called up at one point during the festival.

John had made sandwiches for and was

passing them out to all of us. They were absolutely delicious. John had won lots of points with me with all of his food. I really didn't know him very well before, and he kind of pissed me off a little when he couldn't help with the tent. Everyone has their own talent. He was OK. If he kept making sandwiches like that, I would deal with the tent myself.

He even had a choice of sandwiches, and they were good, too. No Oscar Meyer bologna and cheese here. I hadn't had any, but he also brought some really good beers. If I did want one I was sure he'd gladly give it to me. When all was said and done, John was a good guy. Linda still hadn't really said or done a thing yet, but I didn't dislike her at all.

Chris and Kerry had been having a great time. They loved the music and were just soaking in the scene. They were already pretty hammered though, I didn't know how they would survive two more sets. I couldn't drink like that anymore, if I even ever could.

The second set that day was actually the first set that I got to see with Danny. We had worked our way back to the field just before the music started. It was just Danny, Sabrina and I, somehow we had lost all of the others. It must have been when we had walked past the pinball bar.

We found a good, open spot and sat down. I rolled a couple of joints of Purple Kush. We had all sorts of good pot with us, but the Purple Kush was the best of it and we didn't have a whole lot left. That was one reason Sabrina was so pissed that security had taken some from her the day before.

It was always nice to have a few joints rolled ahead of time. It was harder to roll when the band was playing, the lights were flashing and everyone was dancing. Plus, there was no bad time for a joint of Purple Kush.

Once I finished rolling, we decided to try to work our way through the crowd and get closer to the stage. Sometimes I didn't like the feeling of being trapped up front in a huge crowd, but for one set it wouldn't bother me. Plus, I wasn't tripping, so I would be OK.

We made our way a whole lot closer than I had been yet that weekend, but we were still far enough back where we weren't getting crushed. We even had some room to sit if we really wanted to. These days you always had to check to make sure there were no kids nearby. Kids were going to see some crazy shit, but no need to smoke a joint right in front of them if it could be helped.

The set started with Runaway Jim, the song that the 5k was named after. It was always a nice fun upbeat song and always a good choice to begin a set. The Jam in the middle could end up going just about anywhere. It was usually a rhythmic bass jam that would kick it off, and while most versions only lasted ten minutes at the most, the song had been known to take off into crazy long Type II jams.

A version played in Worchester once lasted a full hour, still Phish's longest official song to date. This time the jam was very simple, and Trey took the time to announce the winners and have them come up on stage to get their trophies. Of course Danny wasn't called up. They also called up the winners of the wiffle ball and Bocci tournaments. Trophies were handed out while Mike kept the groove going.

I lit the first joint. The Purple Kush wasn't the strongest weed in the world, but it still kicked serious ass. The best part of Purple Kush was the taste. It tasted like candy. We passed the joint between us, and to a few of the people around us who seemed interested. There were always people nearby who were interested. When we finished I pulled my cigars out of my pocket and a baggie fell out.

I reached down and grabbed it. It was a pretty large bag of one of the lesser buds that we had. Even though I wasn't tripping, the residual effects were still going on. My pockets were over loaded with crap. I was glad it was the lesser bud, I wouldn't want to lose the Purple...

Suddenly I had a horrible feeling. I pulled everything out of my pockets. There was a ton of crap. I found a few more smaller baggies of weed, but not the Purple. It must have fallen out of my pocket, or still been in my lap, when we got up before.

"I think I may have lost the purple," I hesitantly said to Sabrina. It was her favorite and she had already lost hers. I was afraid that she might punch me.

"Stay right here." She hissed at me with her patented "How have you not yet died of stupid?" look, and she made her way back into the crowd. I wasn't worried about running out of weed, but I really didn't want to be responsible for losing the last of the Purple. I thought we had some back at the hotel, but I wasn't entirely sure.

A few minutes later, I was worried that she still wasn't back. I tried to stop thinking about it and just dance to the music, but I kept glancing back to see if Sabrina was coming. There wasn't much I could do.

At least I had a few joints left. I would have to savor them, or better yet, give them to Sabrina for use at her discretion. Danny gave me his sympathy.

He had just met her but he could tell, Sabrina was probably not a person that a smart man wanted to piss off.

Just as I was sure that she was never coming back, she popped up in front of us, with a huge smile and the baggie of Purple Kush in her hand. "It was easier to find the baggie than it was to find my way back to you guys."

I couldn't believe it, I was sure that it was gone for good. I pulled out another joint and lit it up. Now that I knew we had the rest back, I could enjoy what I had rolled. I had once again narrowly avoided death by an angry European woman.

It ended up being the perfect set for Danny and I to see together. They played a lot of tunes from the era when we first started going to shows. They were playing the more familiar songs, but then one tune started that stumped both Danny and I. Sabrina was no help, not that I expected her to be one.

The song sounded familiar. It was definitely something rare. The bass was funky, with a klezmer feel to it. Finally, when Trey started singing, I recognized it as Scents and Subtle sounds, a song from the Undermind album. It was the album that came out right before they had broken up, and not one I had listened to very much. It reminded me of the break up. After the festival, I would give the album another try. Now, knowing that the band was back, it was a much better listen then it had been.

Everything else they played was recognizable and common, but they were playing well and having fun with the tunes. There was even an instant when we heard Trey make a scratching noise with his pick on the guitar strings. We both instinctively raised our hands in the air and yelled "Aw Fuck!!!"

Sabrina, and a few others nearby, looked at us funny. It was part of a secret language that Phish had introduced to their fans years ago. They had several different signals, the "aw fuck" was supposed to be yelled as if we "just cut our finger."

Many used to think that it may have been a dig at Jerry Garcia and his missing finger. He was still alive when they started doing it, but I don't think it was aimed at him at all. It was just a fun thing to get the crowd to do.

The most obvious and longest lasting signal was the Simpson's Theme. Every time they played it, the crowd was supposed to yell out "D'oh!" My personal favorite was the "We all Fall Down" signal. When they played that, the whole crowd would drop to the ground.

The idea was that most of the people would be Phish fans and would know what was going on, but those who didn't would just be standing there. Then for no reason at all, everyone around them would just fall to the floor, or turn and wave to the sound man, or yell out a random note. The first time it happened around me, it freaked me out.

It was a perfect day, being at the show with Sabrina and Danny. One was a good old friend and the other, a good new one. I hadn't taken any acid since the day before, but we were smoking a lot of weed, even more than usual.

At one point Danny just seemed to disappear. I knew he was right next to me a second before, but then he was gone. Just like that. There was someone else standing and dancing next to me.

I turned to Sabrina, "Where's Danny?"

"What?" She yelled back above the music.

"Danny, Where did he go?" I yelled back.

She pointed to the guy standing next to me, who just seconds before was definitely not Danny. Suddenly, as I was looking at him, his face began to morph and he turned into Danny right in front of my eyes. It was the strangest thing I had ever seen. I knew it had to do with the acid from the day before, but it still threw me for a loop.

I told Danny what had just happened. He just laughed at me. "Same old Chuck."

He had a point. The West Coast tour of 93 had a few of those moments, but none was stranger than what had happened to me at the Santa Cruz Civic Center. Much like that day at the Super Ball, I had tripped the night before, but that night I had stayed clean, except for the weed. That time it was some of the best mushrooms I had ever had in my life.

During the first set that night, I made my way right to the front of the stage. It was easier in those days. The room was half empty. Trey had started a guitar solo and I saw his face morph into Eric Clapton's face. The two of them look a little bit alike, but in my mind he completely turned into Eric Clapton. Only when the solo ended did he turn back into Trey.

Understandably, that had freaked me out, so I went and took a seat in the back of the arena. Unfortunately my legs still wanted to dance, so they ran off and left me, unable to go anywhere until they came back. Luckily they weren't gone for very long. I swore off drugs right then and there. That vow only lasted until later that night, when someone offered me a Valium to help me sleep.

Meanwhile, Phish was giving us one hell of a

set. They were not even halfway through, but I thought it was their best festival yet. Of course I had only been to one other one live.

When they played It's Ice, it reminded me of the show at Big Birch, in Patterson, almost 20 years before. Big Birch was a ski mountain, or hill or "Big Bump" as we called it, not too far away from my house. They had a stage set up at the bottom of the bunny slope in the summer and for a few years they pulled in some good bands.

Phish had opened for Santana a few years before, but that night they had the bunny slope to themselves. During the first set that night, my friend Steve and I decided to hike around a bit on the trails. It was still light out and it was perfect early summer weather.

The music sounded great no matter where on the hill you were. It felt like we were hiking in the woods with the worlds best stereo in our back packs. We were hiking on what were the ski trails in the winter, that cut across the mountain.

At one point we came to a tree that looked right down the center trail to the stage area. We got the idea that it would be cool to climb the tree and watch the show from up there. We weren't the only ones with that idea.

Right before we started to climb, we noticed that all of the best branches were already taken, there were at least twenty people up in the tree already. So we hiked down the trail a bit more and took a seat on what looked like a jump in the winter. Phish was playing It's Ice and it felt perfect. As they hit the long instrumental jam, Steve started doing his own Trey style narration.

"The ice splits open and swallows you whole.

As you sink down you see some bright lights sparkling in the distance. Your air is running out, but you swim for the lights anyway; as you get close you discover that your body is changing. You are now a fish and can breath under water. The lights are coming from the great fish city.

"Suddenly you are surrounded by sharks, and the sharks capture you and take you before the King of Great Fish City, but the King isn't a fish at all, he's an octopus with a great big white beard. He wraps all eight arms around you and pulls you close.

"You think he is going to bite you, but no, he gives you a big, sloppy kiss and congratulates you. He wants you to marry the beautiful Fish Princess. You say yes because you don't have the heart to tell him that you don't want to marry a fish, even though you are now a fish, too.

So the King cheers and everyone cheers and everyone has a great big party." The jam ended right as he finished the story. I never heard the song It's Ice the same way since.

Big Birch wasn't the first show I had seen with Steve, but it was the first show that he didn't get kicked out of for trying to steal drinks. That was at the Roseland Ballroom in New York City several years earlier. I still felt bad for that one, not only did I get to see that whole show, but I got to enjoy my stolen drink while watching the show. We went on to see a few other shows together over the years, enough to make up for that one missed show.

Watkins Glen was turning into the perfect Phish weekend. Police and security, despite what Sabrina thought, had been great at keeping order without being too harsh. That was always important for a good festival. I had learned that the Gathering of the Vibes gave out security jobs as a bonus to the best security guards in the state.

There were a lot of memories that it brought back, but it was also fresh and new. It was its own experience. That was something that Phish always did well. Be new, be exciting, but don't forget what got you here. They were also good at leaving you wanting more, but fulfilled at the same time.

As the sun was setting, I turned and looked behind me. The sky was an amazing swirl of colors behind the Ferris Wheel. I pulled out my disposable camera and took a picture. The girl behind me jokingly starting posing as if I were taking a picture of her, so I took a picture of her.

"I hope you don't mind if I tell everyone on Facebook that we hooked up this weekend." I jokingly yelled to her. She smiled, laughed and just kept dancing. I don't think she heard me, but I took it as permission to post the picture on Facebook, and to tell everyone I hooked up with her. Luckily for her, they came out like crap. It was a disposable camera.

When the set ended, we started making our way back to the tent. We passed by Primate Fiasco once again, this time playing a battle of the bands with the What? Cheer Brigade. We had to stick around for a little while to check them out, both bands were playing great and they drew in a huge crowd. I had never heard the What? Cheer Brigade before, but they were good. Like Primate Fiasco, with a bit more of a marching band feel.

All through the weekend, there was a good chance of running into either band. They were both fun and both good, but this was the first time we had caught them playing together.

Once again Sabrina asked to use my phone. Hers didn't even pretend to work any more, and now she wasn't even getting any texts. I felt bad for Brendan. Here he was with a brand new girlfriend, and she goes off with some other guys to a music festival, sharing a hotel room with one of them no less. I probably wouldn't have liked it too much if a girl I was dating did that. Letting her use my phone to call him was my way of offering some sort of peace of mind to him.

I realized that we hadn't seen our neighbor Shaggy at all since the first day. His tent looked dark. I called out his name, but there was no answer. He was probably just out enjoying the festival. I didn't need to worry about him yet, but I did want to keep it in mind. Festivals and other places with camping were always a little scary. You never knew what was going on in a closed tent.

At the Gathering of the Vibes, Sabrina watched paramedics take a girl out of her tent and try to do CPR to her. Apparently she had overdosed, and no one knew for awhile because she was in a nice quiet tent at a festival. The guy that she was with tried doing CPR himself, but they were on an air mattress. That girl had died. I really hoped Shaggy was OK.

After a 10 minute call, Sabrina handed me back the phone. Either the phone call hadn't gone well, or two days of music and massive amounts of LSD and Molly were starting to catch up to her, but Sabrina was done for the day. She crawled onto the air mattress in the tent and passed out. That was exactly why we had brought the tent.

Reed and Sasha sent a text. They were

almost back. Reed must have been driving like a mad man. I felt bad that they had missed the whole day, but at least they would get to see some music.

Phish had a scheduled third set for the night, and there were rumors flying around that they were going to play a secret late night set at Ball Square. Rumors were never to be trusted entirely, but they did have a long standing tradition of doing late night secret sets during festivals. Something big was going to go down, we could all feel it, but no one knew exactly what was in store.

As we headed back to the field, I heard the beginning of Golden Age, It was one of the most recent songs that they covered. It was originally by a band called TV on the Radio. I had wanted to hear it live since Phish had first played it two years earlier. I finally got my Golden Age and, as hoped, it led into a huge type II jam. The whole set was amazing. They played a lot of their best jam vehicles, like Piper, Tweezer, Twist, and the always fun Harry Hood.

Harry Hood was the perfect example to give when someone asked about Phish and their music. It was never on a studio album, yet everyone knew it. It's always a long song, that was the way it was written. There are well defined segments of the song, yet there is a lot of room for improvisation throughout. It is one of their older and more commonly played songs, yet remains fresh with many interesting versions still to come.

The lyrics, written before the return of Tom Marshall, were nonsensical, or at least had that appearance on the surface. Phish fans with tell you Harry is milk in the fridge. "Where do you go when the lights go out?" The music gives us an instrumental story of the milk's journey once the refrigerator door is shut. "You could feel good about Hood," was the motto of the Hood Dairy that was across the street from the house where Trey and Fish lived in Burlington when the song was written.

"Thank you Mr Minor" were the words written on mail for a former resident. Somehow for Phish fans, all of that together became a reasonable explanation for their lyrics. I still didn't get it though. The music was a deep reggae infused groove, and I got that.

They also threw in a few crowd pleasing covers, like the song known as both 2001 and Also Sprach Zarathustra. It was originally a classical tune by Wagner, reworked by a Brazilian keyboard player, Deodato, and then reworked again by Phish. It was always a fun jam. The crowd also loved it whenever they played anything by the Beatles.

Phish had a great tradition of putting on musical costumes for Halloween. This meant that they would play an entire album, beginning to end. Over the years we were treated to Talking Heads Remain in the Light, The Rolling Stones Exile on Main Street, Velvet Underground's Revolver and Little Feat's Waiting for Columbus. But in 1994 it all started in Glens Falls, New York with the Beatles White Album.

I had never been a big Beatles fan, but I am smart enough to know that they were a great band that wrote some amazing tunes. Phish always had a lot of fun with the Beatles, and this time they gave us a great version of A Day in the Life. When they were done, everyone was hanging out waiting for something to happen.

I wanted to call Bob and leave him my regular

post-show message, but I really didn't want to suck down any nitrous. I had been abusing my body enough all weekend and my head was already spinning. I called him anyway, and at the beep I left him a fake nitrous scream.

It felt dirty and wrong. I didn't like it and I never did it again. I did nitrous again, I just never called Bob after a Phish show. I think Bob may have appreciated it. He's never said anything about missing it though.

Chris, John and their girlfriends took the bus back to the hotel. They had been drinking and it had been a long day.

Reed and Sasha had a really long day already, but they had only seen one set of music. They were ready for more. I was there for the music. There was nowhere else I would rather be.

I went back and checked on Sabrina in the tent. She was still fast asleep and in no rush to go anywhere, So Danny, Reed, Sasha and I made our way back to Ball Square. It was the only place we could think to go, and a bunch of others had the same idea.

There were speakers set up in Ball Square that were playing all sorts of weird noises. Something was coming. Everyone was sure of it. Suddenly a voice came over the sound system announcing that the late night festivities would be starting shortly in Ball Square. We were all looking around. There was no sign of the band. Just people, milling about everywhere. Looking as confused as we were. Where would the band be?

Everyone just assumed they would end up on the top of one of the buildings right in the middle of Ball Square, but I didn't think that looked right. The drum set and other equipment had to be set up somewhere, and I didn't see anything like that on any of the rooftops.

Flags were draped everywhere. It added to the confusion. I was pretty sure that there were fog machines too, but it could have just been my foggy mind. I kept looking around for a spot. Not the Ferris Wheel, not the giant disco ball.

"Where would I pop up if I were Phish?" I asked myself and immediately saw the answer. I was sure they would be at the one building that had been almost completely unused all weekend.

It was the one at the very edge of Ball Square. The one completely in the dark. It simply had the words "Self Storage USA" written on it. There had been too many coincidences already. There was no one there. Everyone was huddled into the center of Ball Square. Every fiber of my being was telling me that Self Storage USA was where they would be.

I pulled everyone over to the building, even though, like everyone else there, they were sure the band would pop up somewhere else. Reed knew that I understood the band well enough to get what they were up to. He trusted my gut when it came to Phish. As soon as I pointed it out, Danny smiled and nodded. If the two old timer's said that was where they were going to be, that's where Reed was going.

Suddenly there were some very psychedelic trance like sounds filling the air. We knew it was the band, but no one could tell where it was coming from. There were lights flashing all over the square. The lights would highlight one roof, the crowd would all flow in that direction. But the spotlight would shine on one building, and then another and the crowd would follow.

I could tell Reed really wanted to follow the lights too, but he resisted. I was proud of him, Reed didn't often resist impulse. When the doors on the "Self Storage" building began to open, I knew we were in the right spot. Reed had been rewarded for his restraint.

There was some sort of thin semi transparent cloth covering the doors, but lights from inside showed the silhouettes of each member of the band. They did a crazy weird jam for about an hour before taking it into a spooky slow version of their song Sleeping Monkey. It's normally a pretty straightforward song, with its moment of humor when Fish takes a vocal solo.

It was the only time I ever remembered hearing intelligible lyrics during one of the secrets sets. They were normal just ambient jams When the music finally came to an end, the doors to the self storage building closed without fanfare. The secret set was over, but it had been the best one yet.

When we got back to the tent, Sabrina was wide awake. She had figured that we were all back at the hotel and that we had left her there, until she heard the music start. Then she knew we were still there somewhere. I had told her about the chances of a secret set on the way up, so it wasn't a complete surprise to her. Sasha and Reed already being back from their ten hour trip was a surprise though.

I offered Danny the option of coming back to the hotel with us, or sleeping in Sabrina's tent on the air mattress. There was plenty of room both places. He decided on the air mattress.

It had been a really long day for me, and Danny had run a 5k on top of that. He needed sleep right then and there and knew that we still had a 20 minute drive back to the hotel, so I didn't blame him. He was fast asleep before we even got in the car.

When we got back to the hotel, the key cards wouldn't work at all. It was my turn, so I went down to the front desk. Even though it was late, Sabrina took my phone and went outside with her cigarettes to give Brendan a call. She insisted Brendan would fit right in with us, he was a night owl, too. If he was still awake, then she might be right about that.

During the long walk to the front desk I didn't pass anyone else trying to get into their own locked rooms, but I was sure it was happening all over the hotel. At least I kind of hoped that we weren't the only ones that had to deal with it. It was late, maybe most people hadn't stayed for the secret set. Chris, Kelly, John and Linda were passed out already. We had tried to knock when we came in.

"Hey, the cards aren't working again," I said as I handed them to the guy behind the desk. He was alone and had just gotten off the phone with someone who was obviously pissed. He looked flustered, I felt bad for him, but Sabrina and I had been trying for five minutes with each of them, and neither key card would unlock our door. I just wanted to get into my room and shower. I had a full day of Festival dirt covering me.

He looked like he knew what I needed before I even said it, so I knew that we couldn't be the only ones having trouble. The woman the day before had told me the locks were getting old and that it was just starting to happen all over the building. The building looked like it was built in the seventies and hadn't been updated since. I was surprised that they had cards instead of keys to begin with.

Destiny Unbound

Something told me that the hotel was usually
not very busy either. It was three floors, and each
floor had multiple wings, but it was at the very
furthest edge of town. As far from all the colleges as
you could get and still be in Ithaca. It was the
cheapest package deal that Phish offered, but
considering we were spending most of our time at
the festival, it wasn't a bad deal.

Reed had made all the arrangements. Reed
always made all the arrangements and he was
usually pretty good at it. He had never been to Ithaca
before, so he couldn't have known. As far as I knew,
he had no problem with his key card though.

The brine shrimp swimming in the puddles in
the parking lot out back should have been the first
hint that they usually didn't fill the whole building. Of
course the key cards weren't working. They probably
hadn't been used since parents weekend the fall
before.

The guy behind the counter didn't look like
your typical behind the counter at a hotel type of guy,
even for the overnight shift. When we checked in,
there was a man and a women in matching dark blue
blazers manning the desk.

They had been very neat and perfect with
their smiles. This guy was wearing a wife-beater t-
shirt and a Pittsburgh Pirates cap. Both of his arms
were covered in tattoos. I liked him more than those
plastic people right away, but he definitely looked out
of place behind the desk.

He took my cards and did some black magic
below the desk. Hopefully that would get me back
into my room again. "Man I hope this works," he said
as he handed me the cards back. I did a noticeable
double take. He confirmed my suspicions, "Sorry,

141

Chuck Howe

people have been having problems all night, and I've never worked the front desk before."

"Really? How did you get stuck doing this alone, on a Saturday night, during a music festival," I asked. It was definitely not the nicest hotel in town, but you would think they would have been a little better prepared for a sold out weekend, maybe the only one all summer.

"The two night people didn't show up tonight. I guess they got sick of dealing with all of this shit last night. I'm the fucking bartender." He pointed to the closed tiki lounge-looking bar across the lobby.

I looked at his hand written name tag, taped to his wife-beater. His name was Rodney, or so he would have us believe. The guy didn't look like a Rodney at all, but then again, what did a Rodney look like? I decided to play along and call him Rodney.

"Thanks Rodney, and good luck tonight," as I headed back to the room, something told me I would be seeing Rodney again. Unfortunately I was right, and it wouldn't take a very long time either.

I made my way up to the second floor, and worked my way through the maze of hallways zig zagging in every direction back to the room. Every now and then I would pass someone trying to get into their room and cursing their key card. I felt better now, knowing for sure that I wasn't the only one having a problem.

It was a full five minute walk back to the room, and when I got there Sabrina was sitting in the hall with a look of murder on her face. She had my phone in her hand, I wasn't sure if the look of murder was over the locked door, or the phone call. Luckily the key card worked right away and we got inside.

142

We packed Kleborp up, and smoked a bowl to celebrate getting through being locked out of our room and not killing anyone over it. It had been a close call.

Everyone was smoking weed in their rooms, we could smell it every time we went to reset our key cards, but we were only smoking tobacco outside for some reason. I was still smoking my big stinky cigars, so that was why I wasn't smoking inside. I think Sabrina was used to going outside to smoke, she did it at home, so she really didn't care.

We should have alternated our smoke breaks like we did the night before, but we were starting to get cocky. Sabrina went out once and her card worked right away when she came back. I went to the vending machine and the door unlocked first swipe when I came back. High on weed and skittles, we decided to go out together for a smoke.

Phish offered free downloads of the show if you had a ticket number. Whether it was the website, or my old laptop, I had to download each track individually. I was downloading the four sets of the day. It would take forever, so I brought my laptop down with me.

The Internet was very slow, everyone else in the hotel was probably downloading the show, too. We could hear either Chris or John snoring away as we passed their room towards the stairs. We sat down next to the puddle and watched as the brine shrimp swam around under the bright parking lot lights.

Sabrina smoked two cigarettes as we chatted away. When she finished her second I snubbed my cigar out and saved the rest for the next day. We laughed again as we passed the others room, we could hear at least three snores now. It was getting really late by then. It was three thirty or four o'clock at least. Most of the hotel was asleep.

We got to the door and Sabrina tried her card. No luck. Again and again she slide her card waiting to see the red light turn to green, telling us we could enter. It refused to go green. Without saying a word she held out her hand for my card. This was getting annoying, and I was a pretty patient guy. If I was getting annoyed, Sabrina must have been out right pissed. Much like Reed, patience was not her greatest strength.

She tried my card again and again. No luck. I took a card from her. The door might have sensed her frustration and was refusing to open because of it, that was as likely a cause as anything else. I tried to think happy thoughts as I slide the card. After I tried twice, Sabrina ripped the card out of my hand and took off for the front desk without another word.

Ten minutes later she came back with an even more of a pissed off look than she had left with. She had the two cards clenched in her fist. Again we kept trying them and again neither card would work. We tried and tried, and when we started getting really pissed, I suggested we go out for another smoke. When we came back in, the cards still didn't work.

We tried to knock on Chris and John's door, but they never woke up. The snoring going on in there was drowning out any noise we were making banging on the door. I took the cards and went back to the front desk. When I got there, Rodney was on the phone with his eyes bugging out.

"Do you see the valve under the toilet? No, I am sorry, there is no one here that can come up right now. Do you see the valve? Ok, turn it. Did it stop? Ok, I'll be up there as soon as I can, I promise." He hung up the phone and looked at me with tears trying to form in his eyes against his wishes. "Please tell me you aren't still locked out."

"We're still locked out." My voice was starting to go. I had done too much screaming and yelling at the shows. It would be completely gone soon, I could feel it. I handed him the cards, he reset them again and handed them back. "And if this doesn't work? Is there some sort of master key you can use to get us in?"

I didn't want to make poor Rodney's life any worse, but it had been a long two days of festival walking and dancing. The walk in the hotel at four in the morning was getting to be too much. I was sure Sabrina felt the same way.

"Ummmmm," I could see his mind racing. "Maybe. I have to run to another room. I'll check on you right after that, I promise." He promised. The poor guy was trying his best, but his promise didn't feel too promising to me.

Sure enough, when I got back, the key cards still didn't work. After ten minutes of Sabrina and I trying, Rodney showed up with a big box full of keys. There was a very small key slot at the bottom of the lock, but I didn't see any tiny keys in the box. We just grabbed random keys and just started trying them.

Nothing worked. Poor Rodney, he was bugging out even more than we were. Suddenly he took a running start and tried to knock the door down with his shoulder. The first hit looked like it hurt, but he slammed against the door a few more times before I stopped him.

"Listen, relax," I said, poor Rodney was about

to fall apart. Physically and mentally. I had to calm him down before he had a stroke and we were left without any employees in the hotel. "I can get us in, if you promise me something."

"What's that?" He asked, now even closer to tears.

"First I need you to go back to the front desk and ignore any calls you might get about a disturbance from over here," I paused. He nodded so I assumed he agreed.

"And then I need you to promise that you will not charge us for any damage that might be done to the screen or window."

That made him look a little more apprehensive, but he hesitantly agreed and made his way back to the front desk. Sabrina and I went outside to assess the situation. The ledge outside of our window was fairly high.

I couldn't get up there on my own and it didn't look like it would even be too easy to for me to get Sabrina up there either. Luckily she was so tiny I could lift her up, even though I wasn't the strongest guy in the world. I could try to get her close, but unfortunately the Ferris Wheel had not cured her fear of heights.

I tried to simply pick her up, but I couldn't get her close enough to the ledge that way. Back in the hallway of the hotel I had seen a small garbage can. I took it outside and flipped it over. If I stood on the garbage can and lifted her up it might work, but the garbage can did not seem sturdy enough to hold me, let alone both of us.

But if Sabrina stepped up onto it, and then got on my shoulders, she could step up on my hands and maybe I could do a kind of cheerleader lift to get her up on the ledge. It was a long shot, but we had to try something. I was just glad she was light.

It actually worked. She was able to reach the ledge. I tried to help push her up, but she started yelling for me to stop. I assumed it was her fear of heights. I didn't think it was all that rational, she wasn't that high up. But fears were never rational, so I stopped.

Finally she said OK and I helped her get up the rest of the way. I was really happy that we got her up there until I saw her approach the window. They purposely made it narrow to prevent jumpers. This was going to be a problem. It couldn't open very wide, and it really didn't look like she would be able to get through it, no matter how tiny she was.

First she had to rip and pull the screen away at the edge of the window, which she easily did. Luckily the glass window was open and she was able to open it a little bit more, but it still didn't look like she could get through. She tried to snake her way in and stopped for a second, I was sure it wouldn't work, yet somehow she kept moving. She made it in and I gave a yell of joy. I ran inside and up to the room where she was waiting for me at the open door.

"Holy shit, I was sure that you were going to get stuck in the window." I still couldn't believe we were inside of our room. "And you seem to have conquered your fear of heights, though it was iffy for a second there."

"I told you to stop lifting me up because I almost put my hand on a dirty syringe, not because I was afraid of heights." She said with a very straight face.

"What?" I thought it was some type of a joke,

but it wasn't very funny. Especially with the talks we had about Michelle. She pointed out of the window. Sure enough, there was a dirty syringe right on the ledge. I was pissed.

Sabrina packed Kleborp with the Purple Kush and we smoked a big bowl to try to calm the nerves. When we finished, Sabrina poured a little water into one of our hotel room glasses for an ashtray and lit a cigarette. "This is a smoking room now bitches," She said loudly out of the window to no one in particular as she sat down and kicked her feet up.

I quickly ran into the bathroom before Sabrina could get in there. She took forever in the shower. I couldn't wait that long. I jumped in and finished my shower before Sabrina even finished her cigarette. When I lit up my cigar, she got up and jumped in the shower, so I stole her seat by the window.

A few minutes later I heard some noise outside. It was Rodney, grabbing the garbage can that I had left outside. He saw me in the window smoking my cigar inside the room, but he just smiled and waved. I wanted to blow up at someone, but poor Rodney didn't deserve it.

He had tried his best and had looked away when that didn't work. I really couldn't have asked for more as far as customer service, given the situation. So I just waved back. I'd wait for the morning staff to come in before I blew up on anyone. It might not have been his fault, but that didn't make me any less pissed.

The sun was going to be coming up soon. It was my favorite time of day again and I was far too worked up to go to sleep. Sabrina had no trouble. She had passed out the moment she hit the bed, with Comedy Central blaring away on the TV. I got online for awhile, but that late at night, no one else was on.

I needed to go for a walk, or do something to try to clear my head. I put on my shorts and reached into the pockets. There was a lot of crap in there, which was strange, because I hadn't tripped that day. I took out everything except my cigars, my wallet, a lighter and a book of matches.

I put the pack of matches in the door jam to keep it from closing all of the way. I wanted to keep the door open, even with Sabrina inside. I wasn't sure she would wake up no matter how hard I banged on the door, and I wasn't going to be locked out again.

I went outside and lit a cigar. I walked around the building, and when I got to the front of the hotel, through the window I could see two people at the front desk yelling at Rodney. When he saw me outside he got a little nervous, as if maybe I had locked myself out again. I gave him a quick wave and kept walking. I could see the relief on his face from outside.

I walked down the street. I knew I didn't want to try any convenience store food again, but I kept walking in that direction anyway. I did end up going in to get a drink, but this time I made sure it was 100 percent juice. The florescent lighting was fucking with me whether I was tripping or not. I had to get out of there quickly.

As it got brighter out, I began to notice all of the flowers on the side of the road. As I walked I would pick one here or there. There were flowers of every color, but the yellow and purple ones looked the best to me, so those were the ones I took. By the time I got back to the hotel, I had a nice little bouquet collected. I went into the bathroom and put some water in my now empty juice bottle. I put the flowers in and walked back into the room.

I put the flowers on top of the TV, it added a nice little bit of color to the room. There might have been a syringe out on the ledge, but at least we had flowers inside. Of course under the flowers was the infomercial about a certain male body part (ear lobes?) that your woman desperately wants to be bigger.

This time I was smart. I left the TV on, but I switched the channel to 24 hour news. Even though I had smoked on my walk, I needed to just sit and have a smoke before going to bed. I packed my orange alien pipe again and took a few deep hits before lighting my cigar.

When I finished I crawled into bed. The TV's light was dancing all over the room, but at least it wasn't the Girls Gone Wild wooing and xylophone or the penis medicine girl. I hoped that the anchor's boring voice would help put me to sleep. It took awhile, but it finally worked.

Destiny Unbound

Sunday, July 3, 2011:

Reba dip a ladle for a taste of her creation
and she knew that what she made
would be the finest in the nation
Bag it, Tag it, Sell it to the butcher in the store

Reba
-Anastasio

Chuck Howe

When I woke up, Sabrina was just coming out of the bathroom. It was the first time all weekend that no one else had to wake us up. She sat down at the little table by the window and lit a cigarette. I had almost forgotten, ours was a smoking room now. So I sat down and I lit a cigar for myself.

"I'm going to go grab breakfast, do you mind staying here so you can let me back in?" She asked. We would not ever be locked out again. I was going to make sure of that.

"No, that's cool." My voice was fading fast, I could barely make it over a whisper. I took a big long drag from my cigar as I packed up Kleborp. I needed a hit of purple kush first and foremost. The cigar made me crave a coffee, but that could wait.

"OK, do you want me to grab you anything while I am down there?" I was thinking it would be nice to have Sabrina bring me a nice breakfast, but I wanted to be hungry. Hungry made angry come more naturally.

"No, I'll go down when you're back. I want to try to get us another room with a door that works. I'll stop by the front desk before I get some food." I took a few hits off of Keborp and smoked my cigar while I got ready for my visit to the front desk.

I made sure not to comb my hair. I wanted to make sure I looked half insane when I got to the front desk. It wouldn't be hard, I was feeling half insane. I threw on my bathrobe and just my bathrobe. Actual clothing would have been too normal. I didn't want normal.

Sabrina came back with a coffee for me, which was a good thing. I needed it more than I had thought. Caffeine would help if I had to really start acting crazy. I gave her my phone so she could call Brendan while I was gone.

I didn't need to tell her why, and I could tell that she appreciated not having to ask me to use it. I snuffed out the cigar, but kept it in my mouth. It was unlit and stinky but it helped to create even more of a look of insanity. I tied the belt of my robe and made my way to the lobby.

There were two people, a man and a woman in matching dark blue blazers, working the front desk. Luckily for Rodney, he was no longer there. It must have been the worst night of his life. Hopefully he was home sleeping, or drinking, or doing whatever it was that Rodney liked doing. I wondered if he would ever come back to work. For his sake, I hoped not.

The young, proper and well kept man was helping a woman who had two kids running circles around her. She looked as frazzled as I felt. I felt bad for her. Not all the guests were Phish-heads. It must have sucked for her to deal with all of our noise all weekend.

I must have looked pretty crazy, with my hair a mess, two days worth of partying under my belt and the rage from the night before still festering in my brain. But I wasn't angry at the little kids, so I gave them a smile and they smiled right back, continuing to play their game of chase and yell.

The young lady behind the desk finished helping the man in front of me. Her hair and smile were perfect, they reminded me of plastic. I had to remind myself that I wasn't angry at her either, none of it was her fault, but she damned well better make things right. If she didn't, then it would be her problem.

As I stepped up to the desk, she kept up her big fake smile, but I thought saw it crack just a little bit before I even started talking to her. The look of uncertainty in her eyes told me that I had already won the psychological battle.

"Hello sir, may I help you this morning?" She had that western New York friendliness to her voice. It was probably real, but sounded very put on to my suburban New York City ears. I was having none of it.

My voice was horse and cracked with three days worth of festival partying and screaming. My eyes were badly bloodshot from getting almost no sleep the night before, I knew I was a scary sight.

Scariest of all must have been the look on my face as I tried to restrain myself from getting angry. It wasn't her fault, I kept reminding myself that I wasn't angry at her. In a hushed, slow and measured voice I responded simply, "I certainly hope so."

I began to tell the story of the night before, the whole time trying to keep from getting too excited. That had only added to the intensity in my face.

Before I even got to the part about the syringe, the smile had already disappeared from her face and was replaced with pure horror. The mother standing next to me reached her hands down and magically corralled her kids behind her as only a mother can.

Maybe I had turned the scary level up a little too much, but the woman behind the counter listened to every word I said. A lot of people would be checking out, but we were staying for one more night, so I told her I wanted a new room, on the first floor, with a lock that worked and I wanted it by the time I got back to my room. Luckily for her, she agreed to take care of everything I asked for.

"And one more thing, Rodney deserves a raise and a big bonus," I finished my rant and she must have let out a deep breath as I turned and walked away.

I could only imagine the look of relief that she and her coworker must have exchanged. I was sure that they were glad that no one was hurt. In fact, everyone in the lobby, including the kids, must have been glad to see me go and I didn't blame them.

I walked into the buffet on my way back and filled an entire plate with bacon to bring back to the room. I grabbed two more cups of coffee and put a bagel in my bathrobe pocket. One of the senior citizens looked at me funny, but when she saw the anger in my face, she wisely decided against saying anything. I felt bad. The poor old lady did nothing wrong. I smiled and offered her a slice of bacon. She just shook her head and walked away.

By the time I got back to the room, Sabrina was on the phone with the front desk. They were just finishing cleaning a new room on the first floor, just like I had asked. The woman at the front desk must have been really happy that Sabrina went to get the key cards for our new room instead of me. Again, I didn't blame her at all.

Someone had to stay back to open the door and Sabrina wanted to pick up more bacon anyway. We had settled into our old room nicely, so it took awhile to pack everything up. I had two whole days worth of pocket collections to go through on my night table. I got to work as soon as she left.

When she got back I had to go out to the car to get Sabrina's bed spread. We had forgotten to bring a "sitting blanket" for the show. I had always been told to remove the bed spread anyway, as hotels usually didn't clean them too often. We brought the hotel's bedspread with us to the festival, and used it as a blanket on the concert field. It was now completely black with dirt, but we put it right back on her bed, as if nothing strange had happened. Take that housekeeping.

Our new room was on the floor directly below our old room. We took turns bringing our things down. At least we knew we could get back in from outside if we were locked out again, but we preferred not to risk it.

Reed showed up as we were finishing moving our stuff and couldn't believe our story. John and Chris had a few problems with their card, but Reed and Sasha had no problems the entire weekend.

He couldn't believe we had so much trouble, so I gave him a card, threw him out of the room, closed the door and told him to try to get back in. He kept trying until Sabrina finally came back up. She was having no more of that locked out nonsense. She immediately threatened to kill us all if she didn't get back in the room in two seconds, so I let both of them in.

When we shut the door for the final time, I felt a little antsy, like "how are they going to open the door now?" but then I remembered that I didn't give a shit. It was the hotel's problem now. I was just glad to have a new room, and one last full day of music ahead of me.

Everyone else went to the show while we were still getting settled in to the new room. Chris and Kerry were going to have to leave early, so they wanted to spend all of the time that they could at the festival.

The key cards worked every single time in the new room. Now that we were on the first floor, it would be a lot easier to get in the window if we did get locked out. I still preferred to get in through the door, so I was happy they were working.

We finally got to the Raceway about 45 minutes after everyone else did, but it was still early. We had plenty of time to hang out and explore before the music would start. John and Chris had fired up the grill and were busy cooking. John offered me a hot dog, but I was still pretty full of bacon.

Danny's back pack was in the tent, but there was no sign of him anywhere. I knew that Danny would show up at some point. He was one guy I never had to worry about. Even when things went wrong he found a way of making it turn out alright.

Sitting out on the front porch of our tent, I felt really peaceful. People were stirring all over, a few of them even packing up their tents already. Shaggy's tent was still up, but no one had seen him since the first day. I had asked a few people at the other tents, but no one else knew where he was either..

I stood outside his tent and tentatively called out his name, but there was no answer. It didn't look like anyone was inside, so I just let it go. He was probably out and about the concert field already. I made a mental note to check on him later though. I didn't want to go into it yet, but I would if I had to. His tent really scared me for some reason.

I have always enjoyed Phish shows that were in a more natural surrounding. They always encouraged camping wherever it was allowed, unfortunately most often it wasn't allowed.

There had been a big stink at the shows in Bethel earlier that year. Town officials cracked down on residents letting Phish heads camp on their lawns. Though camping wasn't allowed at Saratoga Springs either, it had become one of my favorite nature infused venues.

The first time I went to Saratoga, I made the mistake of going for the concert parking. My childhood friend, Rawley, had flow in from England to visit. I had already bought tickets when he said he was coming, so I got an extra one for him.

His father was a musician, so I figured he'd dig seeing a crazy Phish show. He hated it. His favorite part was when the Dude of Life came out and they played one of his more metal sounding tunes. It was a low point of the show, in my opinion.

The Dude of Life, one of Trey's old college buddies who helped write some early Phish tunes, was always funny. Phish had even been his backing band for his own album, but he just never did it for me in a live setting. Luckily he didn't come out often, or stay out for very long anymore.

The lot scene that year was pretty crazy though. We were parked with other concert goers what felt like miles away from the pavilion. Sure it was fun to be in a huge parking lot with a bunch of drinking, smoking, partying fools, but in later years I found out that you could actually park in the picnic areas and smaller parking lots through out the park. One was even right next to the venue.

Going to and from the concert you walked through an ancient forest and followed a peaceful stream that even passed a geyser and natural mineral water fountains. It also helped avoid the post show traffic. We could be out of the park in minutes, rather than hours. Saratoga went from being just another far away venue, to the perfect setting for a Phish show.

Our tent was not within direct view of the racetrack, but we were fairly close to the grandstand. Suddenly, the peace and tranquility of the afternoon in nature was broken. We all looked up when we heard the blast of loud truck horns coming from the track. Everyone jumped up startled. We headed to the Grandstand where a large crowd was gathering, to see what was happening.

There were four tour buses waiting at the starting line of the racetrack. Now that the band members were older and had their own families traveling with them on tour, they each had their own bus. Someone walked out in front of the buses and threw a handkerchief in the air.

I thought it was funny that it wasn't Fishman who started the race. It was the perfect role for him, but then again, he had a long day of music ahead of him. When the handkerchief hit the ground the buses took off.

They all quickly disappeared down the racetrack. A minute or so later they came roaring back from the other direction. Their horns were blaring as they sped by us.

They were really flying, too. I couldn't see the drivers, but it felt like they were going all out racing each other. Pride was at stake on this race. Driving

at such high speeds, they were not only loud, but
displacing a lot of air. We weren't even very close to
the track, but every lap the wind washed over us
shortly after they zoomed by.

They must have flown past us at least ten
times before they all took a slow victory lap. I don't
know who won, but it was fun. Once, eighteen years
earlier, I was driving along route 90 after a show at
the Syracuse Armory. Phish would be playing a
daytime festival in Amherst, Massachusetts the next
day.

Back then the band all traveled in one bus
with a second truck to carry all of their equipment.
Overnight, we were hauling ass to try to make it to
Amherst as soon as possible, and suddenly their bus
and truck flew past us. We were speeding ourselves,
I could only imagine how fast they were going.

I thought for sure that they must have been
two of the drivers at the racetrack, even though I
didn't see either of their faces at either time. It wasn't
until I got home and saw a bunch of videos on
Youtube that I realized that it was the four band
members all driving the buses. They all looked like
pretty good drivers to me. Though Trey would later
break down all of their driving skills for us.

As we made our way back to the tent, we ran
into Danny. He was always a happy guy, but he
looked even happier than usual. I asked him where
he had been and he said, "I didn't know if Sabrina
would be pissed if I brought a girl into her tent, so we
took off early."

He just left it at that and kept walking. He had
been alone, about to pass out when we left him the
night before. I couldn't figure out how he did it, but

once again, that was Danny.

When we got back, Reed asked if Sabrina and I had used the acid that he had given to me the day before. We hadn't. Sabrina had tripped hard on Friday night and didn't want it at all. She finally got a text from the guy who had given her the Molly. He didn't want that back, he had enough of it already, so she was going to stick with that.

I hadn't used mine either, but was thinking about it. I opened up the small pouch Reed had given me and there were two pieces of paper inside. One was twice the size of the other.

"Sweet. I have some for me, but Sasha wanted to trip today, too. I was going to split mine with her, but she'd probably be fine with the small hit."

"She can have the bigger hit," I told him. I was still feeling the effects of the hit I took on Friday. I wasn't still tripping, but I still felt it. I knew that I wasn't going to need all that much to trip out. I probably didn't need any at all, but it was the last day and I felt like having a little more fun.

Reed handed Sasha the bigger hit and she immediately put it on her tongue. Sasha never showed the effects of whatever she was on. She was a lot like Reed that way. I could never tell if Reed was fucked up. I took the smaller hit, and Reed took whatever he had left of his own. Now I knew the final day of Super Ball IX was going to be a blast.

The acid felt like it hit me very fast, much faster than I had expected. We started walking to the concert field for the first set, and I was flying before we even got to the security check point. Everyone made it through security without a problem except for Danny, which was funny since Danny was the only one of us who had nothing on him. He still had that extra bit of smile, and that may have been enough for security.

When he finally made it out, I asked him what the hold up had been. "I don't know man, I think she just wanted to grab my ass, and then she wanted the other woman there to grab my ass." I was pretty sure he was kidding, but it was Danny, so I couldn't be too sure.

Ball Square had been completely transformed over the course of the festival. It had gone from looking like a colonial village, to becoming a Dr. Suessian type of world.

There were the brightly colored flags made by the fans flying everywhere. Now there were giant sculptures and creatures made out of balloons too. The coolest one was a giant fish that was made up of smaller balloons, being held together in a balloon type of netting.

The giant pieces of branded wood that were being made all weekend were now set up everywhere, too. There was art in every direction. The acid was really kicking in. It was hitting hard partly because everything around me was much more psychedelic than it had been at the beginning of the festival. The grounds were like a living morphing being, altered by the crowd, for the crowd.

Reed had made it clear that he wanted to go all the way up front this set, and he wanted all of us to go way up front with him. Reed could be very persuasive. I felt good, so I figured why not go up front. There were 9 of us, and the field was already filling up, but somehow we all managed to find a cool spot right up in front on the Page side of the stage.

Right before the band came on, I was starting

to feel a little claustrophobic. People started closing in all around us as the show time drew closer. The heat of the day was peaking, too. I really didn't like it at all. I felt drained, and I felt trapped.

A tightness was forming in my chest, and I really hoped that Phish would take the stage soon. I needed something to take my mind off of the crowd surrounding me. It wasn't a good sign that I was freaking out so soon. I needed to balance myself.

Chris must have sensed something was wrong, or he may have just been appreciating the day. Either way I was happy, because he came over and put his arm around my shoulders. "This has been an awesome weekend man! I'm glad we got to hang out together."

It was the perfect thing to say to snap me out of the downward spiral that I was finding myself in. He was still a young guy but he had an old soul. He was a good person, and I felt happy to be surrounded by good people.

Phish had been on fire the prior two days. There had only been a few surprises in song selection, but they had been playing everything really well. Even the more common tunes had a fresh flavor to them. The hour long secret set the night before had us looking forward to what might be in store for the final day. We didn't have to wait very long for our first treat.

It was still bright and sunny when the band took the stage. The first notes were soaking in a deep reggae rhythm. They liked jamming out to some reggae, both originals and covers. It was hard to tell what they were playing, and then it came through loud and clear.

Phish was giving us a nice rare treat with a rare rendition of Bob Marley's Soul Shakedown Party. It was one of my favorite Marley tunes, and though I knew they had played it in the past, I had never seen it live. A rarity was a great way to start the day. Plus they could never go wrong playing a Marley cover.

The bass was shaking the ground beneath our feet, the drums were tight. The organ soared, and Trey, though mostly just shucking the guitar, was smiling at the crowd and obviously ready to have a great time. We were going to be in for a treat. Some sets were special, and early on I could tell this would be one of them.

By the time they started playing their tune, "The Curtain," an old rarity that I had not seen live since the West Coast tour in 93, the acid was hitting me really hard. Luckily I was now in a great mood, so it wasn't a problem, yet. I knew I would feel better once the band started. Danny and I were grooving right along. I could see some young guy ask Reed something, Reed was dancing right along but he pointed to Danny and I.

Later Reed would tell me that the guy had asked what they were playing. Reed didn't know, but he could tell Danny and I were happy to hear it, so it must be something old school. As the Curtain ended, the first notes of the next song were unmistakable to us old timers while unrecognizable to most of the kids in the crowd.

The two songs that always segued into each other, Colonel Forbin's Ascent/ Fly Famous Mockingbird were part of what has become known as the Gamehendge Saga. Col. Forbin/Mockingbird, as it became known, tells the story of Col. Forbin searching out the great and knowledgeable Icculus, to help him save the Lizards. Of course the only thing that could save the lizards was "The Helping Friendly Book." Icculus sends the Famous Mockingbird to get it from the Evil King Wilson's Castle.

It was a highlight of Gamehendge, which Trey wrote and Phish recorded as part of his senior project in college. The best part of the song in years past would be the narration in the middle. Like with Harpua, Trey would make up a story on the spot. It usually involved the characters of Gamehendge, but not always.

The song had not been played very often in recent years. Even when we had been treated to the rare appearances, it had lacked the story in the middle. Danny and I must not have been the only ones begging for a story as the typical story time drew close, but it felt that way.

"Tell us a story," we yelled with arms up in the air like holy rollers waiting for Sunday communion. Maybe it was just the acid, but I felt like you could see a wave of joy wash over the crowd as Trey stepped to the microphone.

"It's so strange to be singing this song at this very spot, let me take a minute to tell you why." We went nuts. Trey was going to tell us a story! It was the only thing that the weekend had been missing so far.

The story was about their first long road trip as a band, out to Colorado and passing through the area 25 years earlier. We were told about their early Plymouth Voyager, and that Page was the best driver. Fishman was a great long haul driver. Trey was too distracted by the radio and shiny object on

the side of the road, and the worst driver, Mike.
"Writing in his journal while driving." Eventually the
car broke down right near Watkins Glen.

Of course there was no mechanic around, but
there was a Self Storage Unit, they brought the van
there so their equipment wouldn't be stolen. In my
whole life I think I went to a self storage place once.
Now I was running into them at every turn. What was
it about Self Storage Units?

During Trey's story, the door closed and
locked on them, and they were stuck in the self
storage unit for 25 years. Luckily a leak in the ceiling
gives them water, but they all started to hallucinate
while they jammed and made up stories to pass the
time.

They made up a world where they became
huge rock stars and traveled the world. They played
arenas and sold their merchandise to everyone.
Eventually there was so much stuff in the world that
everyone needed self storage and the whole planet
became covered in self storage buildings. Everything
about the story made perfect sense to me, of course
I was tripping pretty hard, too.

The story ended with the Famous
Mockingbird, who now worked for the post office,
flying in and rescuing the band, much like he
rescued the Helping Friendly Book from the clutches
of the evil King Wilson in Trey's Gamehendge Saga.

Of course when Trey pointed to the sky saying
"Look, here comes the Mockingbird now," everyone
in the crowd turned and looked up into the sky, as if
the bird were actually going to come on cue. But it
took us out of the story and brought us right back
into the song. Trey had done it. He gave us a story. I
didn't think the set could get any better, but the

Famous Mockingbird was followed by the unmistakable opening guitar riff of Destiny Unbound.

Destiny Unbound, written by Mike Gordon, had long been one of my favorite songs. I had one old tape, from Ithaca almost twenty years earlier, that I listened to over and over again that had Destiny Unbound on it. It had appeared a few times in the early 90's, and then just disappeared. For years it was the song that people begged for, held up signs for, chanted the lyrics of and tried anything they could to get the band to play, yet they never would.

Finally they played it right before the break up. They had played it a few more times since, but not very often, and unfortunately, not very well. It made an appearance at their one and only Fenway Park show, but again, it was a real sub par performance. I had never seen it live until the previous summer, 2010, at Jones Beach in Long Island.

It was a late August day that had started out with such promise. After a late afternoon rainstorm, there was a double rainbow coming down from the sky. One end looked like it ended right inside of the theater. I had gone with Reed and our friend Andrew. Andrew hadn't been to very many concerts in the past and it was his first Phish show. Andrew was a spiritual guy, and he took the rainbow as a great sign. Of course he had also taken some acid, but Reed and I agreed with him

Right near the end of the first set, they played Destiny Unbound. Once again, it wasn't a very good version. They still hadn't found the groove that the song needed. The groove that it had back in the early 90's. I was really happy to hear it for the first time, even if it didn't live up to my old Ithaca tape.

At the set break Reed decided he was going to get some food. I didn't need any overpriced concert venue food, so I figured I would stay at the seats, but when Andrew decided to go, too, I figured if we all went it really wouldn't matter if we made it back to our seats or not. I always hated the way Jones Beach was set up, we had to go up a long set of steep steps, just to go down a long set of steep steps.

There really wasn't very much about Jones Beach that I liked at all, and there never had been. I would have avoided it altogether except that Phish usually played really well there. Being right on the water, the sound was terrible in most of the amphitheater. We were lucky that our seats had been in one of the only sections that had good sound.

The bathrooms were all in one place and always had long lines. Bathrooms always sucked at concerts, but they were even worse at Jones Beach. Not only that, the state police who patrolled the parking lot were totally unnecessarily hard-assed. Worst of all was the food. It was bad and over priced. I would have preferred parking lot food, but the Staties were even busting the veggie wrap guys.

After we got our nachos and 12 dollar cups of Bud Light, we made our way back up the steps only to be stopped on our way back down the other steps, trying to get to our seats. There was a big commotion going on and security told us to wait. So we waited. And we waited. We couldn't see what was going on, but there was a lot of buzz in the crowd around us, so we started asking around.

It turned out that someone had jumped off of the balcony and he had landed roughly right where we had been sitting. Security eventually told us to find somewhere else to go, so we moved as far up front as we could get. The view was much better, but the sound sucked.

The next day someone posted a picture of a busted up seat online saying that was where the jumper landed. The seat was number 12. I had been sitting in a seat number 12 when I decided to get up for some crappy food. I couldn't say for sure that it was my seat 12. It could have been a row or two higher or lower. The good news was that even if it wasn't my seat 12, it was unoccupied at the time.

One other person sitting nearby was hurt. The jumper was the most seriously injured, though he did survive. It turned out he was facing jail time up in Maine, and decided to jump instead of going back. Unfortunately he was sent there straight from the hospital, and still faced charges of endangerment in New York for the jump after he served his time up there.

The Destiny Unbound that Phish gave us at Watkins Glen was the best one that I had ever heard them play, live or on tape. It included what would become one of my favorite Type I jams I have heard. It's tough to ever call anything Phish does "the best," but I could call it my favorite.

Trey ripped apart the intro and first couple of verses in all of the best ways. When it came time for the jam however, he held back and let Mike, Page and Fishman form a deep pocket and just groove.

As they jammed, the giant balloon fish that we had seen earlier at Ball Square began making it's way surfing over the crowd. As it approached the stage, powered only by the hands of the fans, the balloon netting that was holding it in form gave way.

What felt like a million balloons of all shapes, sizes and colors were released and they quickly spread out all over the concert field.

Just as that happened, Mike hit his Synth pedal, always a fan favorite, and the bass took on a deep muddy tone that I felt through my whole body. When the song finally ended, I felt physically drained, but the set wasn't even half over yet. As good as the music was the first two days, in my mind both days had already been surpassed.

They followed that with Big Black Furry Creatures from Mars. Their 80's tribute to punk/thrash/alt noise rock. Not my favorite genre of music but they always played it with lots of energy and humor and lighting and stage antics, so it was fun. Plus, now it was a rare treat, not played often at all.

The rest of the set contained mostly older tunes. Wilson, another song from Trey's Gamehendge Saga, was a long time fan favorite. So much so, that in my opinion, the fans had almost killed the song. For years, Phish would do a long introduction to the song, sometimes allowing for really deep explorations. Just before the real rocking part of the song began, the four band members would lightly chant the name Wilson 4 times and then kick it into the song.

All that changed one night in the early 90's at Madison Square Garden. It was their first time playing at the hallowed venue, and as the bass started playing the familiar introduction, the crowd chanted Wilson. Trey loved when the crowd played along with him, and was visually very happy to hear the sellout crowd chanting. He let them chant the four times,and then jumped right into the song.

It was the shortest intro that they had ever played to Wilson, up to that point. Now, every time Mike starts up that familiar bass line, the crowd starts chanting. Trey lets them go four times and then jumps into the song. That beautiful long drawn out intro that used to explore new territory is gone now. Replaced by the crowd singing. I secretly hope that one time, they keep going with the intro until the entire crowd loses it's voice chanting along.

They finished that and then kicked into a playful Mound and then followed with, always a crowd favorite, Reba. A Song I Heard the Ocean Sing was the only song of the set that had been written in the last 10 years, and also one I had never seen live, so I really enjoyed it. The only other first time song for me was a cover of Little Feat's Time Loves a Hero.

I had one tape back in the day with that song on it, and that was the only other time I knew of them playing it. It was another one Danny and I recognized, having grown up listening to the same tapes, and that no one else around us knew.

They ended the set with their long jammed out song David Bowie. It wasn't a cover song originally by David Bowie, it was a Phish original called David Bowie. That was always a point of confusion for many non-fans.

"What song is this?"

"David Bowie."

"Really this is a Bowie song?"

Now imagine having that conversation at a concert during a long loud instrumental jam. David Bowie had a long intro of just Fishman playing his hi-hats. Other band members would jump in to accentuate or jam a little, too. It was an intro that the fans hadn't figured out a way to destroy, yet.

Before the song ended I started feeling claustrophobic, tense again. On top of that, now I was hungry, too. Everyone was into the music. I knew that is was probably the last song of the set, but I didn't want to bother any of them. Still, I felt like I needed to get out, and for some reason, I needed falafel.

I didn't know why I had such an urge for falafel. I had never been a huge fan of it in the past, but then again I had never hated it either. Honestly, I wasn't even really sure exactly what it was. To me they were just bland meatballs without the meat. I wanted a pita and hummus more than anything, but once I got the word falafel stuck in my head, I couldn't get it out without eating some. I think I just needed to be out of the ever tightening crowd that close to the stage more than anything.

My voice was now completely gone, I couldn't tell anyone what was going on. The music was too loud anyway. The set had drained me of the last of my energy. I hadn't been sleeping well, and I needed food and to go lie down on the air mattress, so I left the group and made my way back to the tent.

I thought I had told someone where I was going, but I guess I never did. When I passed the official food vendors who had their booths inside the concert venue itself, I began searching for falafel. It was a little difficult to weave through the crowd, but it was always easier to travel on your own. The signs of food vendors row beckoned me in the distance. At least the band was still playing, so there wouldn't be set break lines yet, if I could get there quick enough.

My voice had been cutting in and out all day.

When I finally found the Gyro guy, I could barely raise it over a whisper. I pointed out all the things that looked best to me. The falafel of course, hummus, tomato, onions, and anything that looked good. Unfortunately everything that looked good also turned my pita into a running, dripping mess.

By the time I was halfway done trying to eat it, I had a blob of hummus and various other juices covering my entire arm. The creamy paste seemed to fill my beard and mustache and it ended up covering my face, or that was how it felt. I needed napkins, but it I couldn't find them. I wasn't really looking for them because I couldn't stop eating. Whatever the hell falafel was, it was perfect.

I immediately felt better, but the acid was still turning my head in circles. I must have been some sight, because a random, kind guy came up to me and handed me a bunch of napkins. Phish-heads were always looking out for trippers like that. Of course, I might have known the guy and in my state had no idea.

I don't think I even finished the gyro, something tells me that whatever was left got thrown out with the napkins. Or maybe it had just disintegrated down my arm. Either way, I was done with it. It had served it's purpose.

I tried to make my way back to the tent. It was just getting dark, and Ball Square was awash in colored lights; with all of the flags hanging around, it caused a ghostly effect. I wasn't sure if there was a fog machine, or if that was all in my head. As I got lost in the fog and flags, music started playing all around me. There was always something going on at Ball Square.

The Primate Fiasco started playing a battle of

the bands with the What? Cheer Brigade, an equally talented horn band, right in front of me. I had seen them both throughout the weekend. This time they were trading licks back and forth. It sounded great, but I still needed to lie down, so I dragged myself away.

I found a water spout and finished washing the gyro off of me. It felt good to get the last of the hummus and other crap removed from my furry face and arms. When I finally felt good and clean, I quickly made my way back to the tent. The air mattress felt like heaven as I collapsed into it.

I didn't fall asleep, at least it didn't think I fell asleep. I felt like I was still aware of my surroundings, but colors swirled on the inside of my eyelids. I could see people having conversations all around me, but I couldn't follow what they were saying. They must have been standing outside of the tent, and my eyes were closed tight, but I could see them, as clear as day.

I could hear the second set begin while I was still lying there, or at least I thought I did. I could swear they played a few songs before I started getting restless. I got up, grabbed my cigars and sat on the grass outside of the tent. It slowly dawned on me that I didn't hear the music anymore. People were walking all around. The set must have been over. I must have fallen asleep and missed the whole set. I assumed that everyone would be heading back to the tent soon.

I lit a cigar and looked up at the sky. The stars were chasing each other all over the place. I thought it was a little odd to still be tripping so hard after so long, but it was fun. I was no longer feeling claustrophobic or even hungry, so I just went with the trip and enjoyed it.

After a short time, I noticed that everyone who was around the tents was starting to walk back toward the concert field, and not away from it. I looked at my phone, it wasn't even 10 o'clock yet. They would be starting the second set any minute.

I had fallen asleep alright, but it was the music that I had dreamed up. Or maybe someone was playing it from a tent nearby, it sounded too real to be made up. Right about the time I was figuring it out, I heard Danny's voice.

"Hey man, just came by to check up on you."

"Just trying to regain an idea of my existence, you know, the usual," I whispered as loud as I could. It really was what I had been doing. I just wasn't sure how successful I had been.

"I'm not thoroughly convinced of my own existence," he said as he sat down beside me. "Reality has lied to me before, I'm just not ready to trust it yet."

I must have really been freaking out when I left the group and had just run off looking for falafel. I thought I had told everyone where I was going, but my voice had been gone all day. I guess I just whispered something that no one heard. Danny had volunteered to come look for me. "Why don't you come back with us for the second set? This is it man, this is the end."

He was right. The weekend had been filled with awesome music and there was only one set to go. I mustered all my energy, which, even with the nap, still wasn't very much, and made my way with Danny to the concert field. I couldn't even try to use my voice to protest any more anyway. I was badly out of shape, and my legs began to rebel on me. I had used them far too much over the weekend. I wasn't used to all of that walking. Danny got the idea from the look on my face every time I took a step, and we slowed way down.

We weren't through security yet when the first notes cut through the air. I didn't recognize the song at all, which was odd, because I even recognized every song that they played when I was dreaming, or when I was listening to a recording earlier, whichever it was.

The song had a big flourishing intro, and I very soon realized Fishman was singing. And then it hit me, even before they got to the chorus. It was a favorite song of mine in my middle school years, a cover that Phish had never played before. In honor of the Super Ball, they played AC/DC's "Big Balls."

"It's my belief that my big balls should be held every night!" Fishman yelled out over the crowd.

"We've got the biggest balls of them all!" everyone screamed together. It was a fun song, and got the crowd fired up and ready for a kick ass night of music.

Jonathon "Henrietta" "Moses Brown, Moses Dewitt and Moses Hephs" Greezy Fisek" "Friar Tuck" "Fish" Fishman was not only a favorite of the crowd, but he was a favorite of the band too. Trey loved him like a brother, it was obvious to everyone. He would write really hard drum parts for songs, just to fuck with Fish, and was always amazed that he could get it every time. Of course Trey did it out of love.

They love him so much that when they learned that Fish hated the song "Hold Your Head Up" by Argent, Page started playing it every time Fish would come out to sing a song. When he got used to that, they changed it up and played "Cold as Ice," by Foreigner, Fish's second least favorite song. He was a small ball of insanity that you couldn't help but love.

What most people knew about Jon Fishman was that he wore a dress and that he played a vacuum cleaner. Both were true, although the vacuum cleaner was making fewer and fewer appearances. In the old days he would come out at least once a show, now it was a rare treat.

Trey would go back and play drums, and Fishman would sing a Syd Barrett tune and then play a spooky vacuum solo. After 500 or so attempts at playing the vacuum, Fish actually started to get pretty good at it. That was no fun, so he started playing Trombone, or Cymbals or washboard. Eventually he would go on to cover Neil Diamond, Prince, and even I Wanna Be Like You from the Jungle Book.

In recent years he hadn't played the vacuum or any other strange instrument as often, but he has been given more and more vocal roles while playing drums, and his singing had greatly improved. Though he was usually just called Fish, he was known by many other nicknames through the years as well. Like Nancy or Henrietta, or Moses, or Greezy Fizek, or Shirley Temple, or Friar Tuck or anything that anyone could think of. He was generally regarded as the most entertaining member of the band by fans, media, and other band members.

In fact, legend has it that the band got their name because Trey said that if he went to a show, he'd spend his whole time watching Fish. Of course, because it was the 80's, and so not to confuse people with Country Joe, they spelled it with a PH, like Phresh. But even in the beginning, Fish was simply the most lovable in a cast of lovable characters.

The dress part was still true. He did lose it for a few years. (He wore regular clothes, although he has never been shy about public nudity either) But the black dress with the red donuts had become his look.

In the old days he would always wear the same dress at every show, usually kept together by duct tape by the end of the tour. Lately though, it seemed like he had a brand new dress every night. They even started selling the Fishman dress at the merchandise booth at shows and in their "Dry Goods" online store.

One of the more frequently asked questions was "What does Fish wear under his dress?" The answer in the old days was nothing. I had seen Fishman's penis more often than any penis that wasn't my own over the years. Luckily he had started wearing boxers at some point, which led to him tucking the dress into his underwear at some show, which then led to another new nickname, "Friar Tuck."

I was still tripping really hard as we approached the concert field. Seeing all of the lights and the crowds of people, I knew I didn't want to try to go back up front near the stage again. The crowds weren't bad all weekend, but I still didn't want to feel trapped in by people. I grabbed Danny, and even with no voice, made it clear I wanted to hang back.

Behind the concert field, not quite at Ball Square, was a nice small, relatively mellow field. There were people sitting all around in small groups, and some by themselves. No one was dancing, but you could enjoy the music and have a conversation back there. It seemed like a much more chill, perfect setting for me.

I let Danny know exactly where I would be sitting. Not that it mattered. Danny was heading off to see the rest of the show, and almost definitely wouldn't be back. I hoped he would find the others. They were in a great spot, even if too claustrophobic for me.

I couldn't see the stage from my new spot, but I could see the Ferris Wheel, which had a light show of it's own. I could also see part of the light show coming from the stage. There must have been speakers nearby too, because the sound was perfect. I sat watching the lights on the Ferris Wheel swirl, not even knowing what song they were playing.

I knew it wasn't Big Balls anymore, or if it was, they had taken it into deep type II territory. It turned out that they were playing Down with Disease. Which, as usually, had become the launching pad for the nice long type II jam. I looked around me, everyone was content but looked as exhausted as I felt. It had been a long, hard rocking weekend.

I felt like I had to get up and walk around for a bit. Slowly, with nowhere in particular to go. In the corner of my eye, I caught a glimpse of a drawing of a tree. A woman was drawing a tree that looked like the one straight ahead of us, except in the drawing, there was a naked woman tangled up in the roots. Suddenly I realized I was standing right over the artist's shoulder, almost on her blanket, as she was drawing. It was as if I were in a deep trance.

The drawing was absolutely beautiful. So was

the artist, sitting in a field and drawing during the show. If I had a voice I would have tried to talk to her, I would have sung to her, I would write poems for her, but luckily I didn't do any of that.

It would have wrecked the scene, and the drawing. I was just tripping out on what she was drawing. I suddenly realized that she hadn't even turned to look at me, or wondered what I was doing. She hadn't noticed me at all and I was almost on top of her.

Being brought back to earth for even a second, I felt a little embarrassed and backed away, hoping to be gone before she noticed or acknowledged me. It worked. I really hoped that she hadn't noticed me. If she had, she was too freaked out to turn around, and I didn't want that.

It had been a long time since I had taken the acid, and if anything, it seemed like it was hitting me even harder now. There was a row of bushes between my field and the concert field. The stage was still completely blocked from view, but I could really get a good look at the light show, and the light show was all that I really needed.

At one point I could swear the music was actually coming from a bush. The bush was playing just for me. Not the band, or even the speakers set up all around me, but from the small hemlock bush. I grabbed a branch and I was about to snap it off as a keepsake, but then I thought better of it.

What if the music really was coming from the bush? If I took the branch, the volume would obviously go down, or it may even mess up the song. So I left the bush alone. I had to. I didn't want to be responsible for fucking the show up for everyone. Instead I made my way back toward the Ferris

Wheel again. I thought that sitting might be fun, I hadn't tried it in a few minutes.

I lined up the lights of the stage with the lights of the Ferris Wheel and took a seat directly in between the two. Right as my butt hit the ground, I recognized the song they were starting to play. It was No Quarter by Led Zeppelin, a song that they had just started covering earlier that summer. Page's electric piano and vocal skills would be on full display. It was perfect for him.

The song immediately made me think of my buddy, Al. When he was a senior in high school, back in 1978, he had gotten a job at Swan Song records, Led Zeppelin's record company. It was a dream job for anyone, let alone a teenager. Every time I sat in his studio I would see the signed picture of Robert Plant that hung on the wall between the two Gold Records that Al got for dance hits in the 80's or 90's.

I missed Al, he had been taken from the world far too soon. I needed to "bone up" with him one last time. Bone up was an expression he used that actually scared me the first time he used it. I wasn't really sure that he meant smoke weed, but luckily he did. It could have gone in a completely different, uncomfortable direction.

Sitting in the field, I went through the junk in my pockets and found the baggie with the worst weed that I had on me. It still wasn't as bad as the weed Al normally had. Even if Al had good weed, he would mix it with bad weed and tobacco to conserve the good weed.

I traded a really nice bud with someone near me for a cigarette. I couldn't put cigar tobacco in the joint. That would be a little too much. It had to be cigarette tobacco. A slim, like Al used to borrow from his wife, would have been best, but I couldn't be choosy. I took whatever they had, and I think they were happy for the bud.

I rolled it up in a nice fat joint and slobbered all over it, just the way he would have done it. Once it dried off enough, I sparked it up. Luckily, No Quarter was such a long jammed out song that they were still playing it by the time it was ready to smoke. I sparked it up and heard a low gravely voice that I hadn't heard in several years right next to me.

"Hey Brother, it's been a while," It was Al, reaching out for the joint, before I even finished taking my first hit. I knew it was impossible. I knew that Al had died. I knew I was tripping, but I also knew that Al was sitting right there, right next to me. I knew it would be a long minute before I got the joint back, and it would be all wet after he slobbered all over it, too. But none of that mattered at all, I was boning up with my friend Al again.

It was great to hear his deep voice with a thick Bronx accent. "You know you've already learned enough to do what you gotta do. I mean, you gotta keep learning, but you can start."

"Start what?" I had no idea what he was talking about.

"I don't know, but whatever it is, I know that you don't think you are ready yet. You are," he coughed up the hit a little, and then took more in. You're ready." He finally handed the joint back to me. It was covered in spit, just like I had predicted. I hadn't tasted the mix of weed, tobacco and Al spit since he had died, it felt good, like I was back home again. "You're on the right track though. The open mics are a good start. You got time, You're still young." You're still young. It was something that he used to tell me all of the time, usually in the context of settling down with a woman.

For the last year I had been playing my own songs at local singer/songwriter open mic nights. A few of them were songs that I had originally recorded with Al. It was just me and my acoustic playing my songs. It felt good.

I was also playing bass and running the open mic jam once a week with Diamond Jim, the one who had originally introduced me to Al. I never knew what song we were going to be playing next, so it really helped me with my music, my improvisational skills and my ability to play with others.

"So music?" I took a small hit and then passed it back to him. It had been a long time since we smoked together, if he wanted to hold on to the joint for awhile, he was more than welcome to it.

"I don't know, but whatever it is, just do it." Al had always been my biggest fan. He loved the funny tunes I would record at his place, or the funny blogs I wrote on Myspace. He always wanted me to do more. Like Reed, "More!" was his mantra, he just went in a slightly different direction than Reed.

Al was always the first one to comment, or give my blog kudos, the Myspace version of the like button.

"I went to the future, dude. You were there. Don't worry, you were doing fine." With that Al gave me a big smile, handed me back the joint, got up and walked back toward the Self Storage building. The ringmaster grabbed him and pushed him into the strange box on the corner of the building. I didn't see if he ever came out or not.

As the syncopated rhythms of the song "Party Time" started up it dawned on me just how hard I was still tripping. I had just hung out with a ghost. I started wandering around again.

Ball Square was oddly deserted, yet still had all the flags hanging in the dark causing creepy shadows. Again it felt like there was a smoke machine going, but that may still have been the acid. I decided to go over to the self storage building to see if Al was around. There were still a few things I wanted to ask him, but he never showed up again. Not even when Phish began playing the song Ghost, which would have been the perfect time.

It dawned on me, Al had been such a good friend, the one thing I already knew for sure was how to be a good friend. I had good friends right there at the concert. Maybe that was my mission. To be a good friend.

There was no reason at all why I wasn't with them. I looked at the concert field and the close to 50,000 people that stood between me and my friends, and I became determined to go rock out with them.

When traveling solo, I could make it to the front of a huge crowd in no time at all. It was one of the advantages of being short. I knew where Reed and everyone else were during the last set. They may have moved, but I had a feeling that they would be close to the same area now. I didn't know if Danny had found them, or was even looking for them, but as I got close, I saw Reed and Danny standing next to each other dancing away.

I jumped up between them and put my arms around both of their shoulders. Reed had always said that he enjoyed seeing shows with me. I figured it was just because I always knew what song they were playing, so I was glad Danny had been there with him to fill my role.

There was more than that though, Danny also had the same pure joy of being at a show that I had. The same love of the music and the musicians playing it. Reed loved that feeling and fed off of it. With all of us together, the rest of the show was just a complete joy.

Unfortunately, Chris and Kerry had already left. They had a much longer ride back to Vermont than we did to New York, and Chris had to work the next morning. The rest of us were off. I had even taken Tuesday off as an additional recovery day.

I was sad that I missed them, but I knew I would see them again soon. I always thought that Chris was a good guy with a big heart, and Kerry had done nothing but make me like her even more all weekend.

Sabrina had gone back to the tent. I was surprised that she had lasted as long as she did. There had been a lot of music during the weekend even for most die hard Phish fans. Plus I was sure that the Molly had probably run it's course. Who knew how much of it she had taken. For me it always led to a hard crash. She was probably crashing really hard.

John and Linda were both still there. They were dancing their asses off to the music. I hadn't noticed how much fun they were having before. Linda must have really loved Phish, or John, for them to still be there and still be as into it. I was just happy to see them both smiling and enjoying the music. Maybe this would end up being one of the shows John went to that was better than the one you went to.

The rest of the set was comprised of mostly newer
material. It was stuff that I didn't know as well, but they were playing great and there was lots of room for jamming.

There was one tune, "What's the Use?" that I had never heard at all before that got me. It was one of the few times that they stumped me as to what song they were playing. It was a cool, mellow instrumental that really grooved with where I was mentally. Trey always knew exactly what my head needed.

Ernesto Guisseppe Anastasio the Third was known to a legion of fans by his nickname, Trey. He was sometimes called Big Red, but usually just Trey. He was more of a nickname giver than a taker. As much as Phish had always been a group effort and would not be the same without any of them, Phish lived and died by Trey's smile, and performance each night. Generally speaking, a good Trey show is a good Phish show. A show where Trey is happy, the fans are happy.

Phish was Trey's vision from the very beginning. He had played in a band in high school with frequent song writing partner Tom Marshall before moving on to the Universty of Vermont. There he met Mike, Fish, and original band member Jeff Holdsworth. Trey was the main songwriter, though Jeff, also a guitarist, and Mike both added a few songs, too. Fish only added the occasional song, but it would usually become a fan favorite.

Eventually Page joined and Jeff left. The rumor had always been that Jeff had found Jesus, and Jesus told him electric Rock music wasn't the way to go. He did come back and join them once, at their 25th anniversary show in Albany. They played Mustang Sally, the first tune Phish played, and Possum and Camel Walk, that were both written by Jeff and still both in Phish's musical rotation.

The first time I saw Phish, I looked at Trey and immediately knew that he was not the hippie or stoner I assumed that he was. He was a nerd. Specifically, he was a music geek. He was the guy everyone knew in high school who liked Frank Zappa and Stravinsky and Abba all at the same time.

He knew about bands before anyone else. He "got" King Crimson. He understood Jazz. He enjoyed classical music. He was a total musical genius and he was a weirdo. He was the perfect man to lead the next generation of freaks.

He studied music, he studied performance, he studied crowd psychology and he studied faces. Every time he walked on stage and began to rip on his guitar he looked at all of the faces in the crowd.

You could see it in his eyes. He was memorizing them, he was watching what bending his notes did to them, and he used that information to perfect his craft. Everyone who has ever gone to a Phish show will say that Trey looked right at them, at least once.

Music is supposed to be fun. Trey understood that. They all did, but Trey wrote most of the songs, and he added fun to his music. They had an insane drummer, that was perfect. Trey wrote that into the live show. He loved to showcase the talents of his band mates. He wrote certain songs in keys he knew would be best for Page to sing, just because he loved Page's voice. Trey was usually the one who led them from one song into the next, and he had done a great job of it all weekend.

The song Meatstick was the next song up, and even though I considered it a newer song, it already had a real history. The most famous version being the closing song at their Millennium Festival held on a Native American Reservation in Florida called Big Cyprus. That night they began their set at 11:50 PM on December 31st 1999 and ended it, with Meatstick, at the first sunrise of the year 2000 just before 8 in the morning.

Trey and Mike had choreographed dances in a few of their songs. They had little funny dances in Guelah Papyrus, the Landlady and they even had a short trampoline routine in their song "You Enjoy Myself." What made Meatstick different was that they encouraged the crowd to join in on the dance.

Much like the Macarena, it was a stupid, simple dance. Also much like the Macarena, people loved it, especially the Japanese. When they played the song on a short tour of Japan, it was so well received that they started singing part of the chorus in Japanese. That made the fans love it even more.

Meatstick added to its history the year before the Super Ball, during their New Years Eve show at Madison Square Garden. One of the band's most loved traditions is the New Years prank. Meatstick, already being a New Years veteran, was going to be central to the prank.

For example, during their New Years Eve coverage of the Millennium show at Big Cyprus, ABC TV decided to go live to Florida and show Phish playing their almost hit song "Heavy Things." Of course Trey had prepped the crowd ahead of time. At a predetermined point, everyone in the crowd yelled "Cheese Cake!" in a very angry voice, for the home audiences confusion.

Another year they put Fish inside of a huge disco ball and fired it out of a cannon. It looked as though he went flying through the roof into the parking lot. His replacement was a woman that Trey pulled out of the crowd. As she came up to the play the drums, she went behind a curtain, when "she" came back out of the other side, it was Fish in the same dress that the woman had been wearing.

For the Madison Square Garden New Year's version of Meatstick, more and more stereotypes came out on stage and started singing the chorus in their own language, as the band played. It started off with four Zulu warriors, and then a Mariachi band. By the time the dancing Rabbis came out, all bets were off. Soon the entire stage was filled with people, dancing and singing. No one noticed, but the band had left.

Suddenly they reappeared, sitting inside of a giant hot dog that hung from the roof across the arena and made it's way over the crowd and to the stage. The Super Ball Meatstick was tame in comparison, but as always, it was always a fun song.

It was still the Third, but it was getting close to midnight when the band walked back on stage for their final encore of the weekend. Another long standing Phish tradition has been the A Capella song. The four of the would get together in front of the stage and sing in 4 part harmonies.

In the early years they sang without microphones. They tried to do it that way as long as they could, but eventually the room outgrew their voices. Usually they would sing an old barber shop tune, like Sweet Adeline, or Carolina. In recent years they had even been writing songs like Grind, to be sung a Capella. In honor of the birth of America, they sang the Star Spangled Banner for us. When they finished, they went back to their instruments and started up their song "First Tube." It was a high energy instrumental, the perfect way to send us all home. About halfway through the song, the fireworks started. They seemed like they were coming from off in the direction of our tent, but they were in an area where the band could watch them too.

Unlike the Clifford Ball, the music and the fireworks were perfectly in synch. The whole weekend had gone down perfectly. Phish had proved that they did, indeed, have the biggest balls of them all.

When they finally left the stage I felt drained, But I was also sad and angry. I didn't want it to be over. I didn't want to go back to the real world. I wanted the Phish festival to last forever.

I was still tripping my face off, and now my voice was so bad that I couldn't even whisper. Walking back to the tent, we passed by the What? Cheer Brigade again. That was what I was going to miss the most, running into random horn bands while walking down the road.

We stopped and gave them a nice long listen. Danny and Reed didn't want the weekend to end either. A crowd grew around the band. People were dancing all over. No one wanted it to end, we all wanted more music. More fun times. Trey had ended the night by joking to start all over again the next day. We would have all taken him up on the offer in a second.

Danny came partway back to the tent with us, but he had to go get his own stuff together and then catch his party bus back to New York City. It had been great to reconnect. He was going to visit some of his family still living in Mount Kisco after he got back to the city, so we made plans to meet up then. I was hoping we might even have a nice jam one night. One thing I knew for sure, I wouldn't be doing any singing.

When we got back to the tent, Sabrina was already busy deflating one of the air mattresses. The fireworks show had woken her up with a literal bang, they were launching the fireworks from an area right behind the tent. At first, poor Sabrina thought she was under attack. Once she escaped out of the tent, she ended up with a perfect view.

We had to break down Chateau Goncalves in the dark. Putting up the monster was definitely harder, but at least we could see what we were doing when we did it. In the dark, it was hard to know what everyone was doing, I was certain that we would forget something or do something wrong. I really didn't want to lose any parts. It was an expensive tent. Sabrina had been nice enough to let us use the tent, we didn't want to destroy it on her.

John and Linda just sat there, not helping at all. It was starting to piss me off. Probably more than it should have. John had bought lots of food and beer and shared it with us all weekend. I think most of the aggravation came from the fact that I was still tripping so hard. I was getting sick of it. I had been tripping all day and it really should have run it's course already. But some of my frustrations came from John and Linda, too.

One of the air mattresses was still full. I thought that it was something they could do to help. It really wasn't very difficult. I put it down in front of John and Linda.

Without being able to say anything, I hoped that they might get the point on their own. They didn't. They sat down on it as if that was why I had brought it over to them. I reached down and opened the plug. Only when it started to deflate on them did they get the idea. And then they acted like deflating an air mattress was the hardest job in the world. Sabrina had to help them out once or twice.

No one had seen Shaggy since the first day. His tent was still up, but it was completely dark. There was no sign of him. Reed and I went to check it out.

Reed called out his name a few times, since I couldn't. There was no answer, so I unzipped the tent. I really didn't expect to find him dead in there, but I couldn't be sure. It would have probably started to stink already if he were dead though.

Luckily he wasn't. He wasn't inside at all. Just as I was zipping up the tent, Shaggy showed up.

"What, were you afraid I was dead?" He asked. He startled us. Both Reed and I jumped a bit and he unzipped his tent.

"Umm." Reed was about to answer but Shaggy just started laughing.

"It's OK, I heard you wondering the other night while I was passing out. Thanks for looking out. Umm, kind of, I guess." It was great to see him alive, that would have really wrecked the weekend. More so for Shaggy, but for all of us, too.

We had almost finished breaking down the

tent when Reed received a text message. He got super excited in the way that only Reed, or a five year old in a candy store, can get. It was from one of the guys that he knew who sold pins. Before we knew it, he had taken off to meet the guy, leaving Sasha behind with us.

I have to admit that some of the pins he collected were really cool. They were all hand made and beautifully painted, but they weren't my thing. Of course Reed loved them, and when he loved something he went all out. At Bethel Woods he had jumped out of a moving car as we were leaving when he saw a pin guy on the side of the road. Someone made a pin for just about every Phish song or Phish joke, and every tour there was a whole new collection available, and of course, Reed had to get them all.

Reed loved the thrill of the hunt. He was always looking for that one pin that he had never seen before. He had a fishing hat that jingles when he walked because it was so full of pins. The guy must have had a pin that Reed could not do without. He was gone before any of us could even offer to go with him.

We packed up Sabrina's car. Reed had taken his keys with him on his quest, so we couldn't load up his car. We moved everything we could to right next to his car though.

The rest of us wanted to go back to the hotel, but we couldn't just leave Reed's stuff sitting out there. It kept getting later and later and there was still no sign of him. We tried calling him and texting. No answer, but he wasn't getting the best reception either..

None of us had a right to be too mad at him.

We would not have been up there at all if not for Reed. John and Linda had a car, too, they could have skipped drinking for one day and drove, or taken the bus if they really wanted to leave on their own schedule.

I also felt bad that Reed had missed most of the show on Saturday. We all knew Reed. We knew he was impulsive, and we knew he lived on his own time. None of us should have been surprised. Still, I wished he would return a text or a call and let us know how long he would be.

There was too much stuff packed inside of Sabrina's car for all five of us to fit in, besides someone had to stay with Reed's stuff. John and Linda were complaining the most about wanting to leave, obviously they weren't going to volunteer to stay behind. Sabrina didn't want my tripping ass driving her car. John and Linda were too drunk. Even Sasha was tripping, though she didn't show the effects. Sabrina would have to drive her car.

Sasha offered to stay, but I wasn't sure how much she meant it. She generally didn't like large crowds or unfamiliar places. Though it had been a really comfortable surrounding all weekend, we really didn't know anyone around us. She had also gotten a lot better at that sort of thing since she had been dating Reed. Reed had no hang ups about anyone or anywhere, so she was getting used to it now.

Sasha kept insisting that she was more than happy to stay behind. She said that we should go, but I knew that she was tripping, too, so I was very unsure of leaving her there alone. I halfheartedly tried to argue with her, but she blew me off and told me to go back to the hotel with Sabrina and the others, so I went. I immediately regretted my decision.

As we started on our way back to the hotel it became obvious to Sabrina and I that John was completely hammered. If I hadn't been tripping so hard I probably would have noticed earlier. He started talking more than he had all weekend and he was talking a lot of shit. I had forgotten that he could be such a mean drunk.

Usually when John was drunk he was funny, but he could be mean as hell, too. I didn't really mind until he started to bad mouth Reed. He didn't say anything too bad and nothing that he wouldn't have said to Reed in person.

It was nothing that Sabrina and I wouldn't say ourselves. Reed would have probably even agreed with most of it.

I was in the front seat, and even if I wanted to, I couldn't say anything to John. I couldn't defend my friend Reed, and that pissed me off. My voice, now completely gone and that just added to my aggravation.

John kept right on going after getting some chuckles from both Sabrina and Linda. He started exaggerating for effect, and that brought even more laughter. Then Sabrina jumped in with a joke of her own.

That pissed me off more than anything. Laughing at "an outsider's" joke about Reed was bad enough, but joining in on the jokes was the final straw. Not that John was even an outsider, he had known Reed for years, it just felt like Sabrina, Reed and I were the Three Musketeers, and that we should defend each other. I couldn't talk, I couldn't defend Reed, I had hoped Sabrina would jump in for me.

I was still tripping hard, getting really pissed, and with no voice, felt like I had no way to express myself. When Sabrina made her joke it was the final straw. I didn't want to blow up with the others in the car, I wanted to keep it "in the family," but I was in a rage.

I was mostly angry with myself, angry for leaving Sasha behind to wait for Reed. I should have stayed. Let them all bad mouth Reed together. Al taught me to be there for my friends. Reed was my friend and I had taken the quick ride back. It was my own damn fault, but it was the others that were pissing me off.

When we got back to the hotel it was nice to have the key card work on its first attempt. Sabrina, happy about getting into the room so easily and not sensing at all how pissed off I was, immediately went and got in the shower. I didn't blame her for that, I had wanted to jump in myself. By the third day the concert field had become a dust bowl. We were covered in sweat and dirt.

I went outside and lit a cigar, hoping it would calm me down a little bit. What I really needed was a drink, but I didn't have anything in the room. I knew that Sasha had a bottle of Jack back in her room. Sasha always had a bottle of Jack somewhere nearby. I really hoped they got back soon. I sent Reed a text telling him to stop by when they did.

I don't know what I was expecting to happen. If maybe I thought Michelle was going to rise from the dead and say goodbye like Al had, but the weekend still felt incomplete. I was going to have to go back to the real world, and I was still tripping extremely hard, much harder than I should have been. I was scared and angry and poor Sabrina had no idea what she was about to walk into.

She came outside and lit a cigarette. She was making small talk but even if I could, I wouldn't have answered her at all. She knew that my voice was gone, so she thought nothing of my silence. I must have looked almost as pissed off as I had at the front desk that morning, but Sabrina didn't notice. The rage was growing, and I felt like I couldn't even say anything without doing permanent damage to my vocal chords. So I just got up and started to walk inside.

"Wait! Give me your phone?" Give me? She didn't even ask. She just said give me. Again, normally that wouldn't piss me off. She really didn't need to ask. It was us, we didn't need formalities with each other. But because I was already pissed, that just pissed me off more. I dropped it in her lap and walked inside without even looking at her. I badly needed to take a piss and then take a shower.

She needed to call her boyfriend. It shouldn't have, but that pissed me off, too. She had repeatedly sworn off of men. She had bad mouthed them up and down for the last two years. I knew why. She had picked some horrible men in the past. Yet now she was swooning over some new guy. It just felt wrong to me, even if I didn't really know why.

Nothing about Brendan had pissed me off before that moment. I had never met the guy, there was no reason to be pissed at him, so I went back to being pissed at her. I sat on the chair next to the window and waited for her to come in. I could hear her voice as she talked on the phone, but I couldn't hear what she was saying, and I really didn't want to. I could make out the sweetness in her voice that sounded nothing like the Sabrina I knew.

I put my hands in my pockets to find that they were absolutely filled with garbage. If I hadn't already known I had tripped hard, that would have told me. There were napkins covered in dried hummus. Two half empty packs of cigars. A couple of cigar butts. Various receipts, I didn't know where those came from, no one gave receipts at Phish shows. I found the roach from the joint I had smoked with Al. That was special. I wanted to keep that, so I tucked it into my wallet.

I pulled out my house keys and put them on the night table. I don't know why I had brought those. It was as if I were purposely trying to lose them. I had the key card for the room, as well as my credit card which was no longer in my wallet for some reason. I put it into it's designated slot in my wallet, across from the roach.

Some of my cash was still in my wallet, the rest of it was crumpled into various pockets. I found a 10 dollar bill mixed in with the napkins. Once my pockets were empty I felt a thousand times lighter. I had hoped I would feel better, but I didn't.

We hadn't been in our new room for very long, so it was still nice and clean, but I had now covered the night table next to my bed with my pocket treasures. There was a half a pack of Lifesavers that I didn't remember buying. It had been a hell of a trip. I still felt it, too, hours later. It should have been over a long time ago. Maybe that was why I was getting so pissed at Sabrina. It must be.

I had never been pissed at Sabrina before. It was hard to believe but true. Even Reed had pissed me off, the day he kept me working on a house when he knew that I had a jam scheduled for that night.

The fact that he ran off to go buy pins and left

his girlfriend sitting there did piss me off a little, but that was just Reed, and that was expected of him. I never expected Sabrina to turn on Reed. She hadn't, of course, but that was the way that I had perceived it.

Sabrina walked in chatting away, not having any idea of how pissed off I was. "God. He's so annoying, wondering when I am going to be home tomorrow. How am I supposed to know, we have late check out?"

I grabbed my phone from her, for the first time she noticed the anger in my eyes. "Some people get what they deserve," I snapped as loud as I could, just slightly over a whisper.

"What?" Sabrina had a look of disbelief in her eyes. She had never seen me pissed off at her before, and she probably had no idea why I was pissed then. I barely knew myself, but the fact that she was confused by my anger pissed me off even more.

"When it comes to relationships, sometimes you get what you deserve." I said, slowly and deliberately, using the very last of my voice. I turned and stormed out of the room. Before I even got a few steps down the hall, I realized that my pockets were empty.

I had no keys or money or cigars. They were all sitting on the night table by my bed, with the rest of my pocket junk. So I turned around, went back and knocked on the door, feeling like a bit of an idiot, but for all of the wrong reasons.

Sabrina answered the door right away. She was probably expecting me to apologize. Instead I went right past her and grabbed some of my stuff. Without thinking I grabbed my house keys, cigars and wallet, but not the key card to the room, and I stormed right back out of the room. I didn't know where I was going yet, but I had to get out, at least until I had settled down a little.

I went out into the parking lot, passed the puddles with the brine shrimp evolving away, to the hill behind the hotel. It was a steep, high, well maintained grass hill. It was maintained better than just about anything else at the hotel, which led me to believe that it was probably the property of the bank that was behind the hotel.

I was sitting with my back to the hotel, but I was in plain view to anyone in the parking lot or rooms on that side of the building. I lit a cigar and waited, I wasn't sure what I was waiting for. After what seemed like only a few minutes, I saw Reed walking up the hill towards me. He had a couple of boxes in his hand.

"So what the fuck happened?" Reed asked. I felt bad immediately. I was supposed to clear the air between Reed and Sabrina this weekend, and I went and blew up on her for all of the wrong reasons. "Sabrina says that you turned into a psycho and then left."

"Yeah, pretty much," I whispered. Even a whisper hurt like hell. The lack of talking had made my vocal chords feel like they had crusted over. I just shook my head. The sun had not yet started it's ascent into the sky, but it would be coming soon. It was usually my favorite time of day.

"What happened?" he asked.

"I don't know man, I just blew up. People were making jokes and having fun and it pissed me off." I was talking so low I don't think Reed heard me, but he got the idea from my face.

"You think it might have something to do with the festival ending? It was a damn good time and we have to go back to reality tomorrow." That was a big part of it, he was right about that.

"Oh sure, but it was the way Sabrina was talking about..." Reed cut me off. Which was probably for the best, I didn't need to tell him Sabrina was talking shit about him when she really wasn't.

"Chuck, do you think maybe you're a little bit in love with her?" he asked.

It was a valid question and it merited some serious thought. The fact was that she was a beautiful girl, and we normally got along really well. When we went to festivals and shows we always had fun. When a scummy looking guy at the Gathering of the Vibes was flirting with her, she grabbed my arm and called me her boyfriend. That actually did feel good.

But was I in love with Sabrina? In my tripping state the thought just kept rolling through my head. A few months earlier when I thought that she might be interested in me, I didn't really want to get involved.

But I did love her as a friend. That was something I took away from Al, to love my friends and let them know it. But that was different than being "in love with her." I had been in love before, it had felt nothing like this.

But was I maybe jealous of Brendan? Was that what kicked off my anger? No, that really wasn't it. If anything I felt a little bad for him. Sabrina, as much as I loved her and though she was awesome, was very set in her ways. She was not about to let some guy change them. I knew that she would fight him tooth and nail over the small stuff.

From what I had heard of him already, he

might have been the perfect person for Sabrina. He was patient and relaxed and he really loved her and he had for a very long time. There was a very good chance that they would work, and I was happy for them. I really was.

I realized that it wasn't Brendan I was jealous of at all. It was Sabrina. I was jealous that she had found someone so good for her without even looking. I was angry that she had a good person in love with her and she was acting so cavalier about it. But that was it. It was just an act. She was falling in love and she was scared shitless about it.

I was angry because that was what I wanted. No, I didn't want it with her, but that was what I wanted in my life. I wanted what she had found.

Reed could tell I was thinking too hard. He handed me the box he was holding. It had a clear top and I could see the coolest set of pins inside. There were twelve guitars, all shaped like Trey's Languedoc. Each one had a location from the summer tour written on it. They all fit like puzzle pieces into a gorgeous wheel, and they all made up what looked like one giant pin.

There were some dazzling colors flowing all over the pins, and in my state it looked even more amazing. All of my anger and confusion dripped away as I got lost in the world of the pin. After what felt like an eternity, but was probably only a minute or two, Reed grabbed my arm and helped me get up.

"Come on man, I'm exhausted and still tripping too, let's go get some sleep." Reed took me back to his room. Sasha was already fast asleep. I had forgotten about the drink that I had wanted earlier, but it probably would have helped a lot if I had thought of it. Reed took some blankets and a pillow and made a little bed for me on the floor, and he was passed out within minutes.

I tried to get to sleep, but it just wasn't going to happen anytime soon. I grabbed my phone and tried to send Sabrina a text apologizing but I just got an error message back. I understood all of her phone frustrations in an instant.

Reed was snoring, loudly, and I knew I wouldn't be able to sleep at all. I could see out of the window that the sun was just starting to come up. I needed to get out and take a walk around. Even though I knew I wouldn't be able to get back in, I quietly made my way out of the room and out of the hotel.

As I walked by the front of the hotel I looked in the window. Rodney wasn't there, or at least he wasn't at the front desk. I was sure that he wouldn't be. There was a woman at the desk by herself. She looked worn out, but not as bad as Rodney had been the night before.

When I got to the street I looked down towards the town and the lights of the convenience store. I really didn't want anything they had to offer, not even the real juice. I looked down the other way, where the road went out of town. It was darker that way, so that was where I went.

The Yellow Barn Self Storage was a five minute drive away on the first night. Not a single car passed me on my walk. I didn't think I would make it anywhere near the spot, but just as the sun really made it's way into the sky I found myself in front of the three steel buildings.

I looked around, I didn't see the rose

anywhere. I didn't expect to, it had been four days since I left it there. I sat against the middle building for a bit before I got up, lit a cigar and took a walk around the buildings. Behind the last building I could just barely make out an old foundation in the ground.

I walked over and rubbed my hands against it. This was it, the old Yellow Barn. I really hadn't thought about the story I wanted to write for the book my internet friends were putting together until that moment. Right then and there I knew that I would have to write the story of Michelle.

It really wasn't a story I wanted to relive, but having already told it to Sabrina, it was now fresh in my mind. I decided right then and there that I would start writing the story as soon as I got home.

With that revelation, I began walking back to the hotel. The walk back felt like it took a lot longer than the walk there, and after all the walking at the festival, I was exhausted by the time I got back. It was about 8 in the morning, so I went to the buffet and chowed down on bacon, pancakes and eggs. The coffee tasted great, but I knew it wouldn't keep me up for too much longer.

After I ate I was ready to pass out, but I didn't really want to wake anyone up. I knew Sabrina and I would be fine after we both got some sleep, but it might not ever happen if I woke her up too early. Luckily the back of her car was unlocked, so I went in and found my sweatshirt.

I went to the pool, found a comfortable lawn chair, and lay down. Using the sweat shirt as a pillow, I closed my eyes. Images were still dancing on the backs of my eyelids, but I was so exhausted that I managed to fall asleep anyway.

Destiny Unbound

Monday, July 4, 2011:

Whoa Fee
You try to live a life
that's completely free
You're racing with the wind
you're flirting with death,
so have a cup of coffee
and catch your breathe

Anastasio

Chuck Howe

I woke up on the beach chair with other hotel guests walking all around me, bringing their luggage to their cars. We had paid for late check out, so I was sure that Sabrina would not be up yet. I dreaded seeing her. I had no idea what I would say to her, but I had to get my shit. Even if I drove back home with Reed, I would still need to get my shit from the room.

Even after sleeping for awhile, I was still tripping. I didn't know how it was possible, but I was, and I was still tripping hard. I had only taken a small amount the day before, but it must have been compounded with what I had taken Friday.

I was still seeing visuals, but my head was a lot clearer than it had been the night before. My voice was still completely gone. It hurt to even breathe through my mouth, let alone try to talk. It would be a few days until I got my voice back.

I must have been wasted when I passed out. Everything I had was on the ground next to the chair. I gathered up my cigars, my phone and the sweatshirt that I had been using as a pillow and made my way back to the room. I knocked softly at first and there was no sound from inside.

I knocked a little harder, and this time I heard a noise. Sabrina eventually got up and opened the door for me, but her eyes were still 90 percent closed. She didn't say a thing. I couldn't tell if she was pissed at me or just pissed at being awake.

"I'm sorry, you know it was the drugs right?" The words came out of my mouth in a harsh whisper before I could even really think about what I was going to say. It was as loud as I could talk and I hoped she had heard me because I didn't know if I could repeat it.

Sabrina didn't say a word. She just gave me a big hug, silently turned and went right back to bed. I plugged my phone in so it would be charged for her to call Brendan and then jumped in the shower. I hadn't been able to shower the night before, and collecting dew on the lawn chair only made my stink worse. That would give Sabrina a little extra sleep time, too.

When I got out of the bathroom, Sabrina and my phone were both gone. I looked out of the window. Now that we were on the first floor she was basically standing right beside it. I went to grab my cigars to join her, but stopped when I heard her voice coming in through the window.

"Again, happy birthday and I'll give you a call as soon as I get home, OK? Bye," I heard her say as she hung up the phone. It was Brendan's birthday and she was up here with us. That sucked for him. We had made all of these plans before they were together, but now I felt really bad for the guy. She was waking up in a hotel room with me on his birthday.

It didn't take us very long to pack up all of our stuff. We had only been in the room for one night, and I didn't even sleep there. I was kind of hoping we could take some time and check out the town. I hadn't been in Ithaca in years, and now I felt good about being there. But that was before I heard Sabrina on the phone.

She had put up with an awful lot from us over the weekend. Poor Brendan had to put up with even more. The quicker the two of them were back together, the better it would be for all of us. We still had a five hour drive ahead of us.

Musically, the weekend had been a wild success. Phish had played a lot of their newer stuff, they busted out a few surprises, gave us a good mix of covers and originals and jammed out hard all three days. Some of the biggest surprises though, were the songs that they didn't play. A band like Phish had hundreds of songs, they couldn't play them all.

For years, their song You Enjoy Myself had been the stereotypical Phish tune. It was played just about every other show, and the fans always loved it. It had all the things that make a Phish song great. It was intricately composed with recognizably familiar movements, yet had plenty of room for improvisation.

There was a section of the song where Mike and Trey jumped on trampolines, while Page ripped a solo on his organ. Each member got to show off their skills with a nice long solo. Best of all were the song's controversial lyrics. The first four words were easily understandable. "Boy, Man, God, Shit," but after that, things got strange.

"What do you say during YEM?" became the most frequently asked question in the Phish universe. In the early days of the newsletter, "the Doniac Schvice," there would be a letter asking about the lyrics in every issue.

"Wash you feetsie, drive me to fierenze," was the closest I could ever come to figuring it out. It was just another one of the jokes they liked to play on their fans, and their fans didn't seem to mind. But the best and often most humorous parts of the song was the very ending, the vocal jam.

With various effects on their voices, the four of them would sing in scat. It was always different and always interesting. They were always able to work different phrases and jokes into it. Sometimes it worked, but it sometimes fell flat.

Sabrina had seen them play it at the PNC show and was not a fan at all. The song had been seen less frequently in recent years, but usually they would play it once on a three night stand. It was still strange that they hadn't played it during the eight sets of music they had given us.

I felt bad leaving Ithaca. We were going to pass the former yellow barn as we drove home. It would be the third time that I had been there, but I never went to the gorge, or any of the restaurants that Michelle and I used to go to.

I had done enough. I had enough fun. We had talked with Reed and Sasha about doing a hike, but now that I knew it was Brendan's birthday, it was more important to get Sabrina back home. It was enough for me to know that Ithaca was still a cool, beautiful town.

For the first part of our trip I just stared out of the window, whispering about how beautiful it all was. I forgot how much I enjoyed the small towns and the big farms. The hills, the streams, the woods, the fields. It was all so beautiful.

My friends who lived in the city always said that I lived out in the country because I lived in Westchester County. While it was true that there was a Llama farm in my town, we were definitely not out in the country. We were suburbs, This, outside of Ithaca, was out in the country. I had no problem with country.

As we passed a beautiful old farmhouse, I

could see myself sitting on the porch, playing banjo and sipping on a big old jug of whiskey. I could see kids running around the corn plants, and "my old lady" yelling at them to be careful. I knew life wouldn't be that easy, but it was a dream, and it felt like it had been awhile since I had a dream.

Traffic was extremely light. Part of it had to do with it being the Fourth of July. Another part of it was that it was Monday, and the Festival had ended the night before. A lot of people had already taken off and headed back home. Even so, the day after the Clifford Ball, it took us three hours just to get out of Plattsburg. The Super Ball was done right, all weekend traffic had been light.

We occasionally passed a car with a Phish sticker or with a group of Phish-Heads in it, but not very often. We made really good time to Route 17, the road we took most of the way back. Even the main roads felt empty. It was almost scary. What if the world had ended, but we didn't know it because we had been at a Phish festival? I was really getting sick of tripping.

Sabrina spent the entire ride home chatting away. Since I couldn't talk and felt like I had talked the whole way up, it was her turn anyway. She was in a great mood and made no mention of the night before. I was hoping that maybe she forgot about it. The texts probably didn't go through, and if she ever did get them she never said anything. I was still tripping pretty hard, I had no idea how she was feeling.

She was finally really opening up about Brendan, too. She was starting to let her guard down a little. Like I thought, Sabrina liked him a lot more

Chuck Howe

than she was letting on at first, it scared her but at the same time, excited her. It had been a long time since she had been in a brand new relationship with someone, and finally it was someone who appeared to be worth it.

The more I heard about Brendan the more I liked him. He was a heavy drinker, but not a smoker at all. That was OK, I found that relationships with one of each tended to be a bit better. He wasn't going to smoke her pot and she wasn't going to drink his beer. It was a little odd that Sabrina, a militant non drinker, would fall for a drinker. Then again, Sabrina had declared herself a militant single woman not to long ago, too.

Brendan had been living up in Vermont for a few years, but now he was back down in the area. Apparently he still had a place in Vermont. The only question about the guy was if he really was back in New York now, or still lived in Vermont. He still had friends in Vermont, and Sabrina loved to snowboard, so she was hoping that they would spend a lot of time up there in the winter anyway.

He was into skiing and kayaking and all sorts of outdoor activities that, other than skiing/snowboarding, I didn't see Sabrina being a fan of. She was trying though. Obviously she thought he was worth it if she was going hiking with him.

Brendan knew Diamond Jim, my drummer, pretty well. We were going to be playing our weekly open jam that Thursday night at a bar right down he road from Sabrina. It was also my birthday, so that would be a great excuse for her to bring him along. We would get Reed and Sasha to come too. Once we all met and got to know one another, I was sure that everything would be fine.

I admitted to Sabrina that when I first heard Brendan's name, I looked him up on Facebook and saw that he was Diamond Jim's friend. I had immediately called Jim and did some snooping. I asked Jim to tell me the worst thing he knew about Brendan. He had to think awhile.

"Well, he drinks. A lot," was Diamond Jim's only answer. I was glad that Sabrina had mentioned that, too. It let me know that she was being completely open.

"Is he an angry drunk, violent, sad?" I asked. I wasn't a big drinker myself, but I have been around enough to know that some are funny, some are mean. Some, like John, were funny and mean.

"He's a sweetheart. A pretty happy guy, drunk or not. I like him, he's a good guy." Diamond Jim was a pretty good judge of people. I trusted him. He knew his fair share of assholes, too, he was even good friends with some of them. He wasn't afraid to call them out as assholes though. If he said Brendan was good people, Brendan was good people. On the ride home, Sabrina just confirmed it for me.

The ride was a lot nicer than I had expected, after the way the night before had ended. We made great time on the way home. As we passed Roscoe, we thought for about two seconds about pulling in. Sabrina was eager to get home and have a birthday dinner with Brendan, I was just eager to get home, so we decided to skip it. Besides, for the first time in my life I felt like I had enough bacon over the course of the weekend, and it was too late in the day for hash browns.

I was trying to go over Michelle's story in my head, whenever Sabrina would take a break from talking. I was glad I told her the story on the way up.

215

I didn't have the voice to do it on the ride home. It had been good to get it all out, and have it fresh in my mind before I even started to write it. I didn't know how I would set the story up or anything, but I figured that would come to me when I sat down to write it. That was what usually happened anyway.

I was so deep in thought I didn't even realize that we were pulling into my driveway. Sabrina must have thought I was asleep as she gently put her hand on my shoulder and told me I was home. I could only smile back as a reply. My throat was almost completely closed up. She helped me unload my stuff and was off to have birthday dinner with her boyfriend.

After she left, I set my laptop up at my desk and sat down ready to get to work. I had a nice cup of tea to help my throat and I was ready to go. I sat there, staring at a blank screen. I waited for the words to come on their own. I waited for my fingers to just start typing, but they never did.

My head was still swimming with the acid. I didn't feel like I was still tripping, but I was still seeing visuals all over the place. I was just more used to tripping now that it had been two days straight and three out of four.

I closed the laptop and picked up my acoustic guitar. I was a much better bass player than I was a guitarist. I could play bass without thought. Guitar still took thought. That was why I liked writing music on a guitar. I had to think about it more, and work on it. I didn't fall back on familiar patterns the way that I might on a bass.

It was the Fourth of July, I felt like I should be doing something to celebrate. I should go see fireworks or something, but I had already seen fireworks and celebrated the Fourth. Sitting on my couch playing guitar, followed by sleeping in my own bed sounded like the best way to celebrate to me.

Some Monday nights I would do a singer/songwriter open mic in town. I liked to play the tunes I wrote there. I wasn't very good at singing or playing guitar, but it was fun and people enjoyed my lyrics. Everyone there was always encouraging, and the talent level really varied. Both the host and the bartender were really good people and over the years it became the real Monday night hot spot.

During the football season it sucked when you would be playing a song and suddenly the guys sitting at the bar would all start to boo. It took a while to realize they were booing the Football game, at least that was what I told myself. Of course if they ever cheered, I assumed that they were cheering for me.

Even though it was Monday, I knew I couldn't go. My voice was gone, and I definitely wasn't good enough at guitar to play instrumentals. I could go and drink and support the others who play, but the weekend was catching up to me fast. I was going to need to be close to my bed. Inspired by the weekend of music though, I started playing a bunch of Phish tunes on guitar.

I was having fun weaving one song into another, the way that they liked to do sometimes. I didn't know how good it sounded, but it was a lot of fun to play, especially with the acid still in my system. I knew what I wanted to do for my birthday gig. I wanted to play a few Phish tunes, solo, on an acoustic, before we started the jam.

I had been threatening my band mates with

opening with a few solo tunes on an acoustic for awhile. What better time to do it than on my birthday. I kept playing the same four or five Phish tunes over and over until I finally drifted off to sleep. Thankfully, this time, in my own bed and without the TV blaring.

That night I had a dream that I was sitting on a street somewhere. It felt like the circle in front of my old high school, but it was different. There were stores behind me.

I was playing my small, shitty, cheap acoustic that was my beater guitar. It was a half sized, classical, nylon string guitar. Most people hated it. I loved it. I had even gotten a full sized nylon string acoustic electric for when I played out. I was busy working on the song Fee when Trey himself came walking up to listen in.

"I always have trouble with the lyrics of that one," Trey told me as I tuned up. I smiled. I never had trouble with the lyrics. What I had trouble with was the c#7 chord.

"I'll bet you that I can get all the words right on the first try," I said to Trey.

"Oh really, what do you want to bet?" He asked. He had the same grin on his face that he did when he was on stage.

As a joke I said, "If I win, I get your old Languedoc guitar, if you win, you get this shitty guitar." Languedoc guitars were selling for 10,000 bucks, if you were lucky enough to get on the waiting list. Even though I knew that it was a dream, I didn't expect him to take the bet. Of course, he did.

I started singing and playing. I sang all of the words right and I even hit the c#7 perfectly. Then I got to the second chorus, and then I flubbed it badly.

Destiny Unbound

The second chorus had different lyrics than
the first, yet I sang "You're racing with the wind
you're flirting with death, so have a cup of coffee and
catch your breathe" instead of "You want to stay with
Milly until you're dead, but you just got a bottle
upside your head." The second I realized my mistake
I stopped playing.

"Fuck!" I yelled out in my dream, and probably
in real life as well. I had been defeated. I held the
guitar up for him, not really expecting him to want
such a piece of crap. He reached down, grabbed my
guitar and walked away strumming the guitar riff to
Julius.

Chuck Howe

Destiny Unbound

Tuesday, July 5, 2011:

And the light is growing brighter now
Purify our souls,
Obstacles are stepping stones
Guide us to our goals

-Light
Anastasio/Marshall

Chuck Howe

I woke up to silence. There was no TV blaring. No girls wooing about their love of going wild, no one telling me that my penis was too small. There were no hotel guests walking past my lawn chair. I woke up in my own bed, alone, silent, happy.

It felt like it had been a long time since I woke up to silence. I had missed it. I wanted to get up and start writing. I was home now and it was time to get back to work. I opened my eyes and looked at the floor as I went to get off the bed, but I stopped.

I looked down. The circular patterns in my oriental rug were spinning like perfectly synchronized gears. I immediately knew that I was still tripping pretty hard. It was starting to get ridiculous. I wanted nothing more than to be done with it. All day long it was all I could think about.

My voice, with the aid of a lot of tea, honey and silence, was slowly starting to come back to me. For the most part, life was getting back to normal. Except, of course, for all of the damned hallucinations.

I sat down and tried to write a few times during the day, but nothing was working. I knew the story that I wanted to tell but I couldn't get it out. That only added to my frustrations. No words were coming to me as I stared at the blank computer screen.

I didn't know how to start, and I really didn't want to get to the meat of it, and didn't know how I was going to end it. I felt like I should have it all, but instead I had nothing. I thought that tripping hard might help me write before going to the Super Ball, but now I wanted nothing more that to stop tripping. I needed to get out of the house, I needed a change of scenery.

I drove over to Reed's house. It was the first time I had tried to drive since I had been back home, and it was a very good thing that Reed lived so close to me. Each car that passed me looked like it was a pirate ship that I was sure was about to attack me. I was terrified by the time I got to his house. I really wanted nothing more than to be done with my trip.

Once I got to Reed's house, I ran inside to escape the encroaching trees, clouds and crickets. The door always stuck when it was humid out, so I had to shoulder my way in, almost falling in the house once I got the door open. I was greeted by a smiling purple cat. At least I knew that the cat wasn't a hallucination.

Maxwell was a British Short Hair cat, and while he was officially called a gray, he would always be a purple cat to me. When he was just a kitten he had a highly visible purple hue to his fur, almost like a deep lavender aura. It had faded away as he got older, but I still saw it.

He was just as friendly and playful as he was when he was a kitten. Maxwell was a cat that just liked to hang out with everyone. He thought that he was just one of the guys, but he would always be a purple kitten to me and I reminded him of it all the time.

"Hi Maxwell, you're a purple cat," I gave him my usual greeting as I picked him up and carried him into the living room with me. He didn't ever protest being picked up, in fact, the moment his feet left the ground he started purring like a Harley. He loved all of the attention that he deservedly received.

I got along well with most cats. Mostly because I knew most cats had a limit. They might put up with some of your shit, but only to a certain point and most cats had no problem letting you know when they were finished with you. Some people couldn't tell, and they woud blame the cat when they crossed the line. I knew. That didn't stop me from crossing the line with some cats, but I didn't blame them for my new battle scar.

Not Maxwell though, he was a cat with no limits. He really didn't care if you picked him up, or grabbed him or pet him or even stepped on him. I never once worried he would bite or scratch. More like a dog than a cat, Maxwell was just happy to be involved.

He liked to be in the center of any group. He was never one to shy away from people. Reed was his obvious favorite, but he liked us all. Even if he did get sick of us, he'd just try to get away. I had never heard him hiss, or protest in any other way, not even when Sabrina was smothering him with hugs and kisses. And Maxwell was the only one we had ever seen Sabrina smother with hugs and kisses.

"I really don't get how you are still tripping, Chuck. I took way more acid than you and I'm fine. It was really clean and not too strong." How much acid Reed had taken was, as always, irrelevant. He could have a ton more of anything than most people and it was hard to notice it have any effect on him. He was a true Viking Warrior of psychedelic drugs.

Because of that I was hoping he might have some tips to help me deal with the trip, but he was stumped. Nothing like that had ever happened to him. He had always tripped and then it was over. My trip just kept going and going. Nothing ever phased Reed too much. Even if anything like that had happened to him, he would have just powered through it.

I had tried sleeping through it. That was his other suggestion, as if I hadn't tried that. Of course I was finding it really hard to fall asleep let alone stay asleep with all of the visions and colors swirling on my eyelids. Even when I did sleep, I was tripping just as hard when I woke up. I even tried eating a roll of Tums because they said Antacid on it.

"I really want to write my story, but I am still tripping so hard that I end up just watching the colors float across my blank screen. I have to do something, and soon." Normally I didn't mind seeing colors and patterns everywhere, but after three days I was getting sick of it.

"You should talk to Andy about it, he meditates and does all that new age shit like that. Plus he's taken more acid than any of us the last few years. If anyone can give you any pointers, it's him." It was a great idea, I didn't know why I hadn't thought of it. I was glad I had gone to Reed. If he couldn't help, I knew he could point me in the right direction.

And Reed was right, Andy was the perfect person to talk to. He had started his journey into the absurd at a later age than most of us, but he understood the spiritual and mental side of the trip in a way that Reed didn't. For Reed the answer was usually to "do more." I didn't think that taking more acid would be much of a help at that point. Andy knew that there were more answers out there than just "do more."

Andy approached his trips as a learning experience. He usually liked to trip alone, and he would meditate while doing so. I didn't know if he had ever experienced such a long trip as the one I was on, but I was sure that he could, at the very least, relate.

Plus, there was a good chance that he might know exactly what to do. Maxwell purred in agreement. He liked Andy too, but Maxwell liked everyone. I put him down and he just flopped over and took a nap where I had dropped him. He was fine where ever he was, just like Reed.

Since my voice was doing much better, I gave Andy a call once I got home. He picked up the phone on the first ring, and told me that Reed had already warned him that I would be calling. We hadn't known each other for very long, but we had clicked right away. He got me, I can't say that I got him, but I was closer to getting him than most.

Andy had a wonderful curiosity for everything about life. I could appreciate that. He was a smart kid, even if he didn't give himself a lot of credit. He had never done well in school, so he thought that made him dumb. But he was always eager to learn more. He wasn't a kid really either, he was only a few years younger than me. He was married and had three kids. If anything, I was still the kid.

I told Andy what was happening and that I really just wanted to calm my mind down. My thoughts were flying through my head much faster than I could process them. I just wanted to be able to slow them down, I knew that there was a good story flowing in that stream somewhere. I had been home for a day already and I needed to come back to earth.

"Do you ever feel like your life is a movie and you are just watching it on a screen?" He asked in his calm, therapeutic way. It was not a question I was expecting. I knew right away that calling him was a good idea.

Andy liked to say that he was the Yoda to Reed's Darth Vader. Though I thought that Andy was wise and strong with the force, I had always believed Yoda to be an evil character. They say that only a Sith deals in absolutes. Every word out of Yoda's mouth was an absolute, therefore, Yoda must have been a Sith master all along. Neither Andy or Reed were very evil, they didn't seem it to me at least.

"Yeah man," I answered, "except that the movie is stuck in fast forward, or maybe there are three different movies playing on the same screen. I can't follow it at all." Just putting it into words was already starting to make me feel a little better.

"That's OK. Close your eyes," he paused as if it would take me more than a second to close my eyes. Thanks to the acid, it did. "Now turn and look up at the projection booth. Who is working the projector?" He had the voice of a hypnotist or therapist.

I try to do what he said but I couldn't see. It was too dark, with a bright stream of light flowing out of the small window onto the screen. The light blinded me to anything else up there, until I saw a face lean over and look out of the small window. The light from the projector hit his face just right for a split second and I saw.

"It's me. I'm the projectionist," I answered suddenly. I had seen myself peering down at me from the window. I got excited. I didn't know what it meant, but it was a start.

"Are you sure? Most people see God," he started to answer back. "Or some sort of higher..."
I cut him off, "Yeah, but I'm an atheist. No one controls my projector but me." I said with joy and purpose. It was true, long ago I had stopped giving credit or placing blame for what happened to me on anyone but myself.

"Well, OK," I could tell he was thinking hard. I hadn't given the answer he wanted, but it was the right answer for me. "Then turn off the other projectors, and slow the fucking movie down yourself." It was true. I was responsible for my view of the world around me. That was about the only thing that I could claim as my own. If I wanted a change, I would have to change.

It was great to talk to Andy. I was still tripping, but now I thought I could control it a little bit better. I couldn't, but at least it felt that way for the time being. It would take some work, but I finally felt like I could turn this thing around. It was a long trip, but at least it wasn't a bad trip, I could be thankful for that.

I called up Bob. He had known right away that my second "Butt Licker" message of the weekend was a fake. It just didn't have the right resonance of a proper nitrous scream.

Bob had never done acid. He couldn't help at all with that, but I figured talking to a friend who wasn't on anything at all might help out. Plus, since he was going to be playing with Jim and I on my birthday, I wanted to go over some of the songs we might end up playing.

I knew that he didn't need any prep. Bob was a great guitarist, he could keep up with anyone who might show up, but it felt good to talk music. It was something I knew about no matter how hard I was tripping.

Talking to him was a nice distraction, but I needed to try to get some work done. I tried to write the story again. When that failed I tried some free thought writing. Nothing came to me. I tried to write an abstract poem and it was just nonsensical words.

When the writing didn't work I decided to switch to the guitar. I wanted to make sure I had my songs down for the jam. They sounded fine to me sitting on my couch, but they would sound a lot different going through a PA system in a bar. I started to sing along, but my voice was still very weak so I mouthed the words to work out the timing. I would get it all down by Thursday night.

I fell asleep pretty easily that night, even though I still saw colors dancing on the inside of my eyelids. I drifted into a dream where I was in New York City and ran into Al on the street. He had worked at the United Nations, doing sound production, right before he had passed away. In the dream it felt like that was where we were, but it was hard to tell in a dream.

"Al," I yelled. "I thought you had died! I went to your funeral and everything," I gave him the biggest hug I had ever given anyone. It was him, exactly as I had known him before he got sick, when his only worry had been his thinning hair.

"Dead? No way man, that was just what Kate had told everyone," his voice had changed. It didn't sound anything like how I remembered it sounding. I looked into his eyes and they didn't look the same to me either. It wasn't him, it was someone pretending to be him. I had almost fallen for it.

"I found a new girl, she's great, you'd love her.

Kate was really pissed about it, so she told everyone I died." I couldn't believe what I was hearing. Kate was his widow. She had been deeply in love with him and she was crushed when he passed away.

In his life, Al had loved Kate with all of his heart, it was obvious to everyone anytime he ever spoke about her. This wasn't right. He had a son too, did she tell him that Al was dead too? She and their son had been everything in the world to him. I knew it was a dream, but it just didn't make any sense. I wanted it to be over, I wanted to be rid of this impostor.

"You could have told me," I started to ague with the dream Al. It definitely was not the Al that I had smoked a joint with at the Super Ball, but I still wanted to believe that maybe he was alive. Maybe he had changed. Maybe he had fallen in love with another woman.

"Whatever man. I'm here now, let's hang out." It wasn't Al. It didn't even look like him at all anymore. I didn't know who it was, but it wasn't him, "Let's smoke some pot?"

That gave him away for certain. Al had never called marijuana "pot." Not even once in the entire time I knew him. If he had said, "Let's bone up" or "Got any bagette," I might have believed it. Even "Ganja" would have been acceptable. Pot was not, so I just walked away.

Chuck Howe

Destiny Unbound

Wednesday, July 6, 2011:

My soul is made of marble
But in her gaze
I crumble into dust
And drift away on the wind
The wind from beyond the mountains

Tela
Anastasio

Chuck Howe

I woke up and I knew that I was still tripping before I even opened up my eyes. I could see red and blue lights dancing across the inside of my eyelids. I was getting really sick of this shit. Sure enough, the wheels on my rug were still spinning. As was my new daily ritual, I steadied myself as I got out of bed, and walked in a crooked line towards the bathroom.

Looking in the mirror was becoming another fun daily adventure. Usually it was me, or some version of me, but sometimes it was someone else looking at me from the other side of the glass. The other person always turned into me after I looked at him or her long enough, but it was still an adventure.

When I was in high school, there were rumors of a kid who was on acid and when he looked in the mirror he never looked away again. As with every story like that, he was the friend of a friend of someone who told the story once long ago.

Everyone always said to avoid looking in the mirror, but that hadn't stopped me in the past, but now I was starting to understand the rumors.

Luckily, this time I was me on the other side of the mirror. There was more of a purple and yellow aura around me than I had ever seen before, but it was definitely me.

"Who is running the projector?" I asked my reflection and my reflection asked back, luckily at the same time as me. I had told Andy I was, but I wasn't sure if I really believed that anymore.

Chuck Howe

It was time to look at my writing project in a new way. If I wasn't going to write it yet, maybe I needed to reload, to read something new, while I was still tripping.

That might give me some sort of inspiration. If anything it would give me a good excuse to run down to the book store. It had been far too long since my last visit, and even longer since my last good purchase.

It wasn't a great bookstore. And I definitely wouldn't call it "my book store." It was a huge crappy chain store, but it was the only book store in town. That wasn't entirely true, there was a Christian bookstore in town, too, but I doubted that they had anything that would interest me.

This chain bookstore had run my favorite independent coffee shop out of town. There cafe workers didn't even know how to draw a decent espresso. Then it ran my favorite bookstore out of business a few years after that. Mine had been an independently owned, expertly staffed, bookstore. The kind you were proud to call yours.

This chain store had a bunch of high school kids who knew as much about classical music as they did about Russian Literature, which was nothing. I once asked about Dostoyevsky and was told that he didn't have any new albums coming out.

I never asked for help there again. If I needed anything, I could look for it myself and find it faster than they could. I knew the store wouldn't last for very much longer. The chain was hurting. Amazon was running everyone who was left out of business. But that made the chain store running my favorite places out of business even sadder.

I begrudgingly drank their double espresso,

cursing the fact that they had gotten it right and I had nothing to bitch about. I checked out their magazines. They had a far superior collection of magazines than anywhere else I had ever seen, even MY old bookstore. So at least I could get pissed about that. I grabbed the latest issue of Gramophone and made my way up the steps to the Books and Music section. I hated the place, and the fact that they had everything I wanted.

I knew what I wanted and where it was, but I didn't go there right away. First I had to go through the CD's. I always check Phish first. Not that I would ever want to buy a Phish CD there, but just to see what they had in stock. They had Billy Breathes, one of their better studio efforts, and three Live Phish CDs, officially released concerts.

Two were the same show, from Japan in 1999, the Third was the Halloween Show in Vegas where they played the entire Velvet Underground album Loaded, in 1998. I didn't need them. Both were good shows, but not impressive enough to purchase. I could download audience recordings of them online for free.

I then went and checked the Jazz CD's. It was more likely I would buy a Charles Mingus or Coleman Hawkins disc I had never seen before than it would be for me to buy a Phish CD. I had enough Phish. I needed more Coltrane. Unfortunately Mingus, Monk and Hawkins all came up dry, so I was off to the Russian literature section, my intended target all along.

I had been reading a lot of Russian writers lately. I had already checked out writers like Tolstoy and Dostoyevsky and was making my way down the list. I had never finished college, so I was trying to read all of the classics on my own. I hated being in a social situation and not knowing references to classic literature. I could quote Peter Griffen, Eric Cartman or Homer Simpson, but not Count Alexei Vronsky, and that was wrong.

I had worked in the music department of the Mount Kisco Book Store and tried to catch up on as many of the classics as I could at the time. I had mostly stayed with American or modern writers, but I tried to mix it up. Once the chain store moved into town I had plenty of time to read.

At one point Penguin did a recall where we had to cut off the covers of most of the paperback classics. We then had to send the covers back to get credit for them and then we were supposed to throw out the books. I ended up with a great collection, all without their covers. Still to this day, most of my best books don't have covers.

I was trying to fill in the gaps in my collection though, and Russians in the 1800's, and even more so, Ukrainians in the 1800's, had piqued my interests lately. I had never read any Nicolai Gogol, but I had heard dark morbid things about him. He sounded perfect, I was there to get his book Dead Souls. You couldn't get darker than an 1800's Ukrainian Author writing about Dead Souls.

I made my way for the furthest, dankest corner of the brightly lit chain store. It wasn't very dank, but it was in the back corner. The only suitable spot in the entire place for Russian Literature. The small section was usually vacant. If there ever was anyone, they looked like they were old enough to have fought in the Russian Revolution. This time I was taken by surprise.

A tall, young, beautiful, black woman stood

there, thumbing through a book. She wasn't right where I was going, but close enough where we smiled at each other as I looked for my book. She was dressed a bit on the conservative side, almost business like, but she had a pretty wild hairstyle and bright colorful makeup. She pulled it off well, it looked more high fashion than like a clown, how most people would look if they tried to pull off the look.

I tried not to be too obvious, but I quickly looked her over. She wasn't as tall as I had thought at first. Her wild hairstyle added a few inches to her height. She was also wearing big platform heels that added at least another six inches. At first I would have thought that she was taller than me, but she was probably at least a good 6 inches shorter than me. Still, she got my attention no matter how tall she was.

I found the book I was looking for, checked out the back cover and started flipping through it even though I already knew that I was going to buy it. It looked really boring and dry. I wasn't sure why, but I thought that was what I needed. I could feel her eyes burning into me and when I looked over, just as I thought, she was staring right at me.

"Ah, I see you're looking at Gogol. I am a big fan of his work." She had a very slight accent. It was hard to place and very faint. I always loved accents and foreign languages, but I didn't want to mention it, because she sounded like she was trying very hard to hide her accent. My voice wasn't entirely back yet, but that may have been for the best. I had a rough sexy voice, and I fully intended to use it to my advantage.

"I have never read anything by him before. I

am trying to make my way through all of the Russians though." I looked down. I tried to see what she was reading, but could only make out the name Fonvizin, a writer that I knew absolutely nothing about. I couldn't even pretend to say something witty, so I just kept quiet. I had learned that lesson in the past.

Her face looked young. I could tell that she was much younger than I was, but she carried herself with a maturity that I liked right off the bat. "I'm Kayla." She held out her hand for me to shake it. I was a little stunned. She was being pretty forward, not that I minded at all.

"I'm Chuck," I answered, stammering a little bit. She had caught me off guard. I kissed her hand, rather than just shaking it. It was my turn to catch her off guard.

"Kayla, I'm almost ready, meet me around back in five minutes?" A very young looking girl, who obviously worked at the store, yelled out as she came around the corner. She had a voice that was naturally too loud for anyone in a bookstore.

She stopped and giggled when she saw us talking and then quickly scampered away, before Kayla could answer her. It made me wonder exactly how young Kayla was. I thought that she was in her late twenties, but I could have been way off. That other girl seemed much younger than Kayla, but Kayla could just look older.

"Well, it was nice to meet you Chuck," She said as she started to follow her friend. The acid still in my system made me a little bolder than I would have normally been. Plus she seemed interested in me, and that was rare, so I couldn't let her get away so easily.

"Wait a minute. Can I see you again sometime?" I asked, feeling a bit like a high school kid. I was hoping my scratchy voice would make my uncertainty sound sexier than it felt. She stopped in her tracks and looked at me with a sly smile.

"Sure you can see me again. I'm always here." She grinned at me. Even though she had come on to me, she didn't plan on making this easy. Again, I wasn't sure if she was being sly or young. If she was just trying to get my attention, it was working.

"No, I mean can I take you to dinner?" I could see her thinking it over. To save face I added, "or maybe you could give me your number, and I can call and we can meet here for coffee or something." That would be a good out for her if she really didn't want to do dinner yet.

"I tell you what, why don't you give me your number? Maybe I'll call you and we can go out for a bite to eat sometime." She quickly answered, as if not even thinking about it. I liked that just fine. Even if she didn't call, I still felt good, like I had accomplished something, like maybe I still had it.

I gave her my number and watched her as she left. Kayla never looked back, but her friend did. I took my Gogol, and my Gramophone and went to the counter to pay.

When I got home I tried to read the book that I had just bought, but it didn't work. The letters kept dancing all over the page. I couldn't get past the first few words before I would get dizzy and I had to put the book down.

Playing guitar was the only thing that was working for me. I picked up my mini guitar and started going over the same few Phish songs I had been playing since getting home from the Super Ball. I should have been using my gigging guitar, and getting used to playing that. I wanted to play them the next night, so I just practiced them over and over again. The mini guitar was just more comfortable to play while on the couch.

The phone rang and I didn't recognize the number. I almost let it go to voice mail. I usually let unknown numbers go to voice mail, but something told me to pick it up. "Hello?" I answered.

"Hello," said the voice with a slight, unidentified accent on the other end. "It's Kayla. I've decided to let you take me out to dinner on Saturday night." It had only been about an hour since I left the book store. This girl was into me, and I really had no idea why, but I didn't care. I was into her, too, so I figured I might as well go with it.

"OK, do you want me to pick you up?" She seemed like the type of girl who would have it all planned out already, so her answer didn't surprise me at all.

"No. I will meet you at Steven's at 8:00. Do you know where that is?" Of course I knew. It was right in town, only about a block away from the bookstore where we met. Everyone who had ever been to Mount Kisco knew where Steven's was. It was one of the only reasons some people ever came to Mount Kisco.

"Yes I do. I'll see you there," I went to say more, but she had already hung up on me without even saying goodbye. She was a weird girl, I was sure of it. But I was still tripping. For all I knew she was perfectly normal and I was the weird one. Well, I knew I was the weird one, but I was starting to think that she might be weird, too. I could only hope.

I went back to playing the guitar but the phone rang again. This time I knew knew the number. It was Andy. He was just calling to see how I was doing. He was a good guy, and genuinely cared about his friends. It was a quality that I had learned to appreciate more and more since Al's passing. I found that my friends were all a lot kinder and sweeter than I would have thought on the surface. I was lucky to be surrounded by good people.

"I'm running the projector right, I guess," I told him all about meeting Kayla. Andy had been married for over ten years and had three kids. He was a little bit jealous of the single life and wanted to hear all about her. Part of it was that he wanted me to be happy, but part of it was that he wanted to hear how the other half lived. I was impressed with myself on this one, so I told him all about her.

"Hey, tomorrow night I'll be doing a little solo set before the band goes on, Sabrina and her new boyfriend will be there. I think Reed and Sasha too, why don't you come?" I was a little embarrassed that I hadn't asked him earlier, but I was still tripping, it was surprising that I had remembered at all.

Andy didn't get out very often, but the bar was right down the road from his house. "Hell yeah," he shouted over the phone to me. "That sounds great! We'll be there!" Andy liked to pick on a guitar, but he was still a beginner. It had taken awhile to get him to go out to see music, but he had been getting more and more into it.

We got him to go to the Vibes, and to a few Phish shows, but he was most impressed with the bar bands. He was amazed that there were local bands that could play Black Crowes or Grateful Dead songs.

He had come to see me play my acoustic tunes a few times, I knew he liked Phish, so I thought he would get a kick out of it. "Great, I'll see you then!" He answered before hanging up.

When I went to bed that night, I noticed my pockets were much less cluttered than they had been since the Super Ball began. I had a receipt for the book, and some random bills and change, but that was it. There wasn't even any cigar wrappers, or the normal ephemera that I would usually find at the end of the day.

That night I had another visitor in my dreams, this time it was Michelle. Where the night before my visitor had looked like Al, but it wasn't him, this visitor didn't look like Michelle at all, but it was her. I didn't know how I could tell, but there was no doubt about it.

It was her voice. It was her smile. It was her eyes and her words, but it was not her face. Her hair was different. She was even a different height and size. I had not seen her in a long time though. Even in my dreams. I wondered if maybe I just didn't recognize her anymore.

There was so much that I wanted to say to her. There was so much that I wanted to hear her say, but none of that happened. She just smiled at me and that made me feel good.

I got the idea. She was right. It was time for me to move on. Had she survived, she wouldn't be the same person today as the girl that I had met twenty years ago. I wasn't the same guy that I was back then either, and that was a good thing.

I had been too hung up on her for far too long.

I had been comparing everything in my life to an ideal that may not have ever been true. I had been comparing everyone to someone who may have been very different than I imagined. I needed to go out and live. She would have been fine with that, in fact, that would have been what she wanted for me. I had to learn to be fine with that, too.

Chuck Howe

Thursday July 7, 2011

When was the last time you picked up a book,
Read the book,
Just read the fucking book

Icculus
Anastasio

Chuck Howe

Destiny Unbound

I woke up and I was still tripping but I didn't
care at all anymore. If that was the way life was
going to be, that was how it would be. No reason to
cry about it anymore. My voice was almost back to
normal, at least it was good enough for me to try
singing later on. Life was good, whether I was
tripping or not.

It was my birthday and as I stood up, for the
first time that I could ever remember, I actually did
feel like I was a year older. My body was creaking
and groaning as much as my head was spinning.

I smoked a bowl, and poured myself some
coffee. I tried to do some writing, but once again, that
didn't work. I tried to read, and that didn't work either.
I played some music, I found that playing guitar was
the only thing that could slow my movie down.

After a few tunes I was feeling closer to
normal. I called Kayla and got her voice mail. I
figured I might as well invite her to the gig that night.
It was always a strange thing to have someone come
to a gig, though. I couldn't give them very much
attention while I was playing, but didn't want to make
anyone feel like I was ignoring them. It was probably
for the best that she didn't pick up. Plus I didn't know
if a first date on my birthday was the best idea in the
world.

I tried singing the songs over and over again.
Singing was the only thing I hadn't been able to
practice all week. I set the PA system up in my
garage so I could practice with amplification. The

249

songs would never be called great, but they were fun. I wasn't a singer in any sense of the word, but it didn't sound that bad at all. I was as close as I was going to get to being ready.

I had to take the night off from the jam the week before, due to the trip up to Ithaca, so I was really in need of a good jam. Playing music was the best way for me to recharge. Diamond Jim and I had been playing with different guitarists every week since Ralph, our old guitarist, had gotten into a fight with the bar owner. Ralph was a great guitarist, but I was always most interested in playing with Diamond Jim. We had been jamming for years, and would probably end up playing together for years more.

For my birthday, I was actually able to get Bob Affeti to come out and play some music. Bob rarely ever played out live, even though he was better than most guitarists working every night. I had played with him as much as anyone else since high school. It was tough to get him out.

Doing an open mic jam was always interesting. There were some nights where I had to play bass the entire night because no other bassists showed up. There were other nights where I only needed to play during our opening three songs, and then there were others itching to jump up and play bass. I was hoping that other bassists would show up to give me a break. Since it was my birthday and I did have a lot of friends coming, it would be nice to hang out with them for a little while.

Reed called. He and Sasha would be coming for sure. That was nice. Reed was a good friend, but he didn't come see me play very often. I had been playing a lot lately, and he just didn't have the time. I didn't blame him, besides, he had come to enough of the early gigs to make up for it. Plus he wasn't really a bar person either.

Sasha was a drinker though, and the bar where I was playing had a pool table, so she would be happy. I just had to make sure to get a few breaks so I could smoke with Reed, and I knew that I would be able to do that no problem. If there were no other bassist, Bob could always take over for a few songs. He always had fun playing instruments other than guitar.

Throughout the day I got plenty of calls from friends and family wishing me a happy birthday. The very best part of Facebook every year is all of the birthday love and well wishes coming from people you would never hope to see on your birthday in real life. People were spread all over the world, but they could all wish me a happy birthday.

All it took was a click on Facebook, but it was nice to know so many people took the time to click and post a birthday wish to me. Even the people that I had never met in person. Not only that, but I was able to get a few people to go to the gig from Facebook. Social media was definitely my friend.

I wanted to respond to every single post, but it would have ended up taking forever. So I just went through and "liked" each post. I went back and checked a few times throughout the day, and liked all the new wishes each time. I felt bad each time one of my writer or artist friends, who would likely be in the book, left me a post. I felt like I should have finished my story by then.

I wanted to write it for them as much as I wanted to write it for me. Still nothing was coming. It was as if I really didn't want to write Michelle's story. Maybe that had been the point of the dream the night before. I was supposed to write my own story, not hers. I still had plenty of time to write it. Plus, it was my birthday, so I wasn't going to worry too much about it yet.

I tried to call Danny. He had said he would be in town for a few days, but I hadn't heard from him since I had gotten back from Ithaca.

He was a good musician, it would be great to have him play, but even if he just wanted to come up it would be fun. He had known Jim and Bob back in school, in fact, he had been pretty good friends with Bob, and I was sure they hadn't seen each other in awhile. The call went to voice mail and I left a message. I just hoped he hadn't gone back to Hawaii yet.

Kayla called me back later in the day. I was glad to hear from her, but she was taking classes at night and couldn't make it. I felt better though. At least I knew she was old enough to be taking classes at night. When I asked her about it, all she said was "Grad School."

That made me feel even better. She was probably in her late twenties, which was around my initial guess. I had been a little bit worried that she might be younger than I thought. Although just about anyone who was younger than me looked like a kid to me, so it was a relief.

I didn't let her know it was my birthday when we were talking. There was no need to make her feel bad about missing out on it if she had to be in class.

I had already celebrated my birthday with my family a few weeks earlier. There were a lot of birthdays in my family around the same time as mine, so we always had one big celebration for all of us. I had a nephew and a cousin with birthdays, and my parents had an anniversary, all within a week of my birthday. I liked doing it that way better anyway. Especially now that there were younger relatives that we could all fawn over.

The bar where I was playing was a good twenty minute drive from my house. I wasn't going to be drinking very much, I never did anyway. I would usually have a beer on my amp that I would nurse all night long.

I might have a shot of something at the beginning of the night, but I would never have too much more than that. Even though it was my birthday I wouldn't go nuts. I figured that since I was still tripping, I should probably avoid drinking too much.

Smoking was another story though. I hadn't been smoking anywhere near as much weed as I usually did since I had gotten back from the festival. Part of that was the tripping, smoking made the trip feel a little bit more intense. I was looking for less intense, not more. The good thing was that when I came down from smoking, the trip did feel a lot less intense.

Most of the time when we played, I would "tune up" in the upper parking lot before we started. Ralph used to tune up with me every time, but Jim and Bob didn't smoke. I was sure that there would be someone who would want to join me for a smoke. If not, I wasn't ever against smoking alone.

I got to the bar nice and early. It was my PA system that we used. I had to set up the microphones as well as my bass and amplifier, and for one night only, my acoustic/electric guitar. The PA only had four inputs. We usually set up three microphones, but mostly used two. That left an input for my guitar, so I was ready to go. We could switch right to band mode after I was done playing without too much change over time.

The restaurant had a decent sized dinner crowd already there most weeks. The band didn't go on until 10, and most of the families that might be in the back dining room were gone by then. Every now and then we'd get a couple of diners who stuck around when they saw us setting up the equipment.

Or some people would ask what type of music we play or say they have to remember to stick around next week as they were walking out of the door. I thought no one ever came back "next week," but two of our biggest fans were a couple that actually did "come back next week."

There were also the regulars who were there just to drink at the bar every night. They would usually bitch about the music and how it cut into their ability to drink. It didn't. It just made their drinking and bitching louder, but they liked Jim and I. We would buy them a drink every now and then, I don't think most of the other bands that played there did that. One of the guys was even named Chuck. Chuck loved us.

Usually, right before the music people started coming in, the place would look fairly empty. Our crowd would start to filter in at around 9:30. Most weeks we would get 10 or 15 people signing up to play. Some weeks more, and some less. Most of the sign ups were guitarists, though there were always a few drummers too. If there were no other bassist, I could usually talk a guitarist into playing my bass if it meant more stage time for them.

Many of the players came almost every week,

and we could guess what they wanted to play before they even signed up. We would always get a few first timers, too, we never knew how that would end up.

Sometimes they were great, sometimes not. At a lot of other jams they might end up being held off to the end. I liked to call people up in the order they signed up. I didn't want to lose a good player because I didn't know their name. We had a few of the "occasional people," too, they would show up every few weeks.

The first timers and the occasional people always brought friends to see them play. The regulars might bring one friend or two, but the first timers would bring 10, another reason to make sure they played. The occasional people would even bring 4 or 5 extra people.

They wanted all of their friends to know that they could play music. I liked them, they were always excited to play. Their friends drank a lot, and the more of them we had, the happier the bartender would be.

There was always a group of bikers there, too. They were never a problem, as far as I could tell. They could be a little bit scary if you didn't know any better, but they were all a part of the same Motor Cycle Club, so there weren't ever any problems between different biker gangs or anything at the bar. If there were any problems at all, they respected the bar and took it outside and I never saw any of it.

I don't know whether they came for the bar, or if they came for us. I assumed it was the bar, but one of the bikers was a guitar player and singer, and he loved to jam out with us every week. One or two of the other guys might play every now and then, but it was mostly just the one guy. He was a lot of fun to

play with, he loved jamming. I liked that. It didn't
matter what type of music, if someone had fun
playing, I liked playing with them.

He was into the Black Crowes, Bob Seagar,
Santana and a few others. He would play three or
four tunes a night, usually taken from the same list of
about 10 songs. "Wicked Game" by Chris Isaac felt
like it might be out of place for him, but he did a great
job with it, and it soon became a favorite of mine. He
always thanked us and gave us hugs after he
played. I didn't mind playing with him one bit.

A few of my friends might have felt a little
uneasy around them, but they had no worries. The
bikers scared some people, but I always treated
them with respect, so I was never very worried. I
tried to treat most people with respect, and that was
what was most important to them. Plus I really liked
checking out all of their bikes and asking about them.
There was nothing a biker liked more than talking
about his bike, and I was always genuinely
impressed.

"So why don't you have a bike?" One guy
asked me as I was fawning over his bike one night.
Much like a guitar, I saw it as a functional work of art.

"Man, I would love to have one, but I know
that it would be the death of me." I answered him
honestly. I could see having a bike in my driveway, it
was seeing me on the bike on the road that worried
me.

"Yeah, but what better way to go." That was
the perfect biker's attitude. I couldn't argue with it
either. There really was nothing like the feeling of
flying down the open road on a bike. I guess I was
just too afraid of dying, whether I was having fun at
the time or not.

We really didn't care who we played with, even when it came to skill level. We were there to have a good time, and help others have a good time. There were older guys, young kids, some chick who liked to sing country tunes, it didn't matter. We had fun and people enjoyed playing with us.

We had been playing together on and off since we were in middle school, so Jim and I were always in time with each other. We had played with a lot of different guitarists and played a lot of different styles over the years. It was hard for anyone to stump us musically, so we could have fun with just about anyone.

We always made sure to encourage all of the musicians. I knew how tough it was to step up in front of friends and play three songs and then have to step down right as they were getting warm. I had been there plenty of times myself. The folks who came out to play deserved some recognition.

Jim and I normally didn't bring in too many of our own friends to come see us play. We had been doing it for a long time so most people who would come, had already seen us play a bunch of times.

I didn't want to be pushy, but if there was something special going on I would let my friends know. I had told some friends that it was my birthday, but they had all told other friends. Before I knew it, the place was packed and I knew almost every one of them.

Diamond Jim and Bob both got to the bar pretty early. Bob didn't have too much setting up to do, just setting up a couple of guitar amps, but Jim had his drum set. He had been using the same drum set for years and had gotten really good at setting it up and breaking it down. If he rushed, he could probably get it set up in under five minutes. He liked to drink a beer and socialize while he did it though, so it always took a little bit longer.

Andy came, so I knew there would be someone to help me "tune up." He brought his wife with him. She was a very nice woman, but she never came out, so I barely knew her at all.

They brought a couple of their friends who I didn't know at all. It was nice of them to bring out even more people. It was great to see the bar was filling up quickly especially with so many friends.

Sabrina and Brendan got there right before I started playing. Brendan looked just like I had expected him to. He was definitely a skier and kayaker and outdoorsman. He was a rugged type of handsome, and he had a smile that made him very likable from the get go. It was always odd to meet people at a gig. I was so busy setting up and thinking about what I was going to play, that I really didn't have any time to get to know him at all.

Sabrina looked beautiful, and a good part of that was her smile. It had been a long time since I had seen her smile like that. That made me like Brendan even more. If he could make her smile like that then he was OK in my book, and she deserved a good smile.

Sasha got to the bar before Reed. I knew she would be first. They came from opposite directions, and Reed was never early. Sasha and Brendan immediately made their way to the pool table.

They were both drinkers, and both pool players. They had known each other back in high school, too, but didn't hang out together very much. He already knew Jim, and Bob had known his brother, too. It was obvious that we would all get

Destiny Unbound

along. Sabrina was right, he was one of us.

Sabrina went out to the parking lot with me and Andy for my pre-show tune up. She even packed Kleborp with some of the Purple for me. She asked me what I thought of Brendan.

"You got yourself a stud." I told her with a smile. "He's cool. I haven't talked to him much, but I like him already. I think everyone does." I knew she didn't need anyone's approval, but she looked glad to get it from me.

"So, where is this Kayla tonight?" Andy asked. I had almost forgotten that I told him about her. Sabrina's eyebrow raised up. I hadn't told her.

"She's in class tonight. We have our first date on Saturday." I answered without saying much more. I didn't want to say much more. I didn't want to jinx anything. I was glad that Sabrina didn't push.

We went back in and I tuned up my acoustic guitar. It was already in tune, but I had to double and triple check. Right before I got up to play my opening songs, Jim came up with shots for he, Bob and I. Jim liked tequila, I usually tried to stay away from it, but it was my birthday, so I downed it with a toast. It burned. I really didn't like tequila.

The place was as crowded as I had ever seen it before. I was actually glad that I had the shot, it helped settle my nerves a little. Usually the bar was pretty sparse when we started, especially if it was nice out and people were sitting out on the deck, smoking.

The bikers had just started showing up as I made my way to the microphone. Everyone at the bar knew me as a bass player. Tom, the biker who always played with us, was really surprised to see

259

me step up to the microphone with a guitar in my hand.

"Hey everyone, thanks for coming out tonight. As some of you know, today is my birthday. So before the band gets up here and then we get a bunch of you up here, I am going to play a few tunes. I spent last weekend at a Phish festival, and got a little bit inspired. I hope this doesn't sound too bad, but don't worry, at least it won't take too long." It was the most that I had ever said into the microphone in the last year that we had been playing at the bar.

I sat on the stool, adjusted the microphone and started to play. I started with Tweezer. The song had a very consistent and familiar opening riff, but could go off in any direction after that. So instead of going into the first verse, I started weaving in the riff for the song Julius, and sang that instead, but bringing it back to the Tweezer riff at the end.

Again, instead of going into the first verse of Tweezer, I started to weave in the guitar riff for the song Taste, and then I sang that. Taste weaved it's way into the song Theme from the Bottom. My fingers felt like they were stumbling a bit and my voice still wasn't back to normal, but I thought that it actually sounded better than when I usually sing. I had no clue how it sounded to the crowd though.

Whenever Phish would play Tweezer live, they would also play Tweezer Reprise later on in the show, usually to close the set or as an encore. The reprise was the same riff, only played a bit faster and in the key of D instead of A. As I finished Theme From the Bottom, I kicked up into Tweezer Reprise. Even though I hadn't sung any of the lyrics to Tweezer, the only lyrics in the Reprise were, "Step into the freezer" and I sang those lyrics building up to the very end.

The ending was similar to the opening riff and should not have been very hard, but it had to be timed and sound exactly right. What made it hard was the build up of the lyrics and the speed of the song leading into it. During practice, I had gotten it right MOST of the time.

The times that I didn't get it right had really bothered me during practice. It sounded horrible when I didn't get it right. At the bar, in front of everyone, I nailed it. It almost didn't matter how the rest of the set had sounded. The fact that I got the very end of it down made me happy. People gave me a good hand, better than usual since the place was already packed.

I put down the guitar, picked up my bass, and I was ready to start the regular set. Jim brought me a beer as he got behind his drums. He had two for himself. He placed one into his cup holder that clipped onto one of his cymbal stands. The other stayed unopened, and he kept it by his seat. He wanted a back up for when the first beer was drained. Diamond Jim was a drinker. I would nurse mine for the rest of the night.

Bob, Jim and I played our three tunes and then we started calling those who had signed up to play. There were three other bassists signed up, which was unusual, but very cool. I would get to spend more time with my friends when the other bassists were playing. There were plenty of people there to help me "tune up" again in the upper parking lot when I was all done playing.

I should have warned the bartender that my

drinking buddies were coming, or maybe it was because it had just been the Fourth of July weekend, but the bar had committed the ultimate bar sin. The bar ran out of Jack Daniels, Sasha's, and many others, favorite drink.

She had been forced to drink Maker's Mark all night. It tasted fine, but unfortunately, she didn't know that it was much stronger than Jack Daniels. She drank the usual amount, but by the end of the night she was hammered. Sasha was a usually big drinker, but normally she handled her liquor well. I had never seen her that drunk before.

Reed needed to get Sasha, and her car, home. She had to be at work in the morning and needed her car to get there. That was the biggest problem with Sasha having a real job. Plus both she and Reed had several pets, so Reed couldn't stay at her place and she couldn't stay with him.

He wanted to drive her car to her place in Connecticut and have me follow them so I could bring him back to his car at the bar afterward. It was my birthday, and it was the middle of the night, I really didn't want to go on a late night mission all over creation. I had just finished playing music, besides, I was still even tripping a little.

I just wanted to go home, but I thought of Al and how he would always do whatever he could to help a friend. I could almost hear him telling me to go. The fact was, I was still wide awake and would be for a long time. There was no reason why I shouldn't do it. So we left the bar for Sasha's house at about 2 in the morning.

Reed had to pull her car over to let Sasha throw up at least three times on the way. I didn't really want to keep following them and have to watch it, so I went on ahead. I hoped to find a spot to get some coffee. There were plenty of towns and gas stations and restaurants, but unfortunately nothing that I passed was open. I ended up waiting in Sasha's driveway for about 20 minutes until they finally pulled in.

It took Reed a few minutes to get her inside and settled down for the night. We made our way back to the bar in record time, but it was still really late by the time we pulled in. I wanted to run inside and see if I could get a cup of coffee, but the bar was already closed. I was going to have to drive home without my caffeine boost.

I was fine on the way home, but I had never had a problem driving late at night. Reed still had to get his own car home, and he had already crashed twice after falling asleep at the wheel. I was afraid he was going to do it again. I didn't want any of my friends to die on my birthday, so I followed him home, blasting my horn every time I saw his car start to drift out of it's lane.

I got home just as it was starting to get light out. The sun hadn't risen yet, but it would soon. It was my favorite time of the day. I stood outside of my door and finished smoking my cigar, taking slow drags while watching as the sky turned lighter shades of black with each drag.

My backyard was adjacent to the Saw Mill Parkway. I lived 45 miles north of New York City. During most of the day I would hear a million cars driving to and from New York City, but not this early in the morning. There would be an occasional car, but for the most part, all I could hear were the birds singing. It sounded like there were a million of them surrounding me. They were calling out over long distances to each other, and though it was hard, you could make out all of the individual birds. It was my favorite time of day.

I could still feel the acid playing with my mind, but the effects were getting much weaker now. It had become a familiar, if not exactly welcome, visitor. I was able to make my trip nothing but background noise now. It was there, but as long as I didn't pay attention to it, it wouldn't annoy me. That was the best birthday gift of them all.

I put my cigar out and walked inside. My laptop sat on top of my coffee table, already open, but in sleep mode. The dark screen looked very scary to me. I was sure there were a bunch of birthday wishes waiting for me on Facebook, but I had a mission to finish first. When I activated the computer, the blank Word page looked out at me, just the way I had left it earlier in the day. It was even more terrifying than the black screen.

My 39th birthday was over. I poured myself a glass of Scotch. It was an 18 year old Glen Livet. It had been first put into a barrel the year that I could finally legally drink. A perfect birthday beverage. I had only had a few drinks all night and then I had driven all over New England. I was entitled to a good drink. When I needed a good drink, I had a Scotch.

I sat down at my computer. My fingers went to work right away. I didn't even have to think about what they were writing, I just let them do their thing. I worked for what felt like days, but when I looked up, the sun hadn't even made it up yet. I got back to typing. I knew the story I wanted to tell so well, I never even had to think about it. My only job was as a typist.

When I finished, I read it over once and made a few corrections. I tried not to take in any of the content, I just wanted to make sure it was well written. I saved it and then went to look for Heather's e-mail address. While it wasn't due for a couple of weeks, I figured if there were any edits or changes needed, I would have plenty of time to do them.

When I looked for her e-mail address on Facebook, I saw that I had 52 notices. Birthdays on Facebook could really make a guy feel loved. That made me think of Kayla. I was feeling all lovey dovey after such an amazing night. I thought that it might be nice if I could be loved by her. I had told myself that I wouldn't, but I broke down and did a search for her, even though I didn't even know her last name.

There were plenty of Kayla's in the area, but none looked like her. Not everyone had a Facebook account, or maybe she had one that was hidden. Plenty of people didn't use their real names, too. I would just have to find out when we were on our date.

By the time I went to bed, the sun was up pretty high in the sky. I felt accomplished. My story had been sent out, it was in the hands of those mysterious writers and artists who lived in my computer, now.

It had been an odd and fantastic birthday. I felt good about playing music. I felt good about writing my story, and I felt good about all of the friends that I had around me. Sasha was home safe. Sabrina was happier than I had ever seen her. Brendan was a good guy, at least he seemed to be so far.

When I emptied my pockets before bed, they were nice and tidy, despite being out all night. No garbage, no tissue, no crumpled up bills. I felt good. I felt complete again. I drifted off to sleep, undisturbed by dreams for the first time since coming home from the Super Ball.

From: Chuck Howe
To: Heather Smith

Here is my Submission, let me know if you want me to make any edits:

Yellow Barn

I pulled over next to three Self Storage buildings. I got out of the car and looked at the sign. "Yellow Barn Road." I had been here twice my freshman year in college and hadn't been back since. I had a feeling it would be gone, but my heart sank a little anyway when I saw there was no yellow barn.

20 Years earlier I walked into the type of bar you only went to if you were depressed, or were under 21 and the bouncers at all the other bars knew your brother, and you had his ID. On the day my ex-girlfriend told me she had a new boyfriend, I was both. The place had darts, the game on TV, a jar of pickled hard boiled eggs and that was it.

I walked in the door and saw two old fucks

crying in their beers. They would be perfect company. But I glanced down to the end of the bar and was immediately caught up in Michelle's giant brown eyes instead. They were staring a hole right through me. I froze. She turned on her barstool still looking right into my eyes and pulled the stool next to her out, the most inviting move a woman has ever made toward me.

A few hours later it was either love or the inability to stand up straight that saw us walking home arms wrapped around each other.

Everything about this girl was perfect. It was the fall of 1991 and all the kids were just starting to get into grunge music. She liked the Dead. She was Canadian and she liked hockey. She had a beautiful laugh and best of all, she was into me.

Everything screamed out for me to kiss her as we got to her dorm. As I moved in she turned her head and I got nothing but cheek. "I want to, but not yet. Call me tomorrow." Somehow, even with no real kiss good night, I floated back to my dorm.

Over the next few weeks we spent almost every free moment with each other. She had friends in Ithaca, which wasn't far, so we went there almost every weekend. On one trip back, we pulled over at a yellow barn. We were in the middle of nowhere and chances were no other cars would pass all night, so we decided to investigate the creepy old place.

A rusted hinge that held a pad lock had already been ripped from the wood and dangled from the door. As we went inside we heard animals scurry away, a big hole in the roof let in the moon giving it the perfect mood lighting. I thought this would be it. She still hadn't let me even give her a real kiss. It had only been a short time, but we were in college, shouldn't we have jumped into bed right away?

We lay down under the hole in the roof to watch the stars in each other's arms. I tried to make a few moves, but was politely blocked each time. I got the idea, and just lay there with her. By the time we got up the sun was shining and we had told each other almost every story we had. When we got back to the car I was feeling great, like I had made a real connection.

A week later on that same stretch of road she seemed very distant.

As we approached the yellow barn I pulled over. She looked at me a bit confused, I motioned for us to go and she just shook her head, a small tear coming out of her large brown eye. "Come on," I said, "You can tell me inside." I couldn't imagine what was wrong. Things seemed to be going so well, right up until we left for Ithaca that Friday. She slowly got out of the car and made her way to the barn.

We just lay there in the quiet for what seemed like an eternity. The moon wasn't as full, so it was darker inside. Clouds covered the sky exposed by the hole. She lifted her head up on her elbow and looked right at me. There was a deep sadness in her eye, but for a second I thought she was going to kiss me.

"I went to the bar that night to get drunk and forget all about love. Then you walked in the door." I went to speak, but she stopped me, "just let me get through this. Richard had called that day." She had told me all about him. He was a lazy asshole from what I could gather. "He told me that he had been a junkie for the last year. I never knew. He found out last month that he is HIV positive." My heart stopped beating. AIDS had been around a few years but still so little was known about it, especially by an 18 year old kid. "I was tested two weeks ago..."

She buried her face deep in my chest and I could feel her body shaking with the spasms of her tears. I just looked up at the blank hole in the ceiling. I tried to think of something to say, but nothing came so I just held her tight. I was afraid I might break a bone, hers or mine. She made strange noises as she muffled her cries with my body. Her face looked completely lost inside of me.

I looked down at her in the dark. I tried to stop myself but a single laugh escaped. Her head immediately jumped up. Her large, beautiful brown bloodshot eyes looked at me through tears. She was confused. She tried to say something but words wouldn't come.

"I'm sorry, for a second there you looked like a lioness feeding on my ripped open heart." I said.

Her look of confusion turned into a small smile. She gave me a quick eye roll and the smile faded, but it was the most beautiful smile I had ever seen. She put her head down and went back to feeding without another word until the black hole in the ceiling began to turn gray.

Chuck Howe

Destiny Unbound

Friday, July 8, 2011

Ice is all he was made of
The bitter blue, and frozen through
He went over to the mound
Reclining down his final thoughts
Were drifting to the time this life had shined

Mound
Gordon

Chuck Howe

I woke up and, for the first time in a week, I didn't feel like I was tripping. It was a miracle. Nothing in my rug looked like it was moving. My head felt clear. I poured a cup of coffee, grabbed a cigar and went outside. It was another beautiful day.

I felt good, better than I had in a long time, and I still had one more day before my big date with Kayla. Finally, I was starting to feel that post festival euphoria that I had been waiting for. I wasn't sure how big of a date it was actually going to be, but I felt ready.

I had only met Kayla once before, and I knew nothing about her. She knew nothing about me. It was entirely possible that we would have nothing in common and the date might end up being a bust. I hadn't been on very many dates recently, so just going on one was big. I was rusty and she was beautiful. It was understandable that I was starting to get a little nervous.

Before I finished my cigar, Powder, the dragonfly, flew over to say hello and suddenly I felt like I was tripping again. I wasn't sure if it was the acid, or just how trippy Powder looked when he flew. Though it was a nice surprise to see Powder being so friendly, I decided to go inside before I went into full relapse.

I went online and checked Facebook. Heather had sent an e-mail saying she received my submission, but nothing about it, I didn't really expect anyone to check it out for awhile. I had a few more birthday wishes. I had online friends from all over the world, so I didn't know if they were stragglers who were late, or if they were on time based on where they lived.

I had long hated time zones. They felt fake to me. I would be fine with 6 PM being when the sun is directly overhead. It was all a conspiracy of Big Clocks and scientists. If there was no time difference between Philadelphia and Berlin, people in those two cities might actually talk about things that mattered instead of spending all their time figuring out the time difference.

Kerry had posted a bunch of pictures from the Super Ball. It was great to see them all, even though it almost felt like I was still there. I was missing it already. There were things that had happened that I was already starting to forget.

I smoked a bowl and I felt the acid in my system again, It was not as strong as it had been before, but it was definitely still there. At least my voice was back to normal now.

My mind started racing again, and filling me with negative thoughts. Although I almost wanted to call Kayla and cancel, I didn't do it. I deserved to go on a date with a beautiful woman. Slowly but surely I would pull myself together.

Just as I was about to close up my laptop, I saw a new message. It was from Heather, she had read my story and loved it. She was going to start looking for art to match with it right away. She said that she wanted it right at the front of the book. I couldn't believe it. I went from not being able to write anything worth reading, to leading off a book filled with writers that I respected. Real writers.

Heather was in the advertising business and had done some amazing illustrated stories that I had seen in her blogs back on Myspace. All of the people involved were top notch, I didn't feel like I even belonged in the book, yet she wanted me right up front.

My confidence got a nice boost. There was no way I was going to cancel the date with Kayla now. If anything I wanted to bump it up to that night. I felt like I couldn't wait another day. I had already invited her to the gig the night before, I didn't want to look desperate. I'd wait and meet her at the restaurant like we planned.

I started writing again. Just a few short stories. Some were complete fiction, some were right out of my life. I wrote them down as quickly as they came to me. It felt really good to get each story out, and each one felt like a great accomplishment. They weren't finished stories, they would need to be rewritten and cleaned up, and some would just end up getting tossed, but they were coming to me easily for the first time in years.

I looked at my guitar, still sitting in the corner where I had brought it in the night before. I loved music. I loved listening to it, I loved playing it. I had fun writing songs, and some people really liked them, but I knew that I wasn't the best musician out there. How much fun would it be to write songs for musicians who were actually good? Maybe I could still play bass, too, I was a better bass player than any other instrument, but the writing was the most important thing.

Al had told me I had all the tools I needed already. I thought he meant musically, but I knew I was far from having all of those tools. He was right though. I had stories, a lot of them. I had an imagination, too. A really good imagination. I could always come up with more stories, and I was having fun. That would lead to even more good stories.

After getting a few more stories down, I tried to read some of my new book, but Gogol was too dry and stuffy. It made me wonder why Kayla had said she liked it. I wanted something outrageous. I needed Hunter S Thompson or even a Far Side Calender. I wanted funny. I didn't know what yet, but something. So I went down to the bookstore to just look around.

I ordered an espresso at the cafe and it sucked, so I was immediately happy that I got to be grumpy about that. It was hit or miss with the espresso there, and that particular espresso was a big miss. As I was leaving the cafe, about to head up the stairs to the book section, I heard someone clearing their throat behind me. I turned and looked, and it was Kayla, with a big smile on her face.

"See, I told you that we would run into each other here again, you didn't need my number." If she hadn't said anything I would have missed her completely. This time she was reading a fashion magazine.

When she realized that I saw what she was reading she looked a little embarrassed. I didn't care, she looked great, more power to the fashion magazine if that's where she got it from. But her embarrassment made her look even cuter.

"No, I guess I didn't need it, but I have it saved now," I patted the phone in my shirt pocket. Outside of the dank corner of the Russian Literature section she looked even better. "Do you mind if I sit down?" I said already pulling out the chair across from her. I was conscious of my voice. I was sure that I sounded different than when we first met. I hated that I was losing my sexy raspy voice, but she didn't seem to notice.

"No, not at all," she answered, smiling as I sat down. The second my butt hit the seat she jumped up and started gathering her scattered things off of the table.

"Well, I had a lovely time, but I have to run to work now." She turned and ran out of the building without another word. She had gotten me again. Even if I had been tripping the other day, I had been right. She was a strange chick, but that was OK, I was a fan of strange.

Through the window I saw her get into a small, blue, Honda hatchback. It was an old car, but it was very well kept and sparkling clean. For some reason I imagined her driving a Cadillac or some big luxury car. As I watched her drive away, my phone rang. It was Danny.

"Hey man, sorry I missed you last night," he said before I could even say hello. "It's been crazy ever since I got back from the festival." He didn't need to apologize. I knew how crazy it could be to go home for the first time in years.

"What are you up to today? I just got to the bookstore, do you want to meet up for a coffee, or get a drink tonight?" It had been great to see him at the Super Ball, it would be nice to hang out for a bit while I wasn't tripping.

"Actually, I'm heading down to the airport now. I just wanted to call and say it was great to see you. That was a blast." I didn't think he would be sticking around New York for too long and I was right. Hawaii was calling him home.

"Yeah man, it was great to see you, too, have a good trip home, and I'll be coming to visit soon." I went upstairs looking for something to read, but ended up just listening to a bunch of albums that I had already heard on their listening stations. You could listen to any album in the place, just by scanning the bar code. That was one more thing I hated about the place.

Later that night I had a dream that I was living in Europe. I had a small studio apartment that was filled to the very top with stuff. It wasn't random stuff. It was all things that I had owned at one point in my life or another.

There were a bunch of G I Joe figures. My old skateboard and helmet, a guitar that I had sold in high school. There was even old clothing that I recognized from my younger days. There was a t-shirt with the chimpanzee "Mucho Macho" on it. There was my lucky striped shirt from high school. My mother had thrown it out when it was in the laundry because it was so badly ripped. Somehow all of the rips were fixed.

There was no junk in the pile, it wasn't junk to me at least. I could see how people could become hoarders, it was all stuff I no longer had, but I think I would have kept it all if I was given the choice, and the storage space, now. It was all good stuff. I wanted all of it.

I was overwhelmed with the feeling of being in a rush. I had to get to the airport. I had to leave forever. I might not ever see any of my vintage stuff again. I had to bring some of it with me, but I couldn't choose what to bring.

In front of me was a single small suitcase, but I was woken up from my slumber by something before I could even start to pack it. My room was dark, the first light of day was seeping through the window, but it was too hard to see. I had fallen asleep at a decent hour for the first time in weeks, but now I was wide awake.

I looked around for the suitcase, it felt like it should be around somewhere. What did I save from my childhood? On the floor, next to the wall I saw it. A small suitcase. I knew that inside of it was my clothing from the Super Ball. I hadn't done any laundry yet. I had been tripping pretty hard since getting home. I would get to it soon enough.

But what if? What if I did pack the suitcase in my dream. What if I did bring it home with me from that small apartment in Europe. I got up and opened it up. I was right, it was my dirty clothes from the Super Ball. I saw some paper towels wrapped around something at the bottom of the bag and I grabbed it. What could it be, could it be from my dream? I unwrapped it. Bacon. Three strips of it.

I sent Sabrina a text. "I just found bacon in my suitcase, should I save it for you?" It was probably my bacon but I really didn't remember packing it.

I didn't expect to hear from her so soon, but within minutes, I got a simple text back. "Yes."

I went back to sleep, trying to go back to the studio apartment in Europe, but it didn't work. So instead I dreamed about titties and bottles of scotch. It was a good night.

Chuck Howe

Destiny Unbound

Saturday, July 9, 2011

And now I know the reason
That I'm feeling so forlorn
 I'll pick you up at eight as usual
Listen for my horn

Horn
Anastasio

Chuck Howe

I woke up knowing that it was date night with Kayla before my eyes even opened. There was no sign of the acid on the back of my eyelids, so I opened them up to see a beautiful world. My rug wasn't moving at all. Life felt great. I jumped out of bed, ready to face the world. I looked out of the window and I saw that it was pouring rain.

That sucked. I really wanted to go out and soak up some sun. It was the first rain in weeks and we really needed it, but it was a torrential downpour. I wanted to go out and enjoy my coffee with the yard pets, but I doubted that they would be out and about on such a nasty day. At least all of the plants would be getting some much needed water, and maybe the grass wouldn't be as brown. Having my coffee and cigar inside was a small price, one I was willing to pay.

I had slept later than I had intended. The clouds must have kept the sun from waking me up. I had wanted to try to get some writing done, but I was feeling a little too anxious. I had a long day ahead of me. I had been given some Xanax for my anxiety, but that usually just knocked me out. I didn't need that. I didn't want to sleep through my date, and I could easily see that happening. That would actually be in perfect keeping with my recent track record.

I had downloaded the entire three days of music from the Super Ball, so I played it with the volume way up. It was good to hear, on second listen, that they were playing as good as I had thought they were at the time. I thought maybe they only sounded so good when I was there because of the acid. It wouldn't have been the first time, but luckily that wasn't the case this time. They really had been playing that well.

I really didn't know very much about Kayla. She was a grad student. She had a job, she drove a Honda and she liked Russian writers. I had ran into her at the bookstore twice in one week.

Had I ever seen her there before? Had she seen me there before? She was very good at hiding in the background, our second meeting proved that. I hadn't seen her before she cleared her throat, maybe she had been watching me for awhile. Maybe she had been waiting for me in Russian Literature on that first day, knowing I would go there eventually. Had she been spying on me for a long time? Did she set the whole thing up?

That was the acid creeping back into my day. Even though I wasn't hallucinating anymore, I could feel it in my head, I was still tripping. The music may not have been helping, so I turned it off. My train of thought was very jumpy.

Obviously she hadn't been stalking me. I had to calm down and get it together before it was time for our date. I tried to call Andy, but he didn't answer. It was OK, he had already given me all the advice I needed. I was running the projector, I could slow it down if I wanted.

When I finished my cigar I went outside, even though it was still pouring. I needed some fresh air, and the rain felt great. It had been hot and dry out for far too long without a break. I let the water soak my clothes and hair. It didn't matter. I was going to be jumping in the shower before I went on my date anyway.

None of my lawn pets were about. It was just me, spinning around in the rain. If any of my neighbors were looking out of their window, they would have thought I was insane. I had lived there long enough, so they probably already thought I was insane anyway. I didn't care. I was having fun playing in the rain and I wasn't going to stop doing it because of what a neighbor might think.

I had some work to do before my date, so eventually I made my way back inside. I needed to do laundry badly. Even though I promised to save it for Sabrina, I threw the nasty old bacon away. If Sabrina really needed the bacon, I could make her some fresh bacon or take her to the diner. At least the Mount Kisco Diner served hash browns all day long, and they never bitched about frying an egg.

I really didn't want all of my clothes smelling like pork. Besides, what if Kayla was a Muslim or Vegetarian, and I showed up with bacon flavored clothes. She probably wasn't either one of those things. Steven's wasn't known for having a very vegetarian friendly menu. And they had a lot of pork products, too. But it would suck if it turned out that I couldn't eat bacon around her. That would almost be a deal breaker.

The rain had been very refreshing. I poured myself some more coffee and pounded it down. Coffee had been a life saver for me during the past week. It was the only thing that did what it was supposed to. Drinking coffee never made me feel like I was tripping. I smoked some weed, but only a little. I needed to balance the anxiety and the trip.

Once I was sufficiently high, I jumped in the shower. The weed got me higher than I had planned, but it worked at calming my mind down. I didn't feel like I was tripping at all anymore. Once out of the shower, I just sat on the couch, smoking weed, and staring at the clock. I didn't turn on the TV or even put on music. I was just waiting for the clock to turn 7:45. Once it did, I leaped into action. It was finally time for my date.

It only took me two minutes to get to Steven's, since I lived right up the hill from it. They didn't take reservations, but I had never had to wait very long to get a table there. Kayla wasn't there yet, I didn't expect her to be, our date still wasn't supposed to start for another fifteen minutes.

I was early enough to get a nice Scotch from the bar, so that was where I made my way. The bartender had worked there forever. He knew what I wanted before I even sat down. That was another reason that I liked Steven's.

Eight O'clock came and went and there was no sign of Kayla. That was OK, I didn't expect her to be right on time. I usually wasn't. None of my friends ever were. Besides, women were supposed to keep a man waiting, especially on a first date. I waited for another ten minutes, but still nothing. I didn't know if I should call her yet. It might seem like I was a little too desperate if I did that.

I waited five more minutes. Still nothing. I looked at my phone. No texts. I was usually the late one. She had turned the tables on me and now I knew how it felt.

Maybe she was always late. I had no clue. If she was normally late that was fine, I would eventually get used to it. I usually wasn't 15 minutes early either. If she was always going to be this late, I wouldn't rush and it would be OK for me to be a little late, too.

I didn't know where she lived either. I didn't know where she was coming from or how far away it was. For all I knew, she could be stuck in traffic trying to get out of the city. Her car was old, even if it was very well taken care of, and that may have been it. She could be broken down somewhere, and if I called and saved her I might even be a hero.

Instead I finished my scotch and ordered another. Even though I wasn't normally a big drinker, it was doing more for my nerves than the weed. Scotch was tasting really good to me the last few days.

Five more minutes passed and there was still no sign of her. She was already 20 minutes late. That felt a bit excessive to me. I was starting to think she might not show up at all. I hoped that she wouldn't stand me up, but I didn't know. She was young, and maybe she had just blown me off. It was getting late, I couldn't be blamed for at least sending her a text. Could I?

Just as I was about to break down and call her, she walked in the door. She looked around to the tables for me, but I was still sitting at the bar. They had a table for us, I had made sure of it. When she saw me at the bar, she gave me a crooked look. I thought maybe it was because I wasn't at a table yet, but as we were led to a table, she looked down at my drink.

"I have only had one drink in my entire life. I didn't like it." She snapped at me, almost angrily. That was not a good sign, or start to things. She sat down before I even had a chance to pull out her chair for her. This was going to be an interesting night for sure.

The next thing I learned about her was that she was a huge fan of Sarah Palin. At first I thought that she was kidding, but she kept going on about what a scumbag Obama was, and how awesome she thought that Sarah Palin was. It was getting bad, but I was able to keep my mouth shut until she mentioned Obama being a socialist.

"Actually, I'm a socialist. Obama is definitely not a socialist." At that point I figured the date was going to be a bust, so I really didn't care anymore. I thought that might get her mad, but she just became more interested.

"Really? You? A Socialist?" she asked with a snicker of derision.

"I'm a dirty liberal hippie. Much more of a socialist than Obama. Look at his cabinet. He's surrounded by the same money whores that Bush and Clinton..." She interrupted before I could say any more.

"Actually, I'm a money whore. Obama is definitely not a money whore." She was horrible. And she was wrong. But she was funny. I liked funny. I should have been out the door already, but I wanted to see what surprises this girl had in store for me next.

"Really? You? A Money Whore?" I asked with a wicked smile. She needed to know I could play this game, too. She gave me a serious look, but broke into laughter. Maybe the date wouldn't be so bad after all.

Kayla had a very interesting and horrifying story. The accent I noticed was from Africa, where she was born. Her mother and two brothers were killed when she was very young, and she and her father escaped to Europe. She didn't offer too much information about it, and I didn't press her. The fact she had told me that much meant a lot to me.

She and her father had been living in America for over ten years. She had finished high school and college, and was now going to grad school. Her goal was to become a Certified Public Accountant. She really was a money whore. It was a strange dream to me, but she was determined to do it.

Despite all of our differences, I liked her. She wasn't on Facebook, in fact, she didn't like computers at all. She used them for school, and she had an e-mail address, but she barely spent anytime on the internet. I had been right, she was very strange. I spent most of my time online, I couldn't imagine living a life without the internet.

We stayed at the restaurant for hours, until it looked like the wait-staff really wanted to go home. I only had the one drink, so there wasn't even going to be a big bar tab to tip on. When they started to give us evil looks, we decided it was time to go, but I didn't want to leave her yet. She was so different than me that I wanted to learn everything about her.

She was a deeply religious woman and couldn't believe that I hadn't been to church in over twenty years. She went all the time. She was part of a prayer group that met once a week, and she went to Sunday Services. I really didn't want to tell her that I was an atheist, but I felt I had no choice after she invited me to go to church with her. She was noticeably upset at that, and it wasn't the first time she was upset at something I had said.

She was the exact opposite of all of the women that I had ever dated in the past. Nothing had ever worked out before, and maybe that was the problem. I was going after women who were too similar to me. I wasn't completely sold on her. After all, she did like Sarah Palin. But maybe, just maybe, I could get past all of that. Maybe we could be good for each other.

I tested the air, seeing if she wanted to come over for coffee. I lived right in town, it turned out she lived about twenty minutes away. She very politely declined, but made sure I understood that she wanted to see me again. I didn't blame her for not coming home with me, it had been a good first date, not a great one, but I had to give it a try. I did get a good night kiss as we parted, and it was a very sweet kiss.

Instead of going home, I went straight to Reed's house. I had to tell someone about the date. Unfortunately, it being after midnight on a Saturday, he was up at Sasha's. Luckily Maxwell was home. He was more interested in me calling him a purple cat and giving him scratches behind the ear than he was about my big date.

By the time I got home, and finished my writing the rain had stopped. The clouds were breaking up and stars were becoming visible overhead. Light was just starting to break on the horizon. It was almost my favorite time of day. I couldn't go to sleep yet. It had been a long time since I went for a walk in my own neighborhood, especially since I had a car in the driveway.

The ground was still wet, and there was a bit of a chill in the air, but it was still the heart of summer. It would be getting warm soon. I didn't need a jacket. I walked to the end of the driveway and looked left and right. I was just walking, no destination in mind, so it really didn't matter which way I went. But in honor of my new friend, I turned right.

That night former Yankee Captain Thurman Munson came to me in a dream. OK, not really, but that would have been pretty cool, right?

Chuck Howe

Epilogue

We got to get on the road,
Our Destiny's unbound
She's the one for me,
We got to get out of town

Destiny Unbound
Gordon

Chuck Howe

My relationship with Kayla did not last for very long. We dated for almost two months, and she broke up with me four times over that period. She always had a good reason, in her own head at least, for the break up.

Once it was because I had a sexy picture with me holding a bunny as my Facebook profile picture. It was one that Heather Smith, the graphic artist, had made for me as a joke. She was good at what she did, and the picture actually looked like me. Kayla wasn't on Facebook, so I always wondered how she knew about it.

She would always call me and apologize a day or two after breaking up with me. I got sick of it pretty quickly though, and as the summer came to an end, she broke up with me again. She was going to be going back to school full time, and she was working close to full time, too. She made it clear that left very little time for me.

I was OK with that, I didn't need very much of her time. I warned her not to end it, that I wouldn't come back if she changed her mind. I told her to take some time and make sure that it was what she really wanted, and then we could decide what to do.

No. She insisted that I would be too much of a distraction to her. I needed to go, and so I did. Of course just like I predicted, she called me a few days later wanting to meet up. I told her that I couldn't. I had met someone new.

Of course I hadn't, but I had enough of her yo

yo dating. At that point I just wanted it to be over, and that was the last time that she ever called me. I was glad that we had given it a try, and I was glad it ended with out too much pain. But I was most glad that the relationship ended for good.

We could have kept trying. I could have taken her back and then we could have broken up every few weeks just to get back together again. I didn't want that. We were too different from one another. We had some fun, but I knew it wasn't working and we ended it before it got too bad. That alone was a real step forward for me.

Uno Kudo Volume 1: Ripped came out in October of 2011 with my story, Yellow Barn, right at the front of it. I was really proud. There were some great stories and poems and Heather had filled it with beautiful artwork. Many of the stories took on a very personal feel. One girl had been a block away from the bombing in Olso, Norway, and her amazing story became a perfect ending for the book.

I still had not met any of the other writers or artists in person, but that was all about to change. Heather had been planning another get together in Brooklyn, and this time I was not going to miss it.

Unfortunately, we were hit with a huge snowstorm that canceled Halloween for the entire city right before her party. A few people who were going to come into town had to cancel. It would have probably been tough for me to get into the city from Westchester even.

Joseph Allen, one of the writers, was a guy that I had wanted to meet for a long time. He was in his early twenties when I first read his work on Myspace. He lived in Jersey back then, but wanted me to go out partying with him and friends every time he came up to the city.

At that point I felt like I was done with my bar hopping days, the last thing I wanted to do was go power drinking with a bunch of kids. Plus, I wasn't very eager to meet any of my online friends. I wasn't eager to see very many of my real life friends at that point either.

As the years moved on, Joseph grew up. He and his girlfriend moved into the city. I didn't chat with him as much, but I still read a lot of his writing and he was still one of my favorite writers. He had matured, and I actually started thinking that going out for drinks with him would be fun. I was excited that he was going to be at Heather's party, but Heather's party never happened.

One of the other writers, Pamela, lived in Brattleboro, Vermont and one day I noticed online that she had scheduled a book signing in a coffee shop up there. It would be a lot of fun to go up there and surprise her. I mentioned it to Joseph and he jumped on the idea right away. I mentioned it to Heather in an e-mail, and really didn't expect her to jump on it, too, but she did.

With three of us coming, we thought that maybe we should warn Pamela, and not just surprise her. It was a good thing we did. There was a Halloween party that had been rescheduled for that Saturday night and she had plenty of room for all of us to stay with her, so we were going up for an extended weekend.

Joseph offered to drive, and he would pick me up since I lived on the way up to Vermont from the city anyway. I was getting really excited. I was finally going to start meeting the people who lived inside my computer. If I was going to start writing more, I needed to start living more. This was the first great chance to live since the Super Ball.

I gathered my things at the end of my driveway as I waited for them. I was just as excited as I had been waiting for Sabrina before leaving for Ithaca.

And also, just like the Ithaca trip, we had a nice long drive ahead of us, so there would be a lot of chatting. I wasn't bringing very much. I had a bag of clothes and my air mattress, but I waited outside with it, even though Joseph had just called and was still twenty minutes away.

I was really excited to finally meet Joseph. I didn't know Pamela at all, but it looked like she was a fun girl from her Facebook page, plus anyone from Vermont had to be pretty cool. Her story in Uno Kudo had been great.

Heather was a sweetheart. I didn't know her well, but I had known her a long time. She was a single mom, and very proud of her daughter, but she had a life of her own, too. I wasn't worried at all about getting along with her. She had a big infectious smile in every picture I had ever seen of her. She always looked beautiful, but pictures on facebook could be deceiving. I know I made sure that I was only tagged in the best pictures of me. So I wasn't really sure what to expect.

Suddenly I saw a car with Joseph's face in the window go zipping right past my house. I lived on a dead end road, so I knew they would be back eventually. Sure enough, they slowly came back a minute later.

They both jumped out of the car as soon as they saw me. Joseph was a big guy with a big smile and he gave me a great big bear hug and then grabbed my bags and brought them to the trunk.

Even though I had seen pictures of her, Heather's beauty caught me off guard. Her smile was just as warm and infectious as I had imagined. She had amazing style, wearing a very short skirt, with crazy patterned tights. She gave me a nice warm hug that felt great.

We had a four hour drive ahead of us. I didn't mind at all. I really enjoyed the company I was with. I can't say for sure that it was love at first sight, but by the end of the car ride, I knew that I wanted to spend a whole lot more time with Heather. I was going to have to start coming up with excuses to go to Brooklyn.

Destiny Unbound

Great thanks go to Aaron, Adam, Ana, Multiple Andys, Bud, Emilie, Erin, Gregg, Kelsey, Khaliah, Kenny, Kim, Lazlo, Luke, Mariano, Mark, Mary, Megan, another Megan, Melissa, Mike, Monica, Neil, Nick, Randy, Rob, Sam, Sammy, Sil, Pat and Todd

Special thanks and a whole lot of gratitude to all of my family and friends.

Gratitude and love to Trey Anastasio, Page MacConnell, Mike Gordon, John Fishman and Tom Marshall, Chris Koruda, Paul Languedoc, Gerry Brown and everyone behind the scenes of a Phish show.

Sources used: Phish.net, Livephish.com, parking lot gossip, memory

Chuck Howe

Chuck Howe is a writer, musician, and humorist from Mount Kisco New York. His stories have appeared in the books Uno Kudo Volume 1 and 2, First Time: Essays, stories and poems, and Thank You. Truly. And also Booze. All available on Amazon.com

His collection of short stories, If I had Wings These Windmills Would be Dead, and the anthology he edited, Too Much: Tales of Excess, are both available from the Unknown Press.

Howe has been an associate editor for Uno Kudo Vol 2 and 4. His second novel, The Battle of Camp Macho Grande is projected for a 2016 release.